Dear Mystery Reader:

In the last few years the number of people fly fishing has grown exponentially, the sport exploding in popularity.

Writer David Leitz was clever enough to recognize that the world of fly fishing—which has a distinctly genteel aura—is the perfect setting for a mystery.

You see, a mystery reader is like a fly fisherman. It takes a great deal of cunning, patience, and strategy to find that fish hidden in that raging river. Like a mystery reader, one tries to anticipate what will happen next. The scenario could unfold any number of ways. But inevitably there is a struggle, a conquering, and a death, all the things we mystery lovers adore most.

If you're new to David Leitz's writing, you've landed a good catch with this book. You might also check out his two previous ones. They will no doubt leave you greatly satisfied, sort of like a delicious meal of rainbow trout.

Yours in mystery,

Dana Isaacson

Dana Edwin Isaacson
Senior Editor
St. Martin's Paperbacks Dead Letter Mysteries

Other titles from St. Martin's Dead Letter Mysteries

OPEN SEASON

Out on the lake, Tommy was now drifting twenty or thirty feet to one side of the big green canoe holding the older men. Bendel was still paddling slowly in the stern, but I could see the flash of Kingfish's rod as he cast out across the flat water. Their voices, now unintelligible, floated across the water. I heard Tommy laugh just as the first booming gunshot echoed across the lake. Bendel seemed to stiffen in his seat. His paddle slid from his hands and floated away.

What I was seeing . . . what was happening . . . didn't register at first. Then a small geyser of water erupted just ahead of the canoe, followed instantly by the explosion of a second shot.

Also by David Leitz

CASTING IN DEAD WATER
DYING TO FLY FISH

FLY FISHING CAN BE FATAL

A Max Addams Fly-Fishing Mystery

 **DAVID LEITZ**

St. Martin's Paperbacks

FLY FISHING CAN BE FATAL

Copyright © 1997 by David E. Leitz.

ISBN: 0-312-96162-6

Printed in the United States of America

St. Martin's Paperbacks edition/April 1997

10 9 8 7 6 5 4 3 2 1

FOR MAXINE AND ED
and a blanket in Foster Park

FLY FISHING CAN
BE FATAL

CHAPTER ONE

I guess I should blame Robert Redford.

He's the one who turned Norman Maclean's novelette *A River Runs Through It* into the beautiful film that we in the fly-fishing business now simply refer to as "The Movie."

Not only did "The Movie" receive critical acclaim and much deserved box-office success, it changed the sport of fly fishing forever.

Today, according to Trout Unlimited and other organizations who keep track of that sort of thing, there are over two million men and women who fly fish in the United States, making it the fastest-growing individual outdoor sport in the country.

I don't doubt it.

If the business at Whitefork, my fly-fishing lodge in northern Vermont, is any indication, the statistics are right. In fact, "The Movie" was still in theaters when the lodge telephone began ringing with reservation requests from fly-fishing aficionados and wannabes as far away as Florida. And it's never stopped. With the exception of the first week of the season when our portion of the Whitefork River is high with snow-melt run off and the color of 2 percent milk, we have no problem filling our six double rooms every day from April to October.

Of course, businesses like mine aren't the only ones who have benefited from "The Movie." Rod, reel, and other equipment manufacturers now run three shifts a day just to keep up with the demand. There are a dozen glossy, well-written magazines devoted exclusively to fly fishing. And you can find videos, self-help audiotapes, computer programs, and even a site on the World Wide Web. Orvis, the old Vermont company that runs the largest and most successful fly-fishing school in the world, is booked two sessions a day, seven days a week, from mid-April to the end of October at all five of their school locations. They alone pump out five thousand new fly rodders a year.

Just about all of it because of Robert Redford.

Today, the person you run into standing crotch-deep in a mountain stream stalking trout with a fly rod can be, and is, anyone and everyone, from doctors to lawyers to sports heroes to policemen. You might find a banker, bus driver, postal worker, garbage collector, Hollywood actor, or as I discovered one snowy evening last March, even the head of New England's most notorious crime family.

I was squatting on the hearth of the lodge's reading-room fireplace cooking four small venison steaks on an iron grate over the coals when I got the phone call.

It was Saturday night and, as she'd been doing for the last few weekends, Ruth Pearlman was staying with me at the lodge. Outside, a typical spring nor'easterly snowstorm roared around the lodge. It had started about three and by six it was coming down so thick you could barely see the yard. To look out the window now at the wall of swirling white, I found it hard to believe we'd be fishing in three weeks. Even Ruth's big Jeep Cherokee was just one more lump of white under the wind-whipped wet snow.

Ruth was curled in the corner of the big leather couch. Her short auburn hair still damp from the shower, she was wearing my blue terry-cloth robe over a faded pink flannel nightgown and dark green wool knee socks. She had gotten herself a glass of red wine and Spotter, my half English setter, half Labrador retriever, lay stretched out beside her, his black-and-white head in her lap. His eyes followed every movement I made with the steaks.

"Isn't this snow going to hurt all our wood, Max?" Ruth asked, referring to the lumber and Sheetrock sitting under tarpaulins in the yard.

"The tarps will protect it," I said.

In a move to better capitalize on the increasing popularity of fly fishing, we were putting an addition on Whitefork Lodge, adding four bedrooms and another bathroom upstairs in the back. I was learning that being your own contractor is not only hard work, it's a nightmare.

Initially, last fall, after finally getting the necessary permits, I hired the old Loon firm of Everett Martin & Sons to do the work. They're more expensive and slower than some of the builders I could have hired, but not only is Lyle—the son who now runs the company—a consummate craftsman and a friend, he and his crew of perfectionists are the ones who rebuilt Whitefork Lodge after the fire. As far as I was concerned, if the upstairs back wall had to be knocked out and the roof raised, I wanted it done by people who knew the building.

Everything had been going just fine until September. Then the problems began. First, the big spruce logs Lyle needed to match the existing exterior walls of the lodge were late in arriving from Canada. Then the historical-landmark designation we so eagerly had sought years before came around and bit us in the ass and Lyle and his crew had to stop while an antiquities committee at the State House debated the impact of our proposed changes. As soon as we got their okay to proceed, we found that Lyle had moved on to another job and we couldn't get him back for at least three weeks. Once he did come back, winter set in. The snow cover was a record one hundred and fifty inches by Christmas and costs began to skyrocket.

Last month, just as Lyle finally moved inside to begin boxing off the rooms in the big empty space behind the sheet of plastic at the top of the stairs, I ran out of money. Getting more from the bank didn't look promising. I had no choice but to try to finish the place myself.

Now every day my housekeeper Stormy Bryant, her brother Rayleen, and I run wiring, struggle with Sheetrock, and pound nails in an attempt to get the rooms finished by opening day of fishing season. Ruth sets aside the never-ending petty politics that are part of her job as the town of Loon's first woman mayor and comes out to help on weekends. We work long days and, although I've tried to keep everyone's spirits up, it had become pretty obvious that without Lyle's professional help we were never going to have the rooms done in time. As a result, I've been turning down reservations for the first week of the season.

Tonight we were tired and sore. I had painful blisters on my hands and Ruth, until her shower, had been covered with sawdust.

The venison I was cooking had been a gift from sheriff's deputy Billy Kendall. Arguably the best marksman and hunter in Loon County, Billy, as usual, had shot two deer the previous November. He was also a brownnoser and had given the deer to Ruth under the pretense it would cheer her up after losing her bid for governor in last fall's gubernatorial election. Jack's Mountain Meats had turned the fat young buck into four Loon Lager beer-case boxes full of assorted chops, steaks, roasts, and ground meat. Ruth, having nowhere to store it, gave it to Stormy, who stacked it in the lodge's big walk-in freezer to save for the day that we had guests who liked wild game.

Neither Ruth nor I are crazy about the taste of venison, but because of the unannounced snowstorm it was the only thing I had to serve that night other than tuna fish or oatmeal. I hoped that the marinade recipe we had found in one of Stormy's cookbooks and the smoke from the wood fire would make it at least palatable.

I had just flipped the meat and was poking at the orange coals under the grill with a pair of tongs when the phone began ringing.

"I'll get it, Max," Ruth said and put down her wine glass. She removed Spotter's head from her lap and padded out to the little narrow table in the hallway where we keep the phone as well as every piece of pocket junk that's carried into the lodge.

I could faintly hear her voice as she answered, and after a minute a louder, "Max? It's for you."

As I entered the hallway, I whispered, "Who?"

She shook her head and put her hand over the mouthpiece. "A man," she whispered. "He wouldn't give me his name. Just says it has to do with reservations for this season."

I took the phone and watched Ruth until she disappeared back into the reading room. "Hello. This is Max Addams."

His name was Donald Collingwood. "I hope I haven't called at a bad time, Mr. Addams." I couldn't place his accent.

I laughed and told him I always had time for someone making reservations.

He didn't seem amused. "I am chief legal counsel to Dantell Corporation in Rhode Island, Mr. Addams," he said. "I would assume you've heard of them."

I hadn't and I told him so. "But, then, there are a lot things we don't know about way up here in Vermont."

"Yes, of course." He cleared his throat. "Well, I've been instructed to obtain reservations at your lodge for Dantell's chairman, Vincent d'Antella, two of his business associates, and a friend. Mr. d'Antella's an avid fly fisherman, and although he usually does his fishing at a private ranch in Montana, this year because of certain business problems he has chosen to stay in New England.''

The name Vincent d'Antella meant no more to me than Dantell Corporation. I opened the drawer in the table. "What dates are you interested in?" I asked as I pulled out the lodge appointment book and opened it.

"Mr. d'Antella asked me to inquire about fishing early in the season."

I turned the pages of the book. "How early?" Just about every page had names scribbled on it, except, of course, the first couple of weeks in April.

"Well, due to commitments later in the summer, Mr. d'Antella plans to fish the first week of the season. That would be around the tenth of April in Vermont. Correct?"

"That's right." I closed the book. "But, I'm sorry, Mr. . . . ? I'm terrible with names.

"Collingwood. Donald Collingwood."

"Mr. Collingwood," I said. "I'm sorry but we're not going to be open the first week of the season this year."

He was silent for a few seconds. "May I ask why?" he finally said.

"We're doing some remodeling." I slid the appointment book back into the drawer. "It's cost us a bit more than we thought and, well, we ran out of money. We're having to finish it ourselves and it's taking longer than we thought."

"I see."

"I do have space later in the summer," I said hopefully, my hand still on the appointment book. "The last week in June looks good."

"No, I'm sorry, Mr. Addams. It is quite important that Mr. d'Antella fish the first week of the season."

"Have you tried John Mowraski's place?" John was a guide and fly-fishing instructor I liked. He had recently opened a small lodge ten miles north of us that took in fly fishermen. "He's right on the river and not a lot of people know about him yet. He might still have room."

"No, I haven't," he said. "And I doubt I will unless he also has a lake. Mr. d'Antella is interested in fishing your lake as much as the Whitefork River." The Whitefork River widened to form ten-acre Sweet Lake directly in front of my lodge.

"Well," I said, closing the drawer, "maybe next year."

"Yes, well, thank you, Mr. Addams. Sorry to bother you."

"No trouble. Hope you try again someday," I said and hung up.

Through no fault of Ruth's, the venison steaks turned out like leather hockey pucks and we left Spotter gnawing on them on the hearth and went to the kitchen to make a couple of tuna-fish-salad sandwiches. While she took a bowl and a can of Starkist from the cupboard, I dug out a jar of mayonnaise and a bottle of Loon Lager from the refrigerator. I sat on a stool at the big chopping-block center island, watched her open the can, and started to tell her about the phone call and how I had to turn down yet more business because of the remodeling when the phone rang again.

I got it on the third ring. It was Collingwood again. "I'm sorry to bother you again, Mr. Addams, but I've just talked to Mr. d'Antella and he insisted that I call you back. He is quite set on fishing at Whitefork Lodge the first week of the season."

"He is, huh?" I laughed. "I told you, I'm not open. The place is torn apart. No way can we can have it finished by . . ."

"Mr. d'Antella would like to know how much money it would take to get the lodge finished in time."

"He what?"

"Mr. d'Antella has suggested that I inquire about renting your entire lodge for his use that week. That way he would get the exclusive use of your waters and the privacy he and his party prefer. If you'll agree, you'd receive a large enough deposit up front to finish your construction."

"In other words, to fish here opening week he'll pay to get our rooms finished?"

"In a manner of speaking, yes. We would assume you'd use the deposit monies to finish your remodeling."

"Why is he so interested in Whitefork Lodge?"

"As I told you, Mr. Addams, Mr. d'Antella is an avid fly fisherman. He is accustomed to fishing in the very best locations. As I also told you, this year it is mandatory he and his party stay in New England. From what he has read and heard, Whitefork Lodge and its variety of water fit Mr. d'Antella's requirements."

I didn't know what to say.

"What do you think, Mr. Addams?" he asked. "Are you interested?"

"Of course, I'm interested," I said. "It's just that it's an unusual offer."

"Wanting to rent Whitefork Lodge for himself?"

"No. We've had guests rent the whole place before. We've had a couple corporate retreats. I've even had a television commercial shot here." I patted my empty breast pocket and wished I hadn't left my cigarettes in the kitchen. "It's just that . . . well, it's almost too good to be true. And you know what they say about that."

"I assure you, Mr. Addams, our offer is very serious."

"Well," I said, "if I can get back the carpenters we had before my money ran out, it might work."

"Is there a chance you might not be able to get them?"

"There's always that chance. There's quite a bit of construction going on in this area right now. We have a big convention coming to town that first week in April." I also knew for a fact that Lyle and his crew were laying new rock-maple bowling alleys at the Loon Bowl.

"But you'll try?"

"Yes. I'll call my carpenter first thing in the morning."

"I've done a little computing, Mr. Addams, and based upon the price list included in your brochure, for the exclusive use of all your rooms, meals for four people for seven days, some instruction for one of Mr. d'Antella's guests, and incidentals, I've arrived at a rough figure of five thousand dollars. Does that sound about right?''

I couldn't add that fast. ''It sounds all right,'' I said. ''I'll have to ask my housekeeper. She's the one who knows all the rates. But you mentioned instruction?''

''Yes, Mr. d'Antella's female friend would like to learn the fundamentals of fly fishing.''

''We charge hourly for instruction. People's learning abilities vary. There's no way I can estimate . . .''

''How much money will you need to finish your construction?''

That I knew. ''Three thousand dollars.''

''All right, Mr. Addams. If it's agreeable to you, why don't we leave it like this. I'll have a check cut for thirty-five hundred and will wait until I hear from you tomorrow about your contractors. If you can get them, I'll send the money via Federal Express and tell Mr. d'Antella that Whitefork Lodge is his for the first week of fishing season. Does that sound fair?''

I told him I thought it sounded quite fair.

''Then, while Mr. d'Antella's party is there, you can keep a tally of your services. Whatever accrues will be paid with the balance owed at the end of the week.''

I told him I thought that was fair too, and after agreeing to talk again late tomorrow morning, we hung up.

Ruth was still in the kitchen. She was sitting at the island eating a dribbling tuna-fish-salad sandwich. She gestured to the one she'd made for me. ''Sit down, Max, and try it. It's not bad''—she smiled—''considering I made it.''

I was too excited to sit down or eat, and instead, I told her all about Collingwood's offer.

When I finished, she licked a finger and said, ''You told him you weren't interested, of course.''

''No. I told him, yes. If I can get Lyle back here, I'm doing it.''

"Max." She brushed the shag of auburn bangs away from her forehead with the back of her hand and studied me. "You don't know who Vincent d'Antella is, do you?"

"Should I?"

"I don't believe it." She laughed derisively. "Vincent d'Antella is the head of New England's largest organized-crime family. Drugs. Prostitution. Extortion. Murder, probably." She was flabbergasted. "I'm amazed, Max. He was on the TV all last winter. Don't you watch anything besides fly-fishing videos?"

I ignored her jab. But, now that she mentioned it, I did remember seeing something on the eleven o'clock news about d'Antella. "Is that old guy who pleaded the Fifth three hundred times before that Senate committee?" I sat on the stool across from her.

"Exactly. And do you remember what he was refusing to talk about?"

I shook my head. "I just remember Peter Jennings saying something about it being close to a Guinness record." I smiled.

She didn't. "There's a war going on in southern New England, Max. A power struggle that your Vincent d'Antella is right in the center of. They want him out, but he won't go."

I sighed and picked up my unfinished beer. "Oh, give me a break, Ruth."

"You don't believe me?"

"Of course I believe you," I said. "But so what? All this guy wants to do here is fly fish."

Her green eyes flashed. "Max." She dropped the sandwich on her plate. "If he comes here, who knows what else will come with him?"

"Oh, c'mon."

"I'm serious, Max."

"Look, Ruth. So am I. I want to get the rooms upstairs finished. With d'Antella's deposit we can stop pounding nails and hire Lyle and his crew back. They'll have it done in a week.''

She stood. ''You can't let Whitefork Lodge be taken over by a bunch of thugs.''

''It's not being taken over by anyone,'' I said, draining the beer. ''He's only going to be here for seven days.''

She walked to the kitchen's swinging door and stood with her forehead against its round window. ''Don't do this to me, Max.''

''You? What am I doing to you?''

She spun around. ''You know what's going on at City Hall. And in town. Earl MacMillan and that CBL bunch of his will have a field day with this.'' She closed her eyes and sighed. ''Me, the mayor who they're already saying is soft on crime, associating with known criminals.''

''Wait a minute. You've lost me. How are you all of a sudden associating with . . . ?''

''You.'' She pointed her finger at me. ''You. You're my boyfriend. Everyone knows that. You rent this place to Vincent d'Antella and I might as well just endorse all the crime in town.'' Her finger was still pointing at me and now she shook it. ''Jeez, Max. This is all I need.'' She turned, pushed the door open with a fist, and stormed out of the room.

I watched the door until it stopped swinging back and forth. Then I got another beer, sat back on the stool, and lit a cigarette. I blew smoke at the ceiling. Damn politics.

City policy dictated that while Ruth campaigned for governor last year, her mayoral duties be shifted to City Council President Earl MacMillan. Earl, a dairy farmer and still part owner of Scotch Hill Dairy Farm, liked being in the mayor's office. More importantly, Loon's ultra-right, ultra-conservative good-old-boy politicos liked having him there. Under the guise of a so-called Citizens' Committee for a Better Loon, together they used Ruth's several months of absence to their advantage. As a result, she returned to find that most of the liquor licenses, land-use deals, and service bids she had vehemently opposed had been spirited through the temporary mayor's office in the name of "Community Betterment." And, if that wasn't bad enough, Earl had now officially declared his candidacy and he and his CBL cronies had begun to do everything in their power to make sure that it would be he who became mayor next election and not Ruth. The CBL platform is simple: Stop the epidemic of crime in Loon.

I wouldn't call it an "epidemic," but like so many small communities in the country, the town of Loon isn't immune to its own versions of big-city lawlessness. Petty theft, spousal abuse, and drugs seem to be the norm these days. Since Ruth's return to office, it's gotten a little out of hand and there isn't a morning when the town doesn't awaken to read about another car theft, break-in, assault, or burglary. Ruth blames the area's high unemployment rate. Earl MacMillan and the CBL, of course, are openly accusing Ruth and her "light hand of naïve female leadership" as being at the root of it all.

"What Loon needs is the hard-nosed brand of get-tough policies only a man can provide," Earl has been telling everyone who will listen. "We have to show these thugs that we mean business and that the town of Loon will not tolerate this kind of flagrant disregard for life and property. We have to send this filth back where it came from."

As head of many of the departments in town, he has begun making it look like he's not just talking. He has lobbied for increases in the pay for the Sheriff's Department and his fire-chief buddies, hired an expensive "crime consultant" supposedly with his own money, and the other day after a homeless man was found stabbed to death in a doorway, Earl jammed temporary legislation through the City Council that repealed Ruth's firearms ordinance and made it legal again to carry any kind of gun within the city limits. As she said sadly a few days after losing the battle, "It's worse than it ever was, Max. The town looks like an armed camp. Every pickup has a rifle or shotgun in its back window again and I've even seen parents picking up their children at school wearing pistols on their hips.''

To me, Earl and the CBL are so transparently political that I find it hard to understand why so many Loon citizens are buying into it. " 'Course you don't understand, Max,'' Stormy says. "You live way out here. But to folks in town this menace is somethin' else. They don't like havin' to lock their doors at night and worry 'bout their loved ones turnin' up raped or stabbed. Earl and them CBL bozos have hit a nerve. And they make it look like they're doin' somethin' 'bout it too.''

I sighed. I knew it was hard for Ruth right now. But it wasn't easy for me either and I really could make good use of d'Antella's money. I doubted my fly-fishing guest would make things any tougher for her than they already were. In the past, no one ever had cared who fished at Whitefork Lodge. Why would this season be any different?

I picked up our plates, grabbed two more Loon Lagers, and carried it all on a tray to the reading room.

Ruth was sitting at my fly-tying table staring into what was left of the fire. Spotter was on the hearth, still diligently gnawing on the leathery venison, and from the looks of it, his old blunt teeth weren't making much progress.

I set the tray in front of her. "Fire's almost out,'' I said.

"Sorry.'' She shook her head as if to clear it. "I wasn't paying attention.'' She pushed the tray away. "I'm not hungry anymore either, Max.''

I crouched beside Spotter and arranged three birch logs on the coals. As the papery bark on the dry wood began to crackle with flame, I looked up at her. "You're not going to tell me that this d'Antella thing is going to ruin our weekend.''

"You have to tell him no, Max."

"Dammit, Ruth," I said. "Earl MacMillan and his CBL might have you walking on eggs, but not me. I'm not going to let anyone tell me who I can or cannot do business with."

"Earl MacMillan isn't telling you," she said. "I'm the one asking."

"As far as I can see, it's the same thing."

"Oh, God, why are you always so stubborn?" She sighed, looking away. "Why do you always have to take the opposite side?"

"Opposite?" I looked back into the fire. "All I want is the new rooms finished."

"So we'll finish them," she said. "We can do it, Max."

I shook my head. "You know as well as I do, we're weeks from having them done doing it ourselves."

"What about your loan? It'll come through."

"Yeah, sure." I'd applied for an increase in my credit line at the Loon Cooperative Bank but was told that because I was behind in the interest payments on the original amount, my chances of getting any more were practically zero. "I have a better chance of hitting the lottery."

She sighed and put her head in her hands.

I stared into the fire.

Ruth and I met just after I bought Whitefork Lodge. I was forty and she just twenty-five. We both had been recently divorced. We dated about a year and then sort of slipped apart for several years while my business grew and she pursued a career in law and politics. About a year after she became Loon's mayor, we rediscovered each other and for the past couple years have spent as much time as we can find together.

I stood and put my hands on her upper arms. "It's not going to happen for a few weeks and then d'Antella will only be here a week. He wants the whole place to himself. No one will be here except him. How's anyone even going to know he's here?"

"Somehow they'll find out."

"From who? Stormy?" I tipped her chin up and looked her in the eyes. "Or do you think I'm going to tell someone?"

She shrugged.

"You know what this can do for me, Ruth." I kissed her forehead.

"Yes." She sighed. "I also know what it could do to me."

I leaned to kiss her again but the phone rang before my lips got there. She hung her head. "Maybe it's Saddam Hussein this time," I heard her say as I walked into the hallway. "Maybe he wants the week after d'Antella."

It wasn't. It was for her. "Some guy," I whispered as I handed her the phone. "Said he wants to talk to the mayor. He sounds pissed." I left her talking in the hall and went back to the sandwiches.

Ruth's about five-foot-five, with a shag of coppery auburn hair feathered around her grass-green eyes, a sprinkle of freckles across her nose, and a dancer's figure she jogs ten miles a day to maintain. As if that's not enough, Ruth loves fly-fishing almost as much as I do and has the most graceful cast I've ever watched. She's funny, businesslike, and sexy all at the same time and I know if one of our long conversations were to turn to the subject of getting married, I'd be hard-pressed to find an excuse not to.

Fortunately, marriage is something neither of us have time for right now. For me, the possibility of becoming a father again just as I'm learning to cope with being a grandfather for the first time isn't exactly a turn-on.

When she rejoined me, her lips were a tight straight line.

I held her plate out to her. "Problems?"

"Yes." She took the plate and stared at it.

"What could possibly be wrong at"—I looked at my watch—"ten o'clock at night?"

"Snow removal," she said. "That was Pete Brock."

"Pete who?"

"He's head of the Loon DPW." She sighed. "Mac-Millan has made him and his crew plow the sidewalks downtown."

I frowned. "I thought you set it up last winter that shop-keepers would shovel their own sidewalks." I took a bite of my sandwich. It was getting soggy. "It's an ordinance, isn't it?"

"Yes." She nodded. "And a very unpopular one." She sat on the edge of the couch and balanced the plate on her knee. "According to Pete, Earl was out there tonight with Easty Flint supervising the whole thing." Easton Flint I knew. Besides being president of the Loon Chamber of Commerce, he was chairman of the Citizens' Committee for a Better Loon. "The *Sentinel* was there too," she said. "Taking pictures."

"I assume you read this Pete guy the riot act."

She shrugged. "What could I say? It wasn't Pete's fault. Technically, as president of the City Council, Earl's his immediate boss. Pete just did what he was told. Besides, I wasn't there, Earl was."

"But you're the mayor, not MacMillan."

She slowly shook her head. "It doesn't make any difference, Max. Right now, all I am is that bitch who won't use city funds to shovel the sidewalks."

"But, how can MacMillan just go and . . . ?"

"Easty will have an excuse. Net net is, they got it done and now Earl will be a hero."

I sighed.

"This is a perfect example of the problem I've got, Max." She looked up at me. "Don't you see? Every chance they get from now until the election they're going to try to make me look bad. And when my boyfriend brings crime boss Vincent d'Antella into town for a week of private fly-fishing, they'll have a field day." She stood and ran her hand through her hair. "I'm tired, Max. I'll have to go in to town first thing in the morning and clear this thing up. If I can.'' She stepped across the room and handed me her plate. ''I'm going to bed. Okay?''

She didn't kiss me good night and I watched her walk out of the room. I looked down at Spotter. The venison steaks were gone and he was carefully licking the hearth bricks between his paws. ''Maybe we'd better sleep in here,'' I said to him, taking a bite from a sandwich.

He slowly raised his head and gave me one of his more-incredulous looks.

''You're right,'' I said quickly. ''That's a dumb idea. We haven't done anything wrong.''

My daughter Sabrina and her husband gave me an antique Seth Thomas schoolroom clock to replace the one we lost when the fire destroyed the original Whitefork Lodge a few years ago. It hangs on the hallway wall above the telephone, surrounded by a rogues' gallery of framed pictures of smiling guests releasing trout. It was just beginning to bong eleven when I banked the fire, placed the screen in front, and stood with my back to the heat, finishing my last cigarette of the day. Then I clicked off the lights.

Spotter had gone out in the snow to the toilet fifteen minutes earlier and now stood in a patch of moonlight on the other side of the hallway at the closed door to my bedroom. He looked at me and yawned.

I carefully opened the door, trying not to awaken Ruth. But Spotter, his toenails clicking loudly on the wide pine boards, trotted in around me, and after two quick turns, plopped with a sigh on the thick braided rug at the foot of the bed. I think he was asleep before I stepped out of my jeans.

The lodge creaked as the temperature dropped and cold settled into the thick log walls. It had stopped snowing and the half-moon outside over the lake illuminated the old, wavy glass in the windows and spread milky white rectangles on the bed. As I slid into the warmth under the thick quilt, Ruth rolled quickly to my side and pressed herself against me. She was naked except for the heavy wool knee socks. She shivered. "It's cold."

I stayed on my back and put my arm under her head, trying not to touch her warm, bare skin with my cold hands. "I thought you'd be asleep."

"I can't. I've been lying here thinking."

"Don't worry. Vincent d'Antella will be long gone before anyone even knows he was here. You'll see."

"That's not what I've been thinking about." She tipped her head back and the moonlight washed over her face. Her green eyes seemed lit from behind. "I wonder if any of it's worth it, Max. What am I trying to prove?"

"I didn't think you were trying to prove anything. You're the mayor."

"It's just that everyone talks about wanting things better, but when you get right down to it, no one wants to try the changes we need to make things better." She sighed. "I mean, I won this job as mayor by the largest margin of votes ever. You remember what the exit polls showed?"

I nodded. Her research showed that for the first time in Loon history, not only did women vote in record numbers, they voted differently than the men.

"So, where did all those women go? Where are they now? It's like they'll speak out only in the privacy of the voting booth." She sighed again and rolled onto her back. "I'm so damn tired of fighting alone."

"I know."

She leaned up on one elbow and looked down at me. "But, dammit, everyone in this town seems determined to keep us in the 1930s. We have a firearm-related injury every week and yet they want their guns in their cars and pickups. They're still handing out liquor licenses like leaflets and we've got one of the highest alcoholism rates in the state. A request from the Vermont Teachers' Association to hold their annual meeting here gets turned down by the City Council, but in three weeks we're opening our arms to a bunch of microbrewers. What's that telling our children, Max?''

I've learned that usually when Ruth asks me a question she isn't looking for a solution. She simply wants me to listen. So I didn't say anything and we both were quiet for a few minutes. Finally she said, ''I'm sorry about tonight. I've lost a lot of control in town and I guess I was just trying to get some back by bullying you.'' Ruth pulled her knees higher and hugged herself to me. ''Who you choose to have out here at the lodge is your business. My problems go much deeper than that.''

''Still,'' I said, ''you were right about what Earl and the CBL could do.''

''I'm hoping you're right that they won't find out.''

''Well,'' I said, ''I intend to do everything in my power to make sure they don't.''

''I know.'' She slid a warm, smooth thigh up on my belly.

''Hey,'' I said. ''What's this?''

She rolled up on top of me and straddled my hips. ''We've never gone to sleep angry at each other,'' she whispered, leaning in and kissing me, ''and we're not going to start tonight.'' The covers fell from her shoulders as she slowly sat upright. Her naked torso was suddenly bathed in the blue-white moonlight. She looked like she'd been dipped in skim milk.

''You should have tried this earlier.'' I gripped her small waist and smiled up at her. ''I'd agree to anything now.''

''I don't want your agreement.'' She leaned over me, holding herself on outstretched arms. Her breasts brushed my lips. ''Just be there if I need you.''

''I'm here.''

''I can tell.'' She slid a hand between her thighs and I felt her fingers find and guide me into her. Then she closed her eyes and twisted her hips. My hands moved to her buttocks and then, as they slowly started to rise and fall under my palms, her mouth found mine and the bed began to creak.

As we lost ourselves in each other in the moonlight, neither of us could have imagined the betrayal, death, and pain our decisions that night would cause.

CHAPTER ✦ TWO

I awoke with Spotter's nose inches from my face, an almost palpable cloud of warm "venison breath" making me hold mine until I could sit up and swing my legs over the side of the bed.

Ruth lifted her head, looked at the clock on the bedside table, and then reburied herself in the covers. "Wake me in an hour," she mumbled. It was six-thirty.

I pulled on my jeans and a sweatshirt, stepped into my old moosehide slippers, and I went out into the hall where I let Spotter out the front door. I stood there behind the glass of the storm door, squinting against the glare of the sun on the fresh snow and watched him bound out through the deep, wet drifts toward the small log barn by the lake we refer to as the workshop. Although much of the snow would be melted by noon, it was a beautiful, picture-postcard morning. Even the tiniest branches were delicately stacked with light, fluffy white, transforming the tangle of birch, maple, and beech trees along the river into a wall of intricate lace. The spruce and hemlocks wore thick robes of it, and except for one window and a corner of a log wall, the guest cabin we had built on the granite ledge overlooking the river was buried in roof-high drifts. A pair of chickadees nervously flitted in under the porch roof, circled, and finding the bird feeder Stormy had hanging there covered with snow, sped off back out across the rolling white toward the woods.

I closed the inner door and, like I do every morning, went into the dining room to make the morning fire and a pot of coffee. Our two fireplaces and the foundation are the only parts of the lodge that were left standing after the fire. The rest of the original 1908 Whitefork Lodge burned to the ground.

It had been built by a Boston shipping tycoon and grandson of Daniel Webster named Thornton Randolph Webster. Like many well-to-do city people at the turn of the century, Thornton wanted a comfortable, rustic-yet-elegant retreat from the sweltering city for his family and friends and he succeeded. He hired the then-famous Adirondack-style architect Wellesly Hinton to design it and when Ruth stumbled upon the old blueprints in the city-hall archives after the fire, with Lyle's help, we copied them almost exactly.

Like the old lodge, the new Whitefork sits on the highest ground on the point where the Whitefork River widens to become Sweet Lake. It is a massive rectangle. Two stories of interlocking logs with a covered porch that runs along the front, it faces west out over the lake. It has giant shuttered windows, two walk-in fieldstone fireplaces, wide, rough-sawn board floors, and beamed ceilings. Webster had spared no expense in the original's construction and, thanks to our fire insurance and a bank loan, we didn't have to either. We found giant old-growth spruce being cut in Canada, so like the original, the new Whitefork is built of three-foot-in-diameter peeled logs flattened by hand on the indoor surfaces and chinked with river clay mixed with straw.

Ruth got us the historic-landmark designation from the state, and the architectural-restoration specialists they sent up to Loon from Montpelier helped Lyle and his crew set the new building on the original riprap foundation of cut and fitted granite boulders. Despite the fact that everything from the foundation up is new, Stormy still claims she can smell the acrid odor of charred timbers.

Untreated wood ages fast and now the new rooms under the big log beams that span the high ceilings are finally getting the weathered look and hand-worn feel of the old lodge. The period furnishings we bought help too. Guests seem to like climbing into the high, carved fruitwood beds and prefer the stately, mirror-fronted armoires to closets. The downstairs has plenty of deep wingback chairs and Oriental rugs, and the walls, like the original lodge, are cluttered with oil and watercolor paintings of fishing scenes as well as the obligatory stuffed trout, deer, and bear heads. Other than the new bathrooms, my apartment, Stormy's more modern kitchen, and the new rooms we're building upstairs, even old Thornton Webster might have a hard time telling that the new Whitefork Lodge isn't the place he built for his family all those years ago.

The coffee gurgled, hissed, and steamed to a finish and I poured myself a mug, arranged three apple-wood logs on the now-crackling kindling, and went to the kitchen to clean up the tuna-fish mess from last night. Stormy and Rayleen would be here at seven to start working upstairs, and although she never said as much, I know she hates to start the day with dirty dishes in the sink.

Just like the original Whitefork Lodge, the first floor of the new one is cut into four basic living areas. My apartment and its bathroom look out over the porch and lake on the left front. The dining room does the same on the right. The hallway runs straight back down the middle from the front door, the full depth of the building. At the back on the right, a doorway leads to the reading room and a small storage room. Another door, just forward of that on the same wall, opens onto the stairs to the cellar. The open stairs to the second floor are in front of that. Stormy and I had fought over the placement of the new kitchen. She wanted it moved from the back-left corner of the downstairs, to up front, across from the dining room.

"Just makes sense, Max," she said. "It should be closer to where folks is eatin'."

I didn't agree. I wanted to be able to look out over the lake from my bedroom. "Besides," I said, "if having the kitchen back there was good enough for Thornton Webster, why should we be any different?"

"Them days," she said, "hotsy-totsies like that had servants to carry all the food down the hall."

I wasn't going to give up my view of the lake, so I had to promise that her new kitchen would have an eight-burner stove, walk-in freezer/pantry, Du Pont Corian counters, a butcher-block food-preparation island, and the two-way swinging door with a round window at eye level before she'd even listen. Then it took a thousand dollars' worth of copper French cookware to get her to agree.

After cleaning up the kitchen, I took Ruth a cup of coffee.

She was already up and in the shower and I set the mug on the back of the toilet. She looked like an impressionistic watercolor behind the wet, pebbly-textured glass of the shower-stall door. The aroma of her herbal shampoo hung in the steamy air.

I put the toilet lid down and sat. "Are you going to wait for Stormy and have some breakfast?"

"No," she said, bending and soaping her feet. "I'll get a bagel or something in town."

"Are you coming back tonight?"

"I don't know." She turned, and tipping her head back, she rinsed the conditioner from her short hair. "But I doubt it. I don't think I'll be very good company anyway."

I laughed. "You finally turned into pretty good company last night."

"Consider yourself lucky." She wiped the haze from the glass and looked out at me. "What do you think Stormy's going to say about having someone like d'Antella around?"

"She hates this mess," I said. "She wants those rooms finished more than I do."

Ruth turned and let the spray hit the back of her neck. "What about Bendel?" Stormy's husband, Bendel, worked for me as a guide during the season.

"Bendel'll love having the guy here. A new face to photograph." Bendel had been a professional photographer when he and Stormy met, so just naturally became the official Whitefork Lodge photographer. In fact, last year we selected twelve of his color shots of the river and had a printer down in Brattleboro turn them into a calendar. Stormy and I mailed them to clients instead of Christmas cards. The two dozen or so that remained were on sale at half-price in what I call the "Shelf Shop" in the reading room, where I also sell tippet, leader, flies I've tied, fly floatant, and Whitefork Lodge patches and T-shirts.

Ruth squeaked off the water and opened the door. "Bendel's due back this weekend, isn't he?" Her normally ivory colored skin was pink.

I nodded and handed her a towel. Bendel had been taking a few freelance assignments during the winter to help us out and was just finishing a catalog photo shoot in New York City. He would be back in Vermont next Friday.

She pressed the towel to her wet breasts. "That coffee for me?"

I handed her the mug and went out into the bedroom, where I threw the quilt up over the bed. There are few things in this world that make less sense to me than making beds. As I jammed the pillows under the quilt, I heard Rayleen's old green International pickup sputter and clank up to the front of the lodge.

I went to the window and peered out. He had the big yellow plow attached to the front and a mountain of snow preceded it. They had obviously dropped the blade just as they turned off of Route 16 and then plowed their way down the lodge's access road. There were a dozen paper grocery bags stacked in the snowy bed behind the cab. I could see Stormy in the passenger seat, and from the glower on her face, today's trip to the lodge, like every day's, had turned into an argument.

The passenger door swung open and Stormy, the morning paper in one hand and a lever-action Winchester thirty-thirty in the other, climbed from truck to the snowy porch. She said something to Rayleen I couldn't hear and then slammed the door. Hard.

Barking puffs of vapor, Spotter came bounding up from the woods through the drifts on the lawn and I watched Stormy stomp the snow from her Bean boots and then stoop to greet the old dog. Meanwhile Rayleen backed up, lowered the plow blade, and began carefully and expertly pushing the deep snow from the area immediately behind Ruth's buried car.

Now that Stormy's married, she and Bendel have taken over the family house in town and Rayleen has moved into a large one-bedroom apartment above the Loon Lanes bowling alleys. He seems quite happy with the arrangement. He says he likes to bowl, but I suspect it's the easy access to the Lanes' little bar that actually really appeals to him.

Toweling her hair, Ruth came up behind me and looked out the window. "They sure are characters, aren't they?" She smiled affectionately.

They are characters all right. To look at them you'd never know they are brother and sister. Or even remotely related. In her late sixties, Stormy is the oldest. A recovering alcoholic who hasn't had a drink in fifteen years, she looks the youngest by at least a decade. Where she's plump, pink, and almost bursting with good health, Rayleen is thin, his face gouged with lines. It's as if he's the one—not her—who used to drink a quart of vodka by noon and now squints through the smoke of two packs of unfiltered Camels a day. Although they're both barely five feet tall, the wooden prosthesis that Rayleen wears gives

him a stooping limp that makes him seem even shorter—
the result of a wartime injury. Stormy wears what seems
like an endless collection of flowing, colorful print caftans
and rarely laced, sixteen-inch Bean boots. I've never seen
Rayleen in anything but a red plaid wool shirt and dun-
garee overalls. I can always tell what kind of day he's
having by the way he wears the greasy baseball cap that
never leaves his head. Both have the same coarse, steel-
gray hair, but where Stormy's is plaited into a long, thick
rope of a braid that sways down the middle of her back,
his tufts uncontrollably out above his ears and through the
little air holes in the cap like feathers leaking from a cheap
pillow.

"I wonder," Ruth said over her shoulder as she walked
back into the bathroom, "if that newspaper of Stormy's
has a story about last night's plowing." She shut the door
and I heard the hum of my electric toothbrush.

I stepped out into the hallway just as Stormy stomped
inside and shut the door. I was going to announce my
good news but she was already talking. "Told that old
fart Rayleen to just let the damn snow melt, but he won't
listen," she said, handing me the paper and setting the
Winchester against the wall. "Wants to plow before we
unload them groceries." She pulled off her parka and
hung it on one of the pegs we have in the beam by the
door. "Channel 32 weatherman last night said this stuff'll
be gone by noon."

"What's open for groceries this early?" I asked, pointing through the window at the bags bouncing in the bed
of the truck. I decided I'd wait until I had them both together before I told them about d'Antella.

She bent and unlaced her boots. "Super Shop's open
twenty-four hours now," she said, kicking one, then the
other into the corner. "Where're my house shoes?"

I shrugged. "In the kitchen, I think."

"My bet is they go back to regular hours, though." She
grabbed the rifle by the barrel, pushed by me, and started

down the hall with Spotter stepping on the heels of her bright red wool socks. "Be safer. All the robberies we got in town." Today's caftan was a gaudy yellow-and-black geometric print. "You feed the dog?" she asked over her shoulder.

"No. He just went out." I followed them.

"Ruth up? She gonna want breakfast too?"

"She's not staying this morning," I said as we pushed through the swinging door. "Some things are going on in town she has to take care of."

Stormy went to the back door, stood on her tiptoes, and hung the rifle on the gun rack we had up there for that purpose. The old, scuffed penny loafers she called her house shoes were in the corner. "Bet Ruth has things to take care of," she snorted, stepping into the loafers. "That damn Earl MacMillan converted another couple dozen folks to his side last night."

"You mean, the sidewalk plowing?"

She nodded and gestured to the newspaper I still had in my hand. "Front page of this mornin's *Sentinel*," she said.

"Kind of early for the rifle, isn't it?" I said. Usually Stormy didn't bring the Winchester until May, when the vegetable garden we had outside the back door was fully planted and the new shoots were most vulnerable to varmints.

"Seen them woodchucks out already," she said. "Soon as this snow's gone, I'm setting out my peas, and this year them overgrown rats ain't gonna eat all my hard work."

While she opened a can of dog food for Spotter I opened the newspaper.

Since being converted to computer by founder Gordon Miller's son, Gordon Junior, our once-quaint weekly newspaper, the *Loon Sentinel*, had become a slick-looking, tabloid-size daily complete with color photographs, national advertising, and an irritating sensational style of reporting. Under a banner headline that read "DOWNTOWN

SAYS NO TO SELF-SHOVELED SNOW,'' there was a color picture of two large smiling men in hooded parkas standing on each side of a smaller man. They were on a sidewalk in downtown Loon. It was dark and obviously taken last night. Behind them, lit by the big display windows of Sam's Sporting Goods store and what I assumed to be the camera's flash, two men in orange coveralls were barely visible behind rooster tails of snow from the snow blowers they pushed. The caption under the picture read, ''Putting your tax dollars where they'll do the most good are (L to R), City Council President Earl MacMillan, CBL Chairman Easty Flint, and Deputy Sheriff William Kendall.'' Under that was a subhead over the story: ''MAC AND EASTY CHALLENGE MAYOR'S ORDINANCE 14.''

I tapped the paper. ''You read this?''

Stormy straightened slowly from putting Spotter's dish of food on the floor. ''Just them headlines,'' she said, lighting one of her stumpy unfiltered Camels, and leaning back against the stove. ''Read it to me. I'd like to hear what that little brat Gordon's got to say.''

I read out loud, ''The snow hit the fan last night when Loon retailers, fed up with the inconvenience of Mayor Pearlman's Ordinance 14, took matters into their own hands. Led by Citizens Committee for a Better Loon Chairman Easton Flint and City Council President Earl MacMillan, retailers enlisted the aid of several DPW employees and town equipment and plowed Main Street sidewalks in clear defiance of Mayor Ruth Pearlman's controversial Ordinance 14. Deputy Sheriff William Kendall and two other members of the Loon County Sheriff's Department provided traffic control during the two-hour process.

''When questioned by this reporter about possible repercussions from the mayor's office concerning Ordinance 14, Easton Flint would only say, 'I think we have a special circumstance here. It's been snowing for three days. Retailers have enough to do these days just protecting their businesses. In my estimation, Ordinance 14 doesn't apply.'

"Earl MacMillan, Mayor Pro Tem while Mayor Pearlman was campaigning for governor last year, put it a different way, 'The inflexibility of Ordinance 14 is just one more example of how out of touch Ruth Pearlman is with the needs of a community like Loon. Leaving retail establishments untended to shovel sidewalks is simply an invitation to criminals. And, as is so typical of her, she could not be found this evening to consult on this problem. Therefore, as City Council president, I made the decision I felt was in the best interest of the safety of my town, the retail community, and my law-abiding neighbors.'

"Deputy Sheriff Kendall saw the plowing from a different perspective. 'Our department needs access to these businesses,' he said. 'If we're to have any effect on this crime wave in the downtown area, we can't have our response time thwarted by several feet of unshoveled wet snow.' "

"Will you listen to that little snot nose Billy Kendall," Stormy said. "Just 'cause Sheriff Ralston's laid up don't give him no call to mouth off." Sheriff Benjamin Ralston had broken both of his legs after losing control of his cruiser in a high-speed chase last winter. Originally in Loon Memorial, he'd been moved to the big hospital down in Montpelier when his compound fractures weren't knitting properly. "The people poor Ruth has to put up with . . ."

"Is that about last night?" Pointing at the newspaper, Ruth pushed through the swinging door into the kitchen. Her hair was still damp. She wore a pair of tan heavy-wool slacks tucked into knee-high laced leather boots. The collar of a pale blue turtleneck protruded from a dark blue cable-knit sweater. She came up behind me and put her hands on my shoulders. "What's it say?" I could feel her breasts on my back.

I pushed the paper out where she could see the headline.

"Oh, damn," she said. "I was afraid of this."

"Max was just readin' it," Stormy said. "Start over, Max."

I felt Ruth shake her head. "No." She backed away. "I'll read it in town. I just came in to say hello, Stormy." She backed up to the swinging door. "And now, good-bye." She smiled weakly. "I have to run."

"It ain't nothin' you can't handle, honey," Stormy said.

"I hope." She stepped through the door and held it open. She looked at me. "You tell her yet, Max?"

"Haven't had the chance."

She looked at Stormy. "You think I've got problems now, wait until you hear what's happening around here in a couple of weeks." Then she let the door swing closed and I could hear her footsteps going down the hall toward the front door.

"Go help her clear that snow from her car," Stormy said. "And then, git right back in here and tell me what she's talkin' about."

I grabbed some gloves and joined Ruth out at her Jeep. While she started it, I cleared the soft, deep snow from her hood, windshield, and rearview mirrors. When the engine was idling smoothly, she rolled down the driver's side window. "Call me," she said with a laugh, "if Stormy talks you out of this thing."

"Fat chance of that." I leaned over and kissed her.

"Just remember, Max"—she put the Jeep in reverse—"I'm counting on you. I'd like this thing with d'Antella not to get out."

There was nothing more I could say, so I just stood there with snow melting puddles in my slippers and watched as she cranked up the window and gunned the engine. Her wheels spun and howled on the ice and then she fishtailed out of the yard and roared up the newly plowed access road.

I got another cup of coffee and took it into the kitchen, where I sat back down at the island. Stormy was in the pantry rearranging the shelves. I could only see her rear end protruding from the door as she bent to the lower shelves. "So, what's this thing Ruth's talkin' about?" she said. "From the look on her face, I'd say she ain't crazy 'bout it."

As I told her about Collingwood's phone call and renting the entire lodge to d'Antella, she slowly backed out of the pantry. By the time I got to the part about the thirty-five hundred dollars up front so we could finish the upstairs, she was standing across from me, her thick forearms crossed over her bosom.

"No wonder Ruth looks upset," she said, pulling a pack of Camels from her caftan pocket. "Town's got enough crime without you bringing it in."

"That's what she said. I'm not bringing any crime in. The guy just wants to fly fish."

She took a cigarette from the pack, stuck it in the corner of her mouth, clinked open her old Zippo, and lit it. "Gotta believe trouble follows his kind, Max."

"I thought you'd be as happy as I am about the money," I said. "Now we can get Lyle and his crew in here and finish those rooms."

"I am happy 'bout the money, Max." She squinted through the smoke at her rough hands. "And my poor, old hands'll sure be happy. But Ruth's right about Mac-Millan." She exhaled a thick cloud of smoke. "He can turn somethin' like this into a damn circus."

"How's he going to know?"

She shrugged. "How's anybody know anythin' in this town? They just do." She stuck the cigarette back in her mouth, turned, and went to the sink. " 'Sides, that little Gordon Miller can smell somethin' like this a mile off." She chuckled and looked at me over her shoulder. "Hell, would surprise me if he didn't know already."

I knew that was impossible. "Ruth wanted me to call them back and tell them no."

Stormy shrugged. "Makes sense to me." Smoke curled around her head.

"It's not right."

" 'Course it's right." She turned and faced me. "We need a mayor like Ruth more than we need them extra rooms done upstairs." She ashed the cigarette in the quahog-shell ashtray in front of me.

"Well, I'm not going to do it."

She shrugged. "It's your lodge, Max Addams. Your girlfriend too. You wanta have Al Capone spendin' a week here fishin', ain't much I can say about it." She narrowed her eyes. "Just don't lose that little girl over it."

"I'm not going to lose her," I mumbled. "She'll see. He'll be in and out of here before anyone knows any different."

She went to the refrigerator, opened it, and took out a dozen eggs and a slab of unsliced cob-smoked bacon. "So, this Collingwood tell you who the three others comin' are?"

I shook my head. "He just said they're two business associates and a friend."

She laughed. "Bodyguards and some bimbo, I'll bet." She pulled a long knife from the rack on the counter. "How hungry are you?"

I shrugged.

"We'll have cheddar omelets 'n' bacon in 'bout thirty minutes." She began cutting thick slices from the bacon. "When you gonna call Lyle?"

I looked at my watch. "Better go do it now." I stood. "Heard from Bendel yet?" Bendel usually called every night when he was away. This trip, no one had heard from him since last week.

"Last night finally," she said, cracking six of the eggs into an aluminum bowl. "Says he's almost done."

"I bet he'll be happy to hear about the money. No more freelance this year."

"Dunno 'bout that," she said, whipping the eggs with a fork. "Think the old lech still likes bein' around all them girls in their underwear."

"Underwear? I thought this was a bathing-suit catalog."

"Look like undies to me." She tossed the fork in the sink.

I laughed. "You're not telling me you're jealous, are you?"

She didn't answer.

There was a thump and Rayleen, carrying two bags of groceries, backed through the swinging door into the kitchen. His cap was pushed back on his head, the bill sticking proudly in the air. "Plowin's done." He set the bags heavily on the island. He looked at Stormy. "Perishable stuff's in these." He turned to me. "Gimme a hand with the rest, huh, Max? I shoveled the porch."

After I pulled on a pair of boots and a jacket, Rayleen and I made four trips from the truck to the kitchen. It was already warmer outside than when Ruth left, and every trip inside we had to dodge through a beaded curtain of ice water falling from the eaves. Stormy set aside the breakfast preparations and was putting things away as fast as we brought them in.

When everything was out of the truck, Rayleen and I took off our boots and coats at the front door and I told him about d'Antella and the money.

"Well, I never heard of him," Rayleen said, unwinding his muffler, "but I ain't gonna complain neither. I'm getting too old for carryin' that Sheetrock anyways."

"Will you call Lyle for me?" I stepped back into my slippers. "See how soon he can put a crew together and get out here? I want the place finished before the season starts."

He raised a bushy gray eyebrow and the creases in his leathery forehead trebled. "Dunno whether Lyle's gonna be able to get right to it, though. Him and mosta his boys

FLY FISHING CAN BE FATAL ≈ 35

is still tied up down't'a the Loon Bowl. Tryin' to get the alleys in 'fore the big beer-makers' convention next month.''

"See what you can do, huh? As long as he can get it done by April tenth.''

He nodded and sniffed the air. You could smell the bacon Stormy was cooking. "I'll call him directly after breakfast, Max.''

We started toward the kitchen. "From what I was told last night, there are going to be four people in d'Antella's party,'' I said. "And, since it sounds like at least one of them needs lessons, you and Bendel will have to decide who does the teaching that week.''

He stopped and, screwing the cap bill down over his eyes, looked at me. "Ain't gonna be me, Max.''

"Why?''

"Told you 'fore Christmas I wasn't gonna be here for openin' day.''

"What?''

"Gotta church retreat, Max. Be gone to midweek. Been planning it since November. And I told ya, least once. Goin' up to Montreal and be baptized again.''

I nodded. I remembered. "The Tears thing, right?''

"Yep. Sacrament of the Tears. Gonna get dipped in the Almighty's own water.'' Ever since the near-death experience in which he lost his right leg, Rayleen has always flirted with one religion or another. And he isn't alone.

In the ten-plus years I've lived up here I've watched our part of northern Vermont become a hotbed of fundamentalist Christian teaching. "God botherers,'' Stormy calls them. Ruth, who has lived up here all her life, says that it started in the sixties with the hippies and their refusal to go to Vietnam. "They ran to Canada,'' she said. "After a while, they got homesick and slowly drifted back down across the border. Old-time Vermonters didn't hassle them, so they set up communes and stayed. Most of

them are in their forties and fifties with families and
homes up here now, and to them, these people and their
crazy religions are entitled to the same tolerance they received.''

I guess the word spread because every loosely organized group from Louisiana to L.A. claiming a direct line
to the Almighty gave northern Vermont a try. Some, like
Rayleen's group, The Lord's Workers, are solvent enough
to lease space in one of the many old, empty brick-factory
buildings in town. Others, like the Bible-thumping Wit-
nesses for the Cross and God's Chosen, pitch big tents in
local farmers' hayfields all summer. When the weather
turns cold, they move south.

Although their arrogance wears a little thin, I don't
mind most of them. And as long as they don't come
knocking on the lodge door preaching their ignorant ra-
tionales for creationism or antiabortion to me or my
guests, they don't really bother me.

But Rayleen was right. He had told me about his Sacrament of the Tears ceremony and I'd been glad he was
only involved in the group's religious side. The Lord's
Workers are quite militant and teach, besides the King
James version of the Bible, survival skills including firearms, explosives, and sharpshooting. It was nice to know
that Rayleen was joining them on a more classic religious
outing rather than a gathering at the quasi-military camp
hidden out at a heavily guarded location north of town.

The Sacrament of the Tears ceremony was being held
just outside of Montreal in a small, salty lake French trap-
pers had named "*Lac Pleurer de Dieu*," which translated
means "Crying God Lake." My geologist friend John
Purcell says that the lake is a result of natural mineral
salts being eroded into the trickle of water that feeds it.
It's this salty waterfall of "tears" that gives it it's name
and, I guess, the proper mystique for The Lord's Workers'
baptismal dunking ritual.

Rayleen rubbed his fingers over the white stubble on

his chin. "Maybe you can get Butch Hull to come 'n' fill in 'til I get back. He could work with Bendel."

Butch Hull was a local insurance adjustor who occasionally took time out from estimating claims to guide out-of-state hunters and fishermen. He had helped us out in the past when the lodge was overflowing with neophytes.

I shook my head. "No. As long as you're back by Wednesday, I think Bendel can handle things." I put my hand on his thin arm. "Just keep d'Antella under your hat, huh? I promised Ruth we'd keep it a secret."

He nodded thoughtfully. "Makes sense to me, all the grief she's been gettin' from Earl MacMillan." He smiled and turned toward the kitchen. "If Lyle asks where we got the money all of a sudden," he said over his shoulder, "I'll tell him somebody died and left it to us."

I stood there and watched him limp toward the kitchen in his stocking feet. Occasionally, Rayleen had a tendency to have one too many Loon Lagers at the bar out at the Starlight after work. Stormy has warned me many times. "You want somethin' kept quiet," she told me, "make good 'n' sure that old fart understands. He's just the same as our daddy was, Max. Couple too many beers and his mouth gets a mind of its own."

After breakfast, Rayleen called Lyle Martin and managed to talk him into finishing the upstairs.

And when Donald Collingwood called just before lunch, I told him we were all set. "Whitefork is all yours for the first week of the season."

He said d'Antella would be delighted. "I'll be calling you in about a week concerning a few other details we'll need to attend to before Mr. d'Antella arrives at Whitefork," he added. "But we needn't worry about that now." Then he thanked me, told me to watch for the check, and we hung up.

The phone rang before I was two steps away. It was Ruth.

"Change your mind?" I asked. "You coming back to-night?"

"No, I can't, Max. But the more I think about this thing with d'Antella, the more I hope you'll seriously consider not doing it."

I laughed. "It's done. I just this minute got off the phone with Collingwood. Lyle's agreed to come back and finish the rooms by opening day and the thirty-five-hundred-dollar check is on its way . . ."

I suddenly realized I was talking to a dead telephone. Ruth had hung up on me.

CHAPTER ♦ THREE

As he said he would, Donald Collingwood called back the next week.

It was Friday. The snow was gone. Only a few gritty pockets remained against the back of the lodge and under the north side of some of the thickest hemlocks and spruce in the damp woods. Nights were still cold enough for maple sugaring and the spider's web of narrow orange plastic tubing still connected the groves of sugar maples on the hillsides to the little weathered sugar houses in the valleys below. Twenty-four hours a day, cupolas on their steep roofs belched sweet, wood-smoky clouds of steam as, inside, hundreds of gallons of clear sap boiled down to quarts of sweet Vermont gold. The ice on the lake had broken up and, overnight it seemed, melted away. It was replaced by rafts of noisy migrating ducks and geese. I now slept with the windows in my room open and at night fell asleep listening to the peeper chorus over the roar of the Whitefork River, swollen milky green with snowmelt. Every morning there were fresh black bear tracks in the mud by the shed that held the garbage cans, and in the evenings a small herd of whitetail deer, ragged with clumps of shedding hair, nervously nibbled at buds on the wild blueberry bushes bordering the lawn in front of the lodge. Hundreds of squabbling northbound robins swooped in to pause and preen in the big beech trees, studding the still-bare branches with noisy spots of orange. From the mountain behind the lodge, the machine gun–like thumping of horny male ruffed grouse echoed out across the lake. And most telling of all, the redwing black-birds were back, their gargled one-note song bouncing around the tall reeds at the mouth of the river. The beginning of fly-fishing season was just two weeks away.

Collingwood's telephone reception was crackly. "I'm on a cell phone at O'Hare. Can you hear me, Mr. Addams?" he said after identifying himself. "I assume you received our check."

"Yes, I hear you, and, yes, we received the check. Thank you." In fact, Lyle and his crew were almost finished. After today, all that remained was hanging the doors, painting, and cleaning up.

"And your construction is on schedule?"

"They should be finished by next Tuesday," I said.

"Good," he said, the crackling now very loud behind his voice. "Two of Mr. d'Antella's party will be arriving at Whitefork the afternoon of the day before he arrives. I'm going to be with them."

"The ninth? Why?"

"I've reviewed the description of Whitefork Lodge in your brochure and I think there are a few security measures needed."

"What kind of security are you talking about?"

"I think two or three small video-surveillance cameras will probably suffice," he said, "but we'll determine that when we get there."

"Cameras? What for?"

"You needn't worry, Mr. Addams. They are miniaturized. No one will ever see them."

"I'm sure they're small," I said. "But why?"

"Mr. d'Antella expects to get the privacy he's paying for, Mr. Addams. My job is to make it happen and video surveillance is the way we do it in a place like Whitefork Lodge.''

''What do we do? Just turn away anybody else who shows up?'' I was worried about how I was going to deal with the few local fly fishermen who just stop by the lodge during the season to fish our waters for the day. I usually charge them a rod fee and some of them have been coming for years.

''You'll have to discourage them somehow, Mr. Addams. Perhaps you can put out a sign. Closed for repairs. No vacancy. Or something like that. Do you have a gate?''

''No.''

''Well, no matter. We can pick up a length of chain on our way to the lodge that day.''

I sighed. A chain? I was going to protest, then thought to myself, Why? There isn't a fly fisherman out there today who isn't getting sick of the crowds and doesn't dream about having a place like our stretch of the Whitefork River all to himself. If Vincent d'Antella could make it happen, who was I to criticize? Besides, I was sure Ruth would be very happy to hear about how careful they were going to be. ''I'll put out a CLOSED FOR REPAIRS sign,'' I said, taking the appointment book from the drawer. ''And spread the word in town.''

''Good,'' he said, the crackling beginning to fade.

''Now''—I opened the book to the first week of April and thumbed a ballpoint—''I need some names.''

''Names? Oh, yes, of course. Besides Mr. d'Antella, there will be Thomas Marchetti and Ralph Garrett. They're the ones arriving with me on the ninth. The female friend is Constance Roth.''

I scribbled the names across the page, underlining Constance Roth and writing ''Instruction: Bendel'' below that.

''Speaking of people, Mr. Addams,'' he said, ''Mr. d'Antella was looking at a list of your employees and he asked me to inquire about your housekeeper's husband, Mr. Domini.''

"Bendel? How do you know about my employees?"

"Don't be offended, Mr. Addams." The crackling stopped. "We always make detailed inquiries about the establishments Mr. d'Antella does business with."

I sighed. "What does he want to know about Bendel?"

"He would just like to know if Mr. Domini speaks Italian."

"I don't know," I said. "But, I don't think so. Not fluent anyway." Although Bendel had been born in northern Italy, he had come to the United States by way of England when he was only six or seven. As a result his accent was decidedly British. He knew some Italian words, but like so many immigrants of his generation, Bendel told me his mother had forbade anything but English in their American home. "Is it important?" I asked Collingwood.

"No," he said. "It's not that important. Mr. d'Antella simply enjoys conversing in Italian at times."

"I intended Bendel to be Constance Roth's instructor. But, I suppose, I could do the teaching and Bendel could . . ."

"No, Mr. Addams. Please don't change your plans. Mr. d'Antella is looking forward to having you as his guide."

"All right. Fine. Anything else?"

"Well," he cleared his throat, "Mr. d'Antella asked me to inquire about one other thing."

"Yes?" I took a deep breath. *What now*? I thought.

"He hopes you won't mind referring to him as 'Kingfish' while he's with you."

"Kingfish?" I tried not to laugh as memories of the *Amos and Andy* radio show played in my head.

"Yes: Kingfish," he said sternly, obviously sensing my amusement.

I grimmed up. "Is using the name Kingfish a part of your security?"

"No, Mr. Addams, it's not." He cleared his throat. "Several years ago, due to his mastery of the fly rod and, so I hear, the number of trout he caught, Mr. d'Antella was nicknamed the 'The Fish King' by a guide in Colorado. Over the years 'Fish King' has somehow been turned around to become 'Kingfish.' "

"Kingfish, huh?"

"I hope you won't mind humoring him, Mr. Addams. It is very unlike Mr. d'Antella's usual persona, but I must admit when he is fishing he seems to like it."

I sighed. "Then Kingfish it is."

"Thank you." He paused and I could hear a public-address announcement in the background. "That's the last call for my plane, Mr. Addams. We'll see you on the ninth."

"Fine. I'll be waiting . . . ," I said, but he was gone. I replaced the phone in its cradle and went out onto the porch in the warm midday sunshine. I lit a cigarette and stood there looking out at the lake. A few fish were rising and the bull's-eye rings left by their feeding dimpled the glassy surface. I waved to Lyle and his three helpers, who were sitting on the back gate of one of the four pickups parked in the yard eating sandwiches and drinking coffee from a big thermos. Spotter, of course, was sitting at their feet, watching every bite. I was glad for their lunch break. As Stormy said after their first full day back on the job, "Good God, Max. Listenin' to that infernal hammerin's almost as tirin' as doing the job ourselves."

It had been a week since Ruth's snow-removal problems, and because of the rapid thaw that next day, what had been intended to hurt her image simply made Mac-Millan look like the political opportunist he was. Had he simply waited twenty-four hours, the snow would have been gone and the taxpayers' money would have been saved. As it was, she was able to turn the entire thing to her favor and last Monday's *Sentinel* carried the new story under the headline, "MACMILLAN MOCKED BY SNOW-MELT." Other than sending me an article about d'Antella torn from a recent *Time* magazine, I hadn't heard from her since she had hung up on me. She had attached a cryptic note on City Hall stationery to the article. "Max," it read, "just so you know what you're getting us into." The "us" was underlined and several of the paragraphs were marked in yellow highlighter, but other than studying the inset picture of d'Antella I had yet to read it. It still lay on my bedside table behind the alarm clock.

Our own personal crime wave in town had been relatively quiet over the week. And other than a burglary at Mike's Package Store on the north side of town, the perpetrators, whoever they were, seemed to be either losing interest in Loon or laying low and plotting something extremely nefarious.

"Max?" Lyle, obviously finished with his lunch, waved to me. "You got a minute, Max? I want to show you something." He opened the door of the truck, lifted a large cardboard box from the passenger seat, and set it on the hood.

I walked out to the truck. Lyle was the antithesis of the rugged, callous-handed construction worker. He was small, to the point of looking delicate, with thinning blond hair held back in a wispy ponytail with a rubber band. His eyebrows were permanently arched high over his big blue eyes, giving him a sort of bewildered look that, until I got to know him, made me feel as if I should tell him everything twice. He had been the art teacher at the high school until cutbacks in the Loon education budget combined with the death of his father turned him into a small businessman. He claims he hates running a construction company, but he's a natural. Not only does he demand quality craftsmanship from his employees, he stays within budget, and amazingly, gets things done on time. Everything, that is, except the home he's still building on a magnificent piece of mountaintop land west of town. Until he does, he, his wife Merriam, and three small daughters live in a big motor home on the site. Asking Lyle how it's progressing is the only time his eyebrows drop.

"What's in the box, Lyle?" I asked, as I joined him at the hood of the pickup. The three helpers gathered around us.

Lyle carefully lifted a strange-shaped object wrapped in newspaper from the box, set it on the hood, and began untying the string holding the paper in place. "I've started carving again," he said. Before Lyle and Merriam were married, he was one of the best bird carvers in the Northeast and had taken blue ribbons in several regional competitions. The beautifully detailed frieze of trout carved deeply into the fronts of both of the lodge's fireplace mantels was his work, as was the carved leaping trout on the banister newel post and the one on my Whitefork Lodge sign up on Route 16.

"Kinda wondered, Max," he said, "if you'd maybe display this in the lodge somewhere." He peeled off the last of the paper to reveal a full-size, almost three-foot-long loon hen and her two chicks intricately carved from a single block of pine. "If one of your sports buys it"—he stepped back and put his hands on his hips—"you can have a commission or something."

I carefully picked up the piece. "I'd be glad to display it, Lyle." It was heavy. The detail was amazing. Each feather was so carefully carved that it appeared it would ruffle if I blew on it. The chicks that he'd carved tucked up next to the hen's wing looked soft enough to squeeze. "It's beautiful. I don't know whether I'll be able to part with it."

Lyle balled the newspaper and tossed it in the box. "Good," he said. "Put it wherever you want, Max." He threw the box into the truck bed. "Anybody says they're interested, have 'em give me a call."

"When do you find time?" I said.

He shrugged. "Oh, it don't take much time, really. Merriam has night-school classes three times a week, so once the girls are in bed I just sit there and whittle."

I laughed. "Well, I'm glad you're almost done here.

Once people see this thing, you'll be too busy carving on commission to do remodeling."

He smiled shyly. "Kinda hope that happens," he said, and then gestured to the men. "Let's go get that ceiling skimmed, boys. Lunch is over."

Carrying the carving, I followed them back into the lodge. They clumped up the stairs to the new bedrooms and I took the bird into the dining room, where I set it in the center of the dining-room table.

I was still admiring the way it seemed to be floating there on the polished surface when the phone rang. It was Ruth.

"Calling to apologize for hanging up on me?" I asked.

"Yes."

"Apology accepted," I said with a laugh. "You should see the carving Lyle just gave me to put on display."

"Really?"

"A beautiful mother loon and two chicks."

"I'm so glad he's carving again. He has such a talent."

"That he does."

"Speaking of talent," she said, "is Bendel back?"

"Yeah, he got back the other day."

"What's he think about d'Antella?"

"He hasn't commented one way or the other."

"You read the article?"

"Not yet," I said. "But I will. On one condition."

"Yes?"

"We have dinner together tonight."

"I can't, Max." I heard papers shuffling. "In fact, I'm not free any day . . . or night . . . until next Friday."

"Friday, huh?" I sighed. "That's the day Collingwood and two of his employees come up to make sure the lodge is secure enough for d'Antella."

"That's the mayor business. If you wanted a regular sex life you shouldn't have become involved with a politician."

"Then it'll have to be Friday," I said. "I guess they'll be gone by dinnertime."

"Good. That's the ninth. Write it down."

We both wrote it on our calendars and then I heard other voices on her end and she had to go. "And read the article, Max," she said just before hanging up.

CHAPTER FOUR

When Collingwood arrived the following Friday, it was unusually hot. Hot for June 9th, much less April 9th. It was the second day of an unseasonable spring heat wave that the National Weather Service was predicting would last at least another week. Already many of the trees had been pushed by the false warmth and the ash, beech, and maples along the river were almost fully leafed out. The tiny Carolina wrens who summered in the porch eaves were hard at work reinforcing last year's nest, and although they looked cute with their little black eyes and long, pointed bills and erect tails, they had all of us ducking as they careened in and out over the steps carrying twigs and tufts of Spotter's fur. Rayleen had left with a busload of believers for Montreal. Lyle and his crew had finally finished, the lumber and construction debris in the yard had been cleaned up and removed, and yesterday the furniture for the new rooms had arrived.

We were ready for Kingfish and his party.

"This d'Antella fellow must live right," Bendel said, as we walked up the lawn to the lodge from the lake. His big black Nikon with the motor-drive bounced on his chest. He not only had helped me carry our two canoes from winter storage in the workshop, hose them down, and tie them on each side of the dock, he had waded out into the water and documented this year's launch for posterity. "If this heat holds, we should have caddis coming off the lake all day every day he's here."

"You have to remember: the name is Kingfish," I said.

"Right, Kingfish." He rolled his big brown eyes. "Kingfish."

Despite the heat we were both in waders. The air temperature might have been in the July-like high seventies, but the water was April's typical testicle-shrinking cold. We did have on short-sleeved shirts and Bendel wore a faded red bandanna tied around his forehead to soak up the sweat.

"I sure appreciate you doing the teaching this week," I said, ducking an exiting blur of wren as we clumped up onto the porch. "I only hope she's not difficult."

"It doesn't make any difference to me, Max," he said, hanging his Nikon by the strap from a peg, sprawling in a rocker, and putting his wet wader boots up on the porch rail. "You've got to remember"—the lines around his big, soft brown eyes deepened into a smile—"I'm a fashion photographer. Difficult women is what I do."

I leaned against an upright and peeled off my waders. A flock of a dozen canvasbacks sped over the lodge and out toward the lake, their stubby, pointed wings beating so fast they whistled.

"Well," I said, "if it's any consolation, I think you'll find that teaching a woman to cast is easier than teaching a man." Men learning to cast a fly rod try to muscle it at first, like they're throwing a rock or baseball. Women, having nothing to prove, take to the graceful rhythm naturally and let the rod do the work. I laughed. "In the classes I've given, the men are still flogging the water when the women are ready to tie on flies and go fishing."

"I'm not worried about it." Bendel leaned his head back on the rocker, closed his eyes, and took a deep breath. "Certainly smells good today, doesn't it?"

It did. The humid air was thick with an almost intoxicating potpourri of pine, wet decaying leaves, and the spicy aroma of the lodge's sun-baked logs.

I've grown to appreciate Bendel's observations. He never seems to tire of the sights, sounds, and smells around the lodge and the river. "If you had spent as much time surrounded by cement as I have, Max," he once told me, "you'd never take any of this for granted." In his mid-sixties and perpetually tan, Bendel is short and stocky, has a barrel chest and remarkably thick white hair pulled back into a six-inch ponytail. Besides the ubiquitous camera around his neck, a tiny diamond stud blinks on his left earlobe and a big black chronograph protrudes from his left wrist. On hot days like this, the heavy copper-link bracelet he wears on his right arm turns the wrist green.

I hadn't cared for Bendel when I first met him. Quite frankly I had suspected his motives when he began to court Stormy. Why would a man who had spent most of his life photographing some of the world's most beautiful women pursue and propose marriage to a tough old Vermonter like her. Oh, I loved Stormy. And she was one in a million, yes. But she was built like a beer keg and had the grace of a small bulldozer. The untimely death of her husband and only child when she was young, a bout with booze, plus years of hard Vermont winters and the company of men summer after summer had, as far as I was concerned, eroded all the feminine softness from her. What was left was as hard as the seamless granite ledge the lodge was built upon.

Bendel saw rock in Stormy also, only a different kind. And when he sensed my suspicions, he took me for a walk down by the river to try to explain his feelings. "Have you ever been to Florence and seen Michelangelo's *David*, Max?" he asked.

I told him I had never been to Europe, much less to Italy.

"No matter." He smiled. "It's displayed in a large four-story-high rotunda at the end of a long, wide corridor. It is a beautiful piece of sculpture, Max, but for me nowhere near as awe-inspiring as the powerful pieces that line the corridor leading up to it. They're massive fifteen- and twenty-foot-tall blocks of white marble, with just the beginnings of women showing in them. From some, only heads and shoulders have been carved out. Others are more complete, with torsos, legs, hips, and breasts. They are all unfinished, of course. But to me they give the impression the women are struggling to free themselves from the stone. They're incredibly powerful." He smiled wistfully this time. "Anita is like that to me, Max. A stone. With a beautiful woman inside."

It was poetic, but I wasn't convinced.

Two days later, however, I did see something I hadn't expected when they announced to me they were getting married. The three of us were in the kitchen and Stormy was perched on a stool, the hem of her caftan above her knees while she laced up her Bean boots. It had never occurred to me she had legs, much less ones as shapely as those now showing, and when she glanced up at Bendel I saw it. Not just in her eyes, but the angle of her head and the color in her cheeks. He was right: she had a softness I hadn't known was there. Suddenly I could see she was very much in love.

"What time do you expect this Collingwood, Max?" Bendel's eyes were still closed and, until he spoke, I thought he'd fallen asleep in the warm sunshine.

I looked at my watch and started to tell him that we could expect Collingwood at anytime now when I heard Stormy yell from the kitchen behind us, "He'll be here in twenty minutes. Called from the Burlington airport while you two was at the dock. Said they was rentin' a car and would be up in an hour. That was fifteen minutes ago."

Bendel and I looked at each other. "I never knew her hearing was that good," I said. Stormy had to be forty feet away from us, down the long, narrow hallway and inside the kitchen with the swinging door closed.

"Me either." He stretched and smiled. "It'll certainly make you think twice about what you say out here on the porch from now on."

I nodded. I don't think there's an evening during the season that a bunch of us don't sit on the porch after the sun goes down, listen to the frogs and swap fish stories. If it's only men, usually the jokes get raunchier in direct proportion to the amount of alcohol consumed. No one has ever held back on the more graphic parts or choice of vulgarities because it has always been assumed that Stormy, way back in the kitchen doing dishes, couldn't possibly hear us. "Jesus," I said. "I hate to think of things she's heard through the years."

"I hate to think what I mighta heard too," she yelled again from the back of the kitchen. "If I cared to listen that is. Soon's I hear them silly laughs you men get when you're talkin' 'bout boobs and butts, I just tune out."

I was stunned. "She just heard me again."

"It must be the acoustics in the hallway," Bendel said, leaning forward in the rocker and peering through the screen door. "Go back there to the kitchen, Max. See if you can hear as well as she does."

I entered the lodge and went back into the kitchen. Stormy was at the island stirring a large pitcher of iced tea. I yelled back down the hall, "Say something, Bendel. In your normal voice."

His voice, just as clear as if he were standing right there beside me, came floating down the hallway. "Max Addams is a self-centered son of a bitch who cares more about trout than people," he said, and then louder, "You hear that, Max?"

"I'll be darned." I laughed. "I heard it." I looked at Stormy. "Bendel's right. It must be some sort of acoustic thing due to the way the new hallway's constructed." As far as I knew, the phenomenon didn't exist before our fire.

"Maybe the logs are different. I'll bet you could hear a pin drop out there from here."

"Or somebody peein' off the porch," she said with a smile.

I think I blushed slightly. "You're kidding?" I had always thought my nightly watering of the rosebush on the far corner of the porch was known only to Spotter.

She shook her head. "You ain't the only one. Rayleen does it too."

"You can tell the difference?"

" 'Course. Rayleen's stream's like Morse code." She smiled again. "Though yours ain't as steady as it used to be either."

Bendel and I were still experimenting with the acoustics of the hallway when Collingwood arrived. "He's here," I heard Bendel whisper from the porch.

By the time Stormy and I joined him, a big red Hertz Thunderbird was parked directly in front of the porch, its rocker panels and tires dripping with mud from the still soupy spots on the access road. There were three of them in the car: two in the front and a thin, erect shadow that I assumed to be Collingwood in the backseat. I went down the steps to greet them.

The front doors opened and two men in their early thirties climbed out. The driver walked stiffly to the grille, pushed his sunglasses back on his head, stretched, and smiled up at me. "Hello, there," he said. "I'm Tommy." His square jaw needed a shave and his hair was a mat of short black curls tight against his equally square skull. A thick weightlifter's neck dropped straight from his ears to his shoulders, and as he crossed his arms over his chest, the fabric in his wrinkled blazer stretched taut over thigh-size biceps. He nodded his head toward the other young man, who was now holding the back door of the car open. "That's Ralph. He's a little carsick."

From what I could see of Ralph, he was tall and thin

with a crisp, dark goatee. His hair, streaked with blond highlights, hung in dirty-looking clumps to the narrow shoulders of a dark green polo shirt. A maze of colorful tattoos started at his wrists and disappeared up into the shirt's sleeves.

Donald Collingwood climbed out of the backseat, obviously very accustomed to doing so. He removed his sunglasses, squinted, and looked at me. "Mr. Addams, I presume?"

"Mr. Collingwood." I extended my hand and we shook. I've met quite a few congressmen and senators since Ruth and I started dating and Collingwood had that same studied look: perfect tan and teeth, graying temples, ice-blue eyes. He wore a crisp dove-gray suit, white shirt, and pale yellow tie with tiny red diamonds on it.

"I didn't picture you with the beard," he said, folding his glasses and sliding them carefully in behind the white handkerchief in his breast pocket.

I smiled. "I didn't picture you so dressed up."

"I have to catch a plane for the West Coast at four-thirty," he said, "for a meeting in Los Angeles tonight." He turned and looked at Stormy. Spotter sat between her legs, his bobbing tongue dripping a small puddle on the floor. "And you are Mrs. Domini?"

"Name's Stormy," she said. "Can I get you fellas some iced tea?"

"In a moment, yes, thank you." His gaze moved to Bendel. "And this is Mr. Domini?"

"Bendel to my friends," Bendel said, coming down the steps. They shook hands.

Collingwood smiled and turned to Tommy and Ralph, who were now at the Thunderbird's open trunk. "Tomaso? Ralph? Before you begin unloading, I would like you to meet our hosts." He put his hand lightly on my shoulder. A gold watch glittered beneath the perfect inch and one half of crisp broadcloth. I could smell hand cream. "This is Mr. Addams, Stormy, and Bendel."

"Call me Max," I said, shaking their hands. Tommy's last name was Marchetti. Ralph's was Garrett and he did look a little pale.

"Nice place, Max." Tommy said, looking up at the lodge. "Could be worse, huh, Ralphie?"

"I don't know how." Ralph was now rubbing his hand on his stomach.

Collingwood looked at Stormy. "Would you have any Pepto-Bismol? Ralph is a bit under the weather."

"Nah." Ralph waved his hand. "I got one of them sensitive stomachs, is all. It don't do planes and cars very well. I'll live."

Tommy laughed. "Ralph's stomach doesn't do anything very well."

"You do look a little green around the gills, young man," Stormy said to him. "Why don't you come inside and let me get you something?"

Ralph looked at Collingwood.

"Go ahead, Ralph," Collingwood said. "Tommy can get the things out."

Ralph went up the steps and followed Stormy into the lodge. "What did you have to eat today?" we heard her say as the screen door slapped shut behind them.

As Collingwood, Bendel, and I went up the steps onto the porch out of the hot sun, Collingwood gave Tommy an almost-imperceptible nod and the young man quickly returned to the trunk.

Collingwood ducked under the two pairs of hanging waders. "Is it always this hot up here in April?"

Bendel pulled a rocker from the wall. "No," he said, gesturing for Collingwood to sit. "Quite the opposite usually."

Collingwood sat in a rocker and carefully arranged the pleats in his trousers. Bendel pulled up another rocker and sat.

"Usually cold as a Presbyterian minister's heart this time a year," Stormy yelled from the kitchen.

Bendel and I looked at each other and laughed.

Collingwood frowned. "Did I say something funny?"

"No," I said. "No. We're laughing about the acoustics. It seems Stormy can hear everything that's said on the porch way back in the kitchen."

"We just discovered it," Bendel said, still chuckling. "In fact, we were experimenting with it when you pulled up."

"We'll have to remember that." Collingwood didn't seem amused or care so I changed the subject.

"Vincent d'Antella must live a charmed life," I said. "Weather like this makes for perfect insect hatches." I sat on the porch rail and lit a cigarette.

"I can imagine," Collingwood said, taking the white handkerchief from his pocket and, without unfolding it, blotted his forehead.

Bendel saw something in the way Tommy unloaded the car and grabbed the camera, put it to his eye, twisted the lens for focus, and clicked off three shots. All I could see was Tommy wrestling two large black fiberboard boxes and two medium-size suitcases out onto the ground and then up onto the porch. "I feel like I should be helping," I said.

"There is something you can do, actually," Collingwood said.

I looked at him. "Name it."

"I'm almost embarrassed to say this." He sighed. "I assumed Tommy and Ralph would have no trouble finding lodging in the town of Loon for tonight." He sighed again. "I didn't think reservations would be necessary but . . ."

"Ain't gonna find nothing available in Loon any night this weekend," Stormy said, holding the screen door open as Ralph sidestepped through, carrying a tray containing a big, sweaty pitcher of iced tea and six rattling glasses. Bendel put down the camera, took the tray, and set it on the narrow table we have placed against the logs at the back of the porch. "New England Microbrewers Convention," she said. "Runs 'til Sunday. Beer-makers got every bed in town." She looked at me. "Coulda filled this place ten times over, ain't that right, Max?"

I nodded. We'd had over thirty calls in the past week inquiring about space. I can only assume microbrewing is to the beer business like fly fishing is to the fishing business.

Collingwood smiled ruefully and looked back at me. "Could I impose upon you, Max, to make room for Tommy and Ralph here at Whitefork Lodge tonight?"

I looked at Stormy.

She shrugged. "All right with me," she said. "Long as they don't expect nothing fancy in the way of meals. We ain't officially open 'til tomorrow."

"They can take their meals in town," Collingwood said. Tommy and Ralph were now standing by the luggage.

"Not while I'm here they won't." She went back to the screen door and pointed at Ralph. "And this one's got more'n just a queasy stomach. My guess is he picked up a bug on that plane ride." She smiled at him. "What he could use is a little homecookin' and a good night's sleep." She opened the door and held it. "Might just as well bring that stuff inside right now," she said to Tommy and looked at me. "Gooda time as any to break in them new rooms, I'd say."

They both looked at Collingwood for an answer.

"I don't think Stormy will have it any other way," he said and smiled at her. "Thank you."

Stormy held the door as Ralph and Tommy hefted the boxes and suitcases into the hall, then the screen door slapped shut and I could hear their feet clumping up the stairs.

I poured a glass full of iced tea and handed it to Collingwood.

"I assume you'll add tonight to the final bill," he said, as he took the glass.

I nodded and poured one for myself and Bendel.

Collingwood sipped the tea and looked out over the lake. "Plenty of room for the helicopter," he said, visibly relaxing. "Plenty of room."

"Helicopter?" *Christ*, I thought, *there goes our secrecy.*

"Yes." He smiled and carefully put his handkerchief on the bottom of the sweating glass. "Mr. d'Antella was not happy about it either."

"We don't have many helicopters around here," I said. "Even if it isn't seen, the noise will certainly draw some attention."

Collingwood studied my face. If I looked concerned, it was because I was. "I don't think you should worry, Max. It's only a small four-passenger Bell Trooper. And Mr. d'Antella will be coming in just after sunrise."

I looked out at the lake. The trees grew right to the waterline and, in some places, in it. "No way he'll get it within twenty yards of the shore," I said to Bendel. "We'll have to ferry him and his baggage in the canoes."

"I'm sorry if this creates a nuisance for you, Max," Collingwood said. "But it is necessary." He drained his iced-tea glass, stood, and straightened his suit jacket. "Now, if you would be good enough to show me a place inside where we can set up the video monitor and VCR, when Tommy and Ralph get downstairs we'll begin unpacking the equipment."

After putting their bags in their rooms and listening to Stormy's rules about overly long showers, the sensitivity of the lodge's septic system, and not succumbing to Spotter's unabashed begging at mealtimes, Tommy and Ralph joined Collingwood, Bendel, and I in the reading room where we watched them set up a small color TV monitor and a VCR on the desk across from the fireplace. I don't know what Stormy gave Ralph but his color had improved.

Then, with Bendel holding the ladder, Ralph climbed up to the porch roof and attached a small video receiving dish while I took Tommy and two of the small video cameras in my Jeep up the access road to where it meets Route 16.

On the way up the road Tommy said, "I hope that this isn't an inconvenience, Max. Our staying tonight, I mean."

I shook my head. "No problem."

"Well, at least we saved you the trouble in the fishing-license area," he said. "We stopped at a place in town and picked up three."

"Three? I thought only Kingfish and his lady friend . . ."

"Ralph and I can share." He shrugged. "Sometimes the only way to cover the old man is to get right out there in the water with him. Fishing's better than just standing around with your thumb up your ass, you know?"

"So you two fly fish also?"

"I try. Ralph? Well, he's not into killing things." He smiled. "Makes him sick to even think about it."

"We don't kill fish here anyway," I said. "It's catch and release or nothing."

"Hmmm." He scratched at his jaw. "I don't know if Kingfish's ever done it that way."

"He'll learn." I parked the Jeep at the top of the access road. Tommy quickly selected a big spruce with a clear view of the entrance to put the camera in and then climbed the tree. I stood at the base of the trunk holding the little camera. We had tied a length of cord around it so he could pull it up when he found the right spot. He had one end attached to his belt loop.

"You always go to this kind of trouble when your boss fishes?" I asked.

"Always." Tommy stomped on a large branch to check its strength.

"He fly-fish a lot?"

He shrugged and deliberately broke off a couple of small branches. "Enough." He tossed the branches out of the tree to the ground.

"It must be difficult to do this kind of thing on some of those big rivers out west."

"You mean because of how open it is?"

"Yeah."

"Actually, it's easier. Need fewer cameras."

I nodded as though I understood.

"It's not nearly as bad as it used to be when Vincent was like those other old guys he knows." He pulled on the cord. "I'll take the camera now, Max."

"What do they do?" I guided the camera up into the tree as far as I could reach and then watched it rise through the thick pine needles toward him. "These other old guys, I mean."

"Palm Springs, Max." Tommy had the camera in his hands now and smiled down at me. "They sit on the beach all day all oiled up with suntan lotion, matching quarters for hundred-dollar bills. All kinds of people around. Hotels full of windows behind them. Boats out in front of them. It's a security nightmare." He rested the camera on a thick branch by his head and aimed it at the access road. "Kingfish used to be right there with them. All winter." He looked through the eyepiece. "Until he discovered fly-fishing."

"When was that?"

"What? The fly-fishing?" He fumbled in his pocket and pulled out a coil of heavy wire and a pair of needle-nose pliers.

"Yeah. When did he start?"

"Four, maybe five years ago," he said, using the wire to attach the camera to the branch. "Just after he saw that *River* movie."

"*A River Runs Through It?*"

"Yeah. That's the one." He crimped off the wire and stuffed it and the pliers back in his pocket. "You see it?" He looked down at me.

I nodded.

Tommy started back down the tree. "Yeah, well, King-fish went nuts for it, you know?" He jumped the last four feet and landed beside me. "I mean"—he dusted his shirt-front—"I knew him when golf was his thing and I'm telling you, Max, it was nothing compared to this fly-fishing gig." He looked at his hands. They were covered with sticky pine pitch. "What the hell's this?"

"Sap's running," I said, ducking out from under the tree. "Stormy's got some soap in the kitchen that'll get it off."

He followed me to the Jeep. There was one more camera on the backseat. The chain was on the floor.

I pointed at the camera. "Where do you want to put this one?"

"Let's see . . ." He leaned on the fender. "Ralph's putting the wide-angle on that cabin you got so we'll have a view of the lake." He rubbed his sticky palms together. "There any other way into this place?"

"Hundreds." I shrugged. "If somebody wants to come through the woods."

He pointed at Route 16. "How far does your property run along this road?"

"A mile or so."

He nodded thoughtfully. "Let's put this camera up in a tree at the other end of your property line," he said. "Road looks pretty straight and level through here. We'll aim it back towards here. That way, if anyone enters the woods from along the road, we'll see them." He hopped up into the Jeep's passenger seat. "We'll put up the the chain last. Okay?"

I nodded, got in, and started the engine. "I'm curious,"

I said, putting it in gear. "Who are you expecting anyway?"

He looked at me and smiled tolerantly. "If we knew that, Max," he said, "we wouldn't need the cameras, would we?"

We bounced out of the dirt access road and I turned left onto the blacktop. "Let me phrase it another way," I said, shifting into second. "Who *might* it be?"

"The way things are right now," he said, laughing, "it could be damn near anybody."

CHAPTER ✦ FIVE

After putting the second camera in a big white oak overlooking Route 16 from the other end of the lodge's property, Tommy and I ran the length of chain from the trunk of a sturdy little maple across the entrance of the access road and padlocked it around the Whitefork Lodge signpost. He handed me the keys. There were two of them. "I kept one," he said, climbing back into the Jeep. "Those are yours."

Back at the lodge, Tommy, who had done most of the work and was covered with perspiration, bark, and sap, went straight upstairs to take a quick shower. I hung the padlock keys on the key rack by the door and I joined Collingwood, Bendel, and Ralph at the rolltop in the reading room. Ralph was sitting, working with the monitor. Collingwood, now in shirtsleeves, and Bendel leaned in from behind.

Bendel saw me first. "Max, come here and look at this." He stepped back to make room for me.

The TV monitor showed a view of Sweet Lake from the camera on top of the cabin and Ralph was fiddling with a small console that allowed him to zoom and pan as well as switch from one camera to the other. He pushed a button and the view changed from the lake to the entrance to the access road. Another push of a button and I could see Route 16 from the white oak where Tommy and I had just put the last camera. Bendel was excited. "Look at that resolution. It's like 35-millimeter."

Ralph mumbled something about "lumes" and "Leica f2 lenses" and, as their talk became more technical, Collingwood and I moved away from the desk and walked into the adjoining dining room. "Well," he said, carefully lifting his suit jacket from the back of a chair, "that's it, Max. Everything's working fine." He slipped on the jacket and smiled. "And Mr. d'Antella's going to like your friend Bendel."

"Bendel's one of a kind."

"So is Mr. d'Antella." He looked out into the hallway. "Something smells good."

I sniffed. "I think Stormy's making meatloaf."

He smiled. "Makes me wish I were staying too. Where's Tommy?"

"Taking a shower."

"Good." He looked at his watch. "I've got a plane to catch." He went back to the reading-room doorway and spoke to Ralph. "Tommy will take me to the airport. You stay and run the tests."

"Yes, sir." I heard Ralph say.

"I want a phone call from one of you tomorrow as soon as they're here and settled in."

"Yes, sir."

Collingwood came back across the room. "Thank you for your cooperation, Max." He shook my hand. "I'm positive Mr. d'Antella will enjoy his stay here."

"Kingfish," I said.

He smiled. "Yes, Kingfish."

Stormy stuck her head into the room. "Max? Can I see you for a sec?"

I smiled at her. "In a minute," I said. "Mr. Collingwood's about to leave and as soon as . . ."

"Now."

I excused myself and followed Stormy down the hall to

FLY FISHING CAN BE FATAL 65

the kitchen. "What the hell's so important?" I asked as the swinging door closed behind me.

Her eyes were red, like she had been crying. "Ruth called 'bout thirty minutes ago." She fumbled with a cigarette, couldn't get it lit, and threw it in the sink.

"And . . . ?"

"Lyle was killed this morning."

"What? You sure?"

She nodded. "He was murdered. Shot right in town."

"But how?"

"Ruth didn't tell me everything. Just that they think Lyle was pickin' up his tools at the bowlin' alley." She turned and looked out the window. "Guess he finished them new lanes late yesterday and forgot some things and . . ." Her shoulders began to shake.

I let her cry quietly for a minute. Long before Whitefork Lodge or working for me, Stormy had been a pediatric nurse. Like Lyle, if you were born in Loon and forty to forty-five years old, she had been there when you came in the world.

She sniffed. "Lyle was two months premature," she said, wiping her eyes on her apron. "He was so tiny. Was nip 'n' tuck there for a while, but the little guy made it. His daddy was so proud. Went right out and painted '& Sons' on that truck of his."

"You call Merriam?"

Stormy nodded and sniffed again. "Takin' her a meatloaf soon's it's done cookin'."

"Why didn't you tell me sooner?"

"Didn't know you was back." She sat on one of the cooking-island stools. "Only just heard your voice and the shower runnin' upstairs a few minutes ago."

"Did Ruth say anything else?"

"Said you two was having dinner at the Loon Hotel and . . ."

"Oh, crap," I said. "I forgot."

"Asked me to tell you to come to her office soon as you

can. Told me she don't think she can get away like she thought, though.''

Bendel stepped into the kitchen, saw the look on Stormy's face, and walked quickly to her. ''Anita? What's wrong?''

As he took Stormy in his arms, I told him about Lyle.

''That's awful,'' he said. ''I mean, I didn't know the young man very well, but what's happening in this town?''

''I was you, Max,'' Stormy said, ''soon's Collingwood's outta here, I'd go. Ruth didn't sound too good.'' She looked at Bendel. ''And you. You're gonna hafta figure out what to do with them boys out there, 'cause I'm taking what was your supper to Lyle's wife.''

''I'll take them to the Starlight,'' he said and looked at me. ''And since Anita and I are moved into the cabin, Max, we'll be here at the lodge in case you don't make it back tonight.'' As they did during the season whenever it wasn't rented, Stormy and Bendel stayed in the cabin out by Sweet Lake instead of having to drive to and from town every morning and night.

Stormy could see me hesitating. ''Go on, Max,'' she said. ''Way things are happenin', who knows when you and Ruth are gonna have another chance to be together?''

I nodded and started to say something when Collingwood's whispered voice, as clear as if he were standing there with us, floated into the room. ''You stay away from her,'' he said. ''You understand?''

''Yes, sir,'' Ralph's voice answered.

''They must be on the porch,'' Bendel whispered.

Stormy put her finger to her lips. ''Shhh!''

We listened.

''I'm counting on you,'' Collingwood said. ''It's over.''

''Yes, sir.''

''Now, where the hell is Tommy?'' Collingwood raised his voice. ''Tommy!'' he shouted. ''Let's go!''

I looked at Bendel and Stormy. They both shrugged.

"You better get out there, Max," Stormy said. "Think he's leavin'."

Smelling like the chunk of pine soap we have in all the guest bathrooms, Tommy came down the stairs just as I got to the screen door and we went out onto the porch together to join Collingwood and Ralph. "Who's taking you to the airport?" he asked Collingwood.

Collingwood snapped his cuffs. "You are, Tomaso," he said and looked at me. "Thank you, Max. And thank Stormy and Bendel again for me." And then, with the three of us following, he briskly went down the porch steps to the Thunderbird. Ralph hurried ahead to the back door, opened it, and Collingwood slid quickly in. Tommy got in the front and revved the big engine. Ralph and I stepped back as the Thunderbird turned around and then, with a spray of wet gravel, roared out of sight up the access road.

I looked at Ralph, hoping something might betray the meaning of what we'd overhead, but his pallid face was blank. "So, how's your stomach?" I asked.

"What's wrecking my stomach hasn't even arrived yet." He clumped back up the porch steps. At the door he stopped and scowled back at me. "Ask me after that chopper sets down tomorrow."

Before I could say anything else, the screen door slapped shut behind him and he was gone.

I went inside too, stripped off my dirty clothes, showered, and dressed in a clean pair of khakis and the dark green linen shirt my daughter had given me last Father's Day. I knew how Lyle's death would depress Ruth, so I trimmed my beard and, though they made my feet cramp, pulled on the tan rough-out cowboy boots she thought were sexy. And although I abhor using the stuff, I even put on a little of the cologne she liked. I looked at myself in the full-length mirror I have on the back of the door by the bed. I thought I looked a little silly. Kind of like a guy on the make. I hoped she noticed. At least, I might get a good laugh out of her.

The town of Loon is twenty minutes down Route 16 and separated from us by the Sunrise Mountain Range of which the massive, camel-humped Morning Mountain behind the lodge is the most prominent. In the autumn, the ride is a favorite with the out-of-state tourists we call ''leaf peepers.'' The series of tight switchbacks that follow Gracey Gorge down to the town afford spectacular views of the town, with its white church steeples, the glistening Whitefork River, the neat sprawl of buildings that house the Loon Lagering Company, and pointing at you from behind the Whitefork Dam in the distance, the long, thin finger of water called Monday Lake.

Gawking at the Fall scenery, however, most tourists never see the other Loon, Vermont, that's hidden behind the screen of flaming red and gold trees. But it's there, and on any spring day like this one, when fewer leaves block the view, the pockets of our rural poverty are painfully visible. Scrap-wood shanties and mobile homes crooked on crumbling foundations sit in small filthy clearings cluttered with rusted cars, piles of rotting firewood, broken children's toys, and torn plastic bags of uncollected garbage. Scrawny dogs, dirty children, and chickens dig together in the dirt under clotheslines full of oversize underwear, formless housedresses, and tattered baby clothes. If you look hard, you can see the men, scrawny with sunken eyes and angry stares, looking back as you pass. And the women, if they're visible, are pale and either sadly overweight or heavy with child. As far as Ruth is concerned, it's become Vermont's biggest problem and was the major issue in her campaign for governor. ''Scratch the surface of anything that goes wrong in this state,'' she said in speech after speech, ''and you'll find at the root of it the apathy, anger, and frustration caused by joblessness and poverty.'' For me, the squalor is an embarrassment and the directions I give to customers coming to the lodge for the first time are carefully written to bring them up the uninhabited, pristine roads of the Green Mountain National Forest.

Poverty not withstanding, on Friday it's not unusual to find Loon's Main Street crowded. Today, with what I guessed to be the influx of home brewers attending the New England Microbrewers Association Convention being held at the Loon Lager headquarters, it was a zoo. Except for our Fourth of July parade, I'd never seen the sidewalks so full of people. A red, white, and blue banner reading "WELCOME N.E.M.B.A." was stretched across the street and, held in place by guywires, a three-story-tall inflated Loon Lager beer bottle stood on the roof of the bandstand in the middle of the town square. It was as if Lyle's murder had never happened.

There were no spaces left in the City Hall lot where I usually parked and I had to drive around the giant beer bottle three times until a diagonal slot opened up in front of the movie theater. It was only a two-block hike to Ruth's office, so I grabbed it.

Gary Carrier, the owner of the newly converted three-screen multiplex, was up at the face of the blank marquee on a rickety twelve-foot stepladder. There was a jagged hole the size of a man's head in the white plastic near his shoulder. He was juggling oversized black plastic letters and when he saw me he shouted down, "Hey, Max. How's the river look out by your place?" Gary is one of the fly fishermen who usually pays a day rate to fish my section of the Whitefork in early April. "I was thinkin' about sneakin' out tomorrow mornin', soon as I get my license."

I shielded my eyes from the sun and shook my head. "You'll have to find some other place for opening day, Gary," I yelled back. "We're not going to be open to the public until next weekend."

"What's the matter?"

"River's too high out there." A small lie, but not far from the truth. "And muddy."

He shrugged. "Too bad."

"Come on out in a week. It should be perfect." I pointed to the hole in the marquee. "What happened to the sign?"

"Who knows?" He shook his head as if trying to understand it all. "Wasn't this way yesterday. Deputy Kendall thinks it was probably that same bunch that shot Lyle."

"Any more information on that?"

He shook his head. "Question is, Why? Lyle never hurt nobody. Kept to himself mostly. Sure did good work. He did your place after the fire, didn't he?"

"Yeah. And just finished adding some new rooms."

"Yep." Gary nodded and pointed up the street toward the Loon Bowl. "They think Lyle was pickin' up his tools from the bowling alley. He and his boys just finished in there yesterday. Musta surprised somebody inside. I heard the new alleys he just put in are all trashed now too." He lowered his voice and leaned his forearms on the top of the ladder. "Some folks are sayin', maybe he was shot 'cause he saw who it was. You know?"

"Jesus."

"Yep. It's sure got everybody freakin' out, I'll tell you." He looked around. "I think a lot of us'd be closed today if it wasn't for all these conventioneers coming in."

I nodded. "Hard to tell anyone was killed."

"Wouldn't be if you could see the inside of the bowling alley," he said. "Blood everywhere. Shot him with a deer rifle, they think. Soft-nose bullets, anyway. A real mess. Damn near tore his head clean off." He sighed as if picturing it. "Yeah, 'course I didn't know Lyle that well, but I think things have gone just about far enough now." He gestured at the hole in the marquee. "We're all feelin' it." Gary straightened and rearranged the stack of letters on the top of the ladder. "Just between you and me, Max, your friend the mayor better figure out a way to stop this bullshit or she's gonna be out of a job come November."

I didn't say anything and looked up the street.

He picked up a letter G and waved it. "I gotta get this sign up, Max. Murder or no murder, I have a four o'clock matinee today."

I mumbled, "Good luck," and started up the street toward City Hall and the town offices.

It's unusual for a small town like Loon to get a convention and everyone was trying to capitalize on it. In fact, there was so much brewer convention–related signage along the street that it almost obliterated the bright blue, metal CBL "CRIME WATCH" signs bolted to every other signpost along the curb. "Lot of good that did Lyle," I said to myself as I dodged around a name-tagged foursome. They gave me a dirty look.

Just about every storefront had posters taped to its windows welcoming the microbrewers. I passed The Triangle bar. "YOU MAKE IT, WE'LL SERVE IT THIS WEEKEND" read the sign beneath the lit neon LOON LAGER in the small window. Across the street, Woolworth's and Ace Hardware had brewer-themed sales going in progress.

The Loon Bowl was next on my side and I tried not to look at the yellow police tape X-ed across the entrance as I passed. I was afraid I'd see blood.

At the newly renovated Loon Hotel, my forward progress was stopped by a clot of men and women on the sidewalk unloading luggage from the trunks of several double-parked cars. The bright red Victorian-style bed-and-breakfast sits back from the street and the big ornate sign in the small yard had a NO VACANCY shingle hanging beneath it. John Quinn, the new owner, was out on the long gingerbread porch sorting a pile of suitcases. He saw me. "Too bad about Lyle, huh, Max?" he yelled. Lyle had done much of John's renovation also.

I waved and nodded.

"See you and Ruth for dinner? Right?"

"Who knows?" I shouted.

"Don't let this worry you." He gestured at the crowd. "Dining room'll be nice and quiet."

"I'm sure it will," I said and wound my way through the crowd, past Freddie's Lunch. It's open twenty-four hours year-round and I looked in the open doorway at the crowd and could see Freddie's seventeen-year-old daughter Janine listlessly cooking burgers at the grill behind the counter. Along with being the captain of the Loon High School cheerleading squad, I knew she regularly baby-sat for Lyle's little girls. She glanced my way and I waved, but her mind was somewhere else today. She didn't see me.

Next door, was Judy's Booknook, Loon's only bookstore. Owner Judy Bowman was standing mid-sidewalk, hands on her ample hips. She was squinting around the smoke from a long, thin cigarette with a long gray ash, studying the display of books in her store window. "What d'ya think, Max?" She nodded her head toward the window as I approached. "Think it looks fishy enough?" The ash fell from the cigarette into the pills on her ratty green sweater. She didn't brush it off.

I stopped, stood beside her, and looked at the window. In an attempt to tie reading to local interests or events, Judy's windows changed almost weekly. This one was her attempt to tie into the beginning of fishing season, and several fishing rods, a stuffed trout, waders, and wicker creels competed for space with a couple of dozen hard-and soft-cover books. A hand-lettered sign hanging from an oversized hook attached to an old bamboo rod in the middle of it all read "THIS SEASON, CATCH THE READING HABIT."

I told her it was nice. "But, how come you're not tying in with the convention?"

She made a face. "I hate beer." She stepped back and looked at me. "You know about Lyle?"

"Ruth called."

"How's she holding up?" Judy was one of Ruth's more loyal supporters.

"That's where I'm going now. What's wrong with her?"

She shrugged. "They had an emergency City Council meeting this morning," she said. "Ruth took a lot of heat from MacMillan and that crime consultant of his." She dropped the cigarette on the sidewalk and stepped on it. "She wants to bring in the state police and they're dead set against it."

"Why? After this thing with Lyle I'd think . . ."

She shook her head. "I guess the idiots think they're within days of arresting someone." Aside from Stormy, Judy is probably MacMillan's most vociferous critic.

"You mean, they might know who killed Lyle?"

"Who knows? All they have is the car used in the liquor-store thing the other night. I guess it was stolen down in Rhode Island. Billy Kendall found it abandoned out by the dam." The Whitefork Dam was three miles north. Until it was built in 1947, the river went over its banks and into town every spring. There's a brass plaque just under the second-floor windows on the Loon Library commemorating the highest of the high-water marks. "Personally, though," she continued, "I don't believe it's the car at all. I think this shit we've got here is home-grown." She shook her head in disgust. "MacMillan just doesn't want to admit it. Especially since he was the idiot who repealed Ruth's firearm ordinance." She stooped and picked up her cigarette butt. "But that's nothing, Max. Get this. Sheriff Ralston's not coming back for six more weeks now and . . ."

"Six more weeks? Who's going to be running the Sheriff's Department in the meantime?"

"That's what I was going to tell you." She rolled her eyes. "MacMillan put Billy Kendall in charge this morning."

"You've got to be kidding? He can do that?"

"Of course he can. Sheriff's Department is under him."
She laughed. "Can you imagine? Billy Kendall running
the Sheriff's Department?" As a teenager, Billy Kendall
was probably one of the most notorious troublemakers in
Loon. Now, at the tender age of twenty-five, he's the high-
est-ranking deputy in the Sheriff's Department and, like a
reformed smoker or one of Rayleen's born-agains, a bigger pain in the ass than he ever was. "My bet is," Judy
continued, "it's going to be a toss-up as to what's
worse—the crime around here or Billy messing up everybody's lives trying to solve it." She smiled wearily. "Just
be glad, Max, you're way out there on the river where he
can't bother you."

Judy and I talked a few minutes more and then she told
me to give Ruth a hug for her and we said good-bye. I
crossed the street, hurried by the four display windows of
Sam's Sporting Goods, sidestepped the water dripping
from two big air conditioners humming in the office windows of The *Loon Sentinel* directly above, cut across the
Sunoco lot, and entered City Hall through the side door.

Ruth's office is on the second floor in the front and I
took the worn granite steps two at a time. The door to her
outer office was open and her staff of three white-haired
women were clacking away on their computer keyboards
when I walked in. The door to Ruth's private office was
closed.

I knew them all but caught Pauline Tritch's eye first. I
gestured to the closed door. "She busy, Pauline?" I asked.
"She called and asked me to meet her here."

Pauline looked over the tops of her glasses, smiled
weakly, and nodded. "In a meeting, Max." Her eyes were
red and swollen. Her son Danny and Lyle had grown up
together.

"I'll wait," I said.

"No. Go on in. She squinted at the big clock on the
wall. "She'll appreciate the interruption. They're well past
how long they had booked."

I shrugged, carefully opened the door, and peeked in.

Across the twenty feet of maroon carpet, Ruth was sitting at her big wood desk facing my direction. Two men, both in suits, stood at the front, their backs toward me. I couldn't tell who the fat one was. The tall guy with the broad shoulders and collar-length silver hair was Earl MacMillan and he was stabbing his finger across the desk at her. "If you expect us to sit still while you scare off the first big boon to business this town has had in ten years," he was saying, "then you don't know me . . ."

I rapped my knuckles loudly on the door.

Ruth saw me and closed her eyes. I could almost hear her sigh of relief. MacMillan and the fat man spun around and glared. Earl's glare turned into a frown. "Excuse me, Max," he growled, "but we're having a meeting here. You want to wait outside until . . . ?"

I looked at my watch. "Your time's up, Earl."

He spun and looked back at Ruth who was just standing. "Get this guy out of here, Ruth," he said with a jerk of his head in my direction, "I'm not finished yet."

She smiled wearily at him. "Yes you are, Earl. We can finish this tomorrow." She looked at me. "Come in, Max. Mr. MacMillan and Mr. Bernstein were just leaving."

"No, dammit." MacMillan balled his fists. "I want your promise on this now."

I took a few steps into the room. "Are you deaf, Earl?" I said. "The mayor wants you out of here, and if you're half as smart as you think you . . ."

Ruth held up her hand to silence me and looked at MacMillan. "As I've been telling you for the last half hour," she said with amazing calm, "I gave you my answer this morning, Earl. Lyle's death has changed the rules. Loon law enforcement has had several months to solve all of this and, except for a rusted-out Chevrolet from Rhode Island, they haven't the slightest lead. I owe it to the people of this community to see to it that they have more protection than a twenty-five-year-old boy still wet behind the ears can provide. As mayor I am going to request Vermont State Police assistance until this thing is solved.'' She leaned on the desk with both hands and narrowed her eyes. ''I expect your unqualified support.''

He grabbed a folder of papers from the desktop and shoved them into the fat man's arms. ''You're making a mistake, Ruth.'' He was pointing again. ''The citizens of Loon do not want marshal law. It's a disgrace to the memory of that young man and an affront to his fine family.'' His voice was going up a decibel a word. ''They're Loon natives. I knew his father and his grandfather. They deserve a local effort to find and punish these murderers.''

''Good-bye, Earl.'' She wasn't looking at him any longer and was typing something into the computer on her desk.

The fat man stuffed the folder of papers in his bulging soft-leather briefcase and, hugging it in his arms, waddled by me and out the door. He smelled of sour, nervous perspiration. MacMillan wasn't in that big of a hurry and he walked slowly across the room, breathing hard. When he got abreast of me, he stopped, his dark blue eyes flashing. ''You going to be open this winter, Max?'' He glared at me.

I shook my head. ''I hadn't planned on it. Why?''

''Maybe you should think about it,'' he said, jerking his silver mane toward Ruth. ''I can guarantee you that your girlfriend's going to be looking for employment after the November election.'' He pushed by me and out the door.

I started after him.

''Max! No!'' Ruth came around the desk and grabbed my arm. ''That's all I need.'' When she was sure MacMillan was gone, she released me, went to the door, and looked at the women in the outer office. ''You can all go,'' she said. ''I'll lock up.''

As soon as she closed the door, I grabbed and kissed

her. "I've missed you," I said, letting my hands slide down to her buttocks.

"Max, stop it." She pushed herself from me and went back across the room to her desk. "I'm not in the mood." She looked tired but great. She was wearing a fitted glen-plaid suit. The string of pearls I'd given her last year for her thirty-seventh birthday hung loosely on her off-white silk blouse. The skirt stopped at the back of her knees. I hadn't seen her in anything this short in quite a while, and even though she had a run from her heel to the back of her knee, I couldn't help but notice how good her legs looked all dressed up.

She went around behind the desk and slumped in her chair. The blinds were closed over the window behind it. Her collection of hard hats, each one bearing the logo of a different area construction or logging company, sat in a row on the deep windowsill beside a leggy red geranium. There was a cut-glass vase of fresh daffodils on the desk beside her computer monitor. A pile of manila file folders were stacked neatly on the other side next to the multiline telephone.

I sat in one of the two wooden chairs across from her. "You look great in that suit," I said. "It's sexy."

Her hand moved to the throat of the blouse.

"Of course, I know what's underneath." I smiled.

She didn't smile back.

"Who was the fat guy?"

"That was MacMillan's hotshot crime consultant," she said, leaning forward and carefully typing something into the computer keyboard again. "His name is Avery Bernstein."

"He smells."

"This whole thing stinks, Max."

"I ran into Judy on the street. She said they gave you a hard time this morning."

"It just goes on." She sighed and slumped back in the chair again.

"Anything official being done for Merriam and the girls?"

She nodded. "But not until Monday. Earl talked the *Sentinel* into holding the story until the convention's over. Then, I think, we'll start a fund for Lyle's daughters' college education." She crossed her legs under the desk. "I called Merriam immediately, but she just screamed at me and hung up."

"Screamed?"

She sighed. "Everyone's screaming at me these days, Max."

"Sounds to me like you've got the right idea, though."

"You mean the state police?"

I nodded.

"It's probably the only way Lyle's murder or any of this will ever be solved." She shook her head. "Judy tell you about Billy Kendall, too?"

"Yeah." I laughed.

"Unbelievable, isn't it?" She rubbed her temples. "MacMillan thinks a child barely out of reform school's going to solve all of this." She sighed long and hard. "You figure it out." She leaned forward again and resumed typing on the keyboard.

"What's with the computer?" I asked.

"Think Earl's my only problem?" She hit the ENTER key and turned the computer monitor around on its base so I could see the screen. "Can you read those names I highlighted on the screen there?"

I didn't have my reading glasses with me and even squinting couldn't focus. "Nope." I shook my head. "You read them. Who are they?"

She turned the monitor back around and read, "Thomas J. Marchetti, 13 Ocean Court, Westerly, Rhode Island. Constance Anne Roth, 152 East 62nd Street, New York City. And"—she looked at me from under her fringe of bangs, her eyes like green ice—"Vincent Salvadore d'Antella, Seaview, Newport, Rhode Island."

I leaned forward. "What!? What are they . . . ?"

"They bought seven-day fishing licenses this morning at Sam's, Max." Her face was now unreadable. "Computer flagged two of them because they have arrest records."

"But how did they get in a . . . what are they doing in your computer?"

"Sam's, like all official licensing agents, is now required to be tied into a main terminal in Montpelier through its cash registers. It's supposed to help Fish and Game ferret out known poachers."

I turned the monitor back toward myself and squinted at the screen. "MacMillan and fatty know?"

"No one knows yet but me." She turned the screen back toward her. "But procedure is to inform local law enforcement as soon as I receive something like this."

"You're going to tell Billy Kendall?"

She sighed and leaned back in the chair. "I'm supposed to inform local law enforcement. Whoever it is."

"But are you?"

"I don't know what to do."

"Who would know if you didn't do anything?"

She shrugged. "No one, probably." She tilted forward and put her forearms on the desk. "But if I don't and somehow someone finds out that I didn't, I'm really screwed. It would be interpreted that I have something to hide." She smiled weakly. "Which, in this case, is the truth."

"Does this mean d'Antella can't fish when he gets here?"

She rolled her eyes. "That's all you care about?"

"No, that's not all I care about but . . ."

"Yes, of course he can fish."

I pointed at the screen. "Then how do you make sure no one sees this?"

"Just delete it. It's only E-mail."

"Jesus," I said. "Then get rid of it."

She stood and turned to the window blinds. "Can't you see what's happening, Max?" She leaned and peered between the slats.

"I guess not."

"That computer says your guests bought those licenses at eight A.M. this morning."

"So?"

She spun around. "So, it means they were in town around the time Lyle was murdered."

"Oh, Jesus, Ruth." I stood this time. "Give me a break. You think they had something to do with Lyle?"

"Of course not, dammit. But someone will."

"Then delete it."

Now she was mad and she pointed a shaking finger at the computer. "That's misuse of the power of my office. I do that and I censor information that theoretically affects this entire town." She ran her hand through her hair. "I could be impeached."

"Oh, C'mon, Ruth. That's ridic . . ."

"C'mon, Ruth?" She stepped toward me and slammed her fist on the heavy desktop. I swear the computer jumped. "I've been listening to 'C'mon, Ruth' since March. Since that Collingwood person first called. I told you this wouldn't work, Max. I asked you to cancel them. I tried to tell you how bad this could be for me. Dammit!" She hit the desk again and this time the computer did jump. "I sent you that article, which I know you never read. Did you?"

I didn't answer.

"Did you?"

"Shhh." I held up my hand and looked back over my shoulder toward the office door, half expecting Pauline to come running in.

"Don't shush me," she hissed, sitting hard in the chair and staring at me. "Everyone's gone." She was breathing heavily. I stared back and watched the red color in her face slowly fade. Finally, her voice calmer, she said,

"Now I know why you're so good at what you do, Max. You're totally oblivious to everything else."

"Look," I said, sitting back in the chair, "I just spent most of the day helping d'Antella's bodyguards put up surveillance cameras all around the lodge. We've got a CLOSED sign out on Route 16 and a locked chain up at the end of the access road. The guy's arriving by helicopter at sunrise. Nobody's going to be able get within a half mile of him much less know he's there." I pointed at the computer. "Of course these people have records. But you let Billy Kendall see that thing and . . ."

"Why did you let them buy licenses in town?"

"I didn't know they had until after they had done it. They thought they were doing me a favor."

"Some favor."

"So?"

"So what?"

"So delete the names," I said.

She sighed and shook her head. "I'm not sure I can, Max."

"Hell." I stood and reached for the computer. "I'll do it."

"Don't you dare, Max Addams." She pointed at my chair. "Sit down." I sat and we looked at each other again. Finally she said, "I have to think about it, Max. I've got to find a way around it."

It was my turn to sigh. "Will you let me know if you decide not to delete the names?" She nodded and we were silent for another minute. Finally I looked at my watch and said, "I think we'd better go. Our reservations were for six-thirty."

She shook her head. "I don't feel like it anymore, Max. Besides, if I go out there, I'll just be hounded with questions."

"You have to eat."

"No I don't."

"Then how about just a drink?"

She shook her head again.

"A quickie on the desk?" I smiled and lifted one foot so she could see. "I'll keep the boots on."

She didn't even crack a smile at my attempt at humor.

I stood. "Well, then I guess I'll go back out to the lodge."

She nodded, but I don't think she really heard me. She was staring at the computer screen, tapping her fingernail lightly on the keyboard. I walked backward to the door, hoping she'd look up. She didn't and I slipped out and closed it quietly behind me.

The outer office wasn't empty.

Pauline was still at her desk. She looked up, her eyes wide behind her glasses. "Oh, it's you, Max. You startled me."

"Sorry," I said. "Ruth and I thought you'd gone."

"I'm leaving in a minute." She smiled and gestured to the papers on the desk in front of her. "Was just assembling some information for our new acting sheriff—he's such a nice boy."

CHAPTER 🦑 SIX

After canceling the dinner reservations at the hotel, I got back in the Jeep and drove straight out to the Starlight. If Bendel wasn't there yet with Tommy and Ralph, I didn't care. I didn't feel like schmoozing with clients anyway. What I did feel like was sitting at the bar and maybe getting a little drunk.

The Starlight is four miles north of Whitefork Lodge on Route 16. There's a circular sign high on a pole out by the road that stays lit day and night and reads STARLIGHT in blue neon script. The "R" in STARLIGHT has been missing for as long as I can remember, making it read pretty much the way a lot of the locals pronounce it. The establishment itself is a one-story building that sits perpendicular to the highway at the back of a large unpaved parking lot carved out of the trees. Built initially during World War II to house a radar installation, the building has been just about everything from a body shop and used-car dealership in the fifties to a topless disco in the sixties. Skip Willits and his Vietnamese wife, Lo Ming, bought it in the early eighties from the Vermont Department of Highways, which was using it to store snowplows, and they turned it into a bar and restaurant. Through good honest food, free pouring, and fair prices, the Starlight quickly became the home away from home for just about every pickup owner in the area. In fact, on any Friday and Saturday night, no matter what the weather, the parking lot overflows and trucks crowd the shoulders of both sides of Route 16 for a mile in each direction.

Tonight was no exception, but I drove into the jammed lot anyway on the chance that even though Ruth hadn't succumbed to my magic perhaps my parking karma was still intact. It was and I found a space being vacated beside the big Dumpster behind the building. I also found the red Thunderbird parked directly in front when I walked back around to the entrance.

Saturday night at the Starlight always features live country-and-western music from eight o'clock until closing. Friday night features music also, but thanks to Lo Ming, a mixture of bands perform—everything from bluegrass to jazz to good old loud rock 'n' roll. The only problem with Friday night at the Starlight is that you never know exactly what you're going to be listening to until you get there.

Tonight, the sign at the front door exclaimed in big glitter-encrusted black letters that the featured entertainment was a group called the Johnson Boys. They were from the southern Vermont town of Brattleboro. Written in red script diagonally across the middle of the sign was a quote I assumed to be from one of the Johnson Boys: "We ain't the best band in Vermont, but we sure as hell are the most popular," it said. I could hear their voices, electric guitars, and feel the vibrations of their thumping bass before I even opened the door.

Although it was just going down, the sun was still bright and it took me a few seconds to become accustomed to the comparative darkness inside the windowless Starlight. As I stepped into the long room, I was hit with the thick aroma of stale beer, people's bodies, cigarette smoke, and fried food. The Johnson Boys had just kicked into high gear with a song called "Honey Truck" and the wall-to-wall crowd was clapping, stomping, and banging beer pitchers in time with the music.

The Starlight is basically one long, deep room. When he remodeled, Skip tore down the tacky acoustical ceiling and exposed the big oak ceiling beams. Through the years they've been obliterated again by customer memorabilia: ties, business cards, photographs, and literally hundreds of baseball caps bearing logos from companies as diverse as IBM, AT&T, and Harley-Davidson to Loon Lager, Cersosimo Lumber, and somewhere up there, even an old cap with Whitefork Lodge printed on it.

If it's raining or the trout aren't cooperating during the week, I'll occasionally bring sports up to the Starlight for lunch. The sandwiches are hearty, the beer cold, and Skip makes them feel at home. But because Ruth hates big crowds and music so loud you have to yell to carry on a conversation, I seldom join the revelry on a Friday or Saturday night. As a result, I was amazed not only at the size of the crowd but at the number of wives, dates, and unattached women I pushed by on my way through the crowded room to the bar, which runs almost the depth of the room on the left.

I figured I'd nurse a Loon Lager alone for a while and then look around the room for Bendel and Kingfish's bodyguards.

The bar was packed three-deep in places and I had to wedge my shoulder sideways just to get my forearm and a five-dollar bill on the wet mahogany. Skip and Lo Ming's exotic, almond-eyed twenty-five-year-old daughter, Kate, was working this end and smiled when she saw who the arm and five were attached to. "Hello, Max," she yelled over the Johnson Boys. "Want a Loon?"

I held up two fingers.

Holding her long black hair out of the way with one hand, she reached into the cooler behind the bar, pulled out two dripping wet bottles, snapped the caps, and ex-

pertly slid them in front of me. "Looking for Bendel?"
she shouted.

"Yeah." I nodded and mouthed, "Eventually."

"When you're ready"—she pointed—"he's in a booth
over there."

I looked and caught a glimpse of Ralph and Tommy
through the crowd. They were squeezed into one of the
dozen booths Skip had running the length of the far wall.
I didn't see Bendel.

"Isn't that Bendel dancing?" she said.

I studied the spirited group on Skip's twelve square feet
of wood-grained linoleum dance floor. Kate was right.
There he was, eyes closed, arms flailing, white ponytail
bobbing in time with the music, dancing with a tall bru-
nette in an equally animated, bright green T-shirt with
AGAINST ABORTION? DON'T HAVE ONE! written in large
white letters on the front.

"I like that aftershave you've got on, Max," Kate said
as she made change for the guy on my right. "What's it
called?"

"A mistake." I looked up and down the bar. There
wasn't anyone I knew well enough to talk to . . . as if I
could have anyway over the Johnson Boys' din . . . so I
leaned my back to the bar, sipped one of the beers, and
watched Bendel and the rest of the dancers.

I was worried about Ruth. Lyle's murder was one thing,
but if the confrontation I'd witnessed in her office was a
sample of what she'd been going through with MacMillan
every day since losing her bid for governor, no wonder
she didn't need the potential grief d'Antella represented.
And now it was too late. I'd spent his money. The security
was in place. He'd be here in the morning. On top of that,
I was worried about what she was going to do with the
names in her computer. She'd never delete them. She took
her job too seriously for that. But she would never give
them to Billy Kendall either. That would be the same as
handing the whole thing to MacMillan. I sipped my beer

and lit a cigarette. It wasn't that I was disappointed I wasn't able to help her; it was that I sensed she didn't think I was capable. She had been deeply troubled by her dilemma. And what had I done? I'd suggested we get laid on her desk.

"Max?" Kate was back and leaned across the bar behind me. She put her mouth by my ear. "Who are the cute guys with Bendel?"

"Sports."

"They single?"

I shrugged.

"If they get tired of looking at trout, send them up here." She laughed. "I'm on every afternoon next week. Two to eight."

I looked over my shoulder to tell her I doubted they'd have time, but she was already gone and down at the other end of the bar drawing the first of several pitchers of beer for a line of very harried-looking waitresses.

I finished my first beer at the same time the Johnson Boys finished their set. The dance floor began to empty immediately and, taking advantage of the clear pathway to the booths, I grabbed my full beer and headed over. On the small stage, one of the band members, a young man with a black knit watchcap pulled down over his ears, took the microphone from its stand. Whistles bounced off the walls as the room thundered with applause. "Thank you," he said. Feedback made the microphone squeal for a second. "Thank you," he said again and the applause faded. "I'm Buck Johnson and my brothers and me are gonna take a break and have ourselves some Loon Lagers"—he smiled—"before all you good folks drink 'em all. Be back in fifteen or so." He turned his back on the new surge of applause and joined the others, who were lighting cigarettes and putting guitars in cases.

I dodged the rest of the way to the booth.

Bendel, his face red and slick with perspiration, was back in his seat and saw me first. "I thought you were eating in town with Ruth, Max." He was on one side, Tommy and Ralph were shoulder to shoulder on the other.

"Fell through," I said, grabbing an empty chair from a nearby table and sitting at the end of the booth. "Doesn't look like you ate yet," I said, pointing to the two or three rounds of beer bottles already in front of them.

Bendel shook his head.

I had already decided I wasn't going to mention anything about the names in the computer and I didn't want to talk about Ruth or Stormy, so I looked at Ralph. He was sipping a bottle of Budweiser. "You obviously must feel better."

He shrugged.

"Told him, that big brewery swill isn't going to help that stomach of his," Bendel said. "The least he could do is try one of our own." He lifted a half-full Loon Lager from the bunch on the table.

I took a pull on mine and looked at Tommy. He was drinking a Loon Lager. "It has a very unique taste," he said, "doesn't it?"

"Maple syrup," Bendel said. "Or at least that's what Stormy's brother says. He used to work at the brewery."

"It's good, Ralph," Tommy said. "You really ought to try it." He looked at me. "Old Kingfish is a nut for beer." He smiled. "He's gonna love this stuff."

"Most sports do," I said, lighting a cigarette. "In fact, the way some of our customers load up their cars with it on their way out of town, we sometimes wonder if they come for our brookies or the beer."

We all laughed except Ralph. He was looking at something over my shoulder. "Unless I don't know my cops," he said, barely moving his lips, "here comes trouble."

I turned and looked. It was Deputy Billy Kendall, the brim of his Smokey hat set straight on his square head, coming across the dance floor. As usual, it was his tiny eyes in that flat expanse of face that you noticed first—

sort of like two small-caliber bullet holes side by side in a block of wood. His light brown uniform was pressed crisp, his collar buttoned, and his tie straight. His badge, brass, and boots gleamed. I don't know whether it's all the cop gear he wears, his weightlifter bulk, or just his way of posturing, but he always walks like he's got a load in his pants. He nodded when he saw me looking. "Howdy, Max," he said, his leather belts creaking like a saddle as he came up to the table. He touched his hat brim. "Howdy, Mr. Domini." He smiled and put a big, freckled hand on the back of the booth. "How are you gentlemen tonight?" He looked from Tommy and Ralph to me. "Who's your company, Max?"

I introduced Tommy and Ralph to Billy. "Billy's acting sheriff in Loon right now," I added.

"Yep," he said, putting his other hand heavily on my shoulder. He looked down at me. "Don't wanta bother you, Max," he said, "but I got a couple things I want to ask you about."

"Like?"

"Well," he said. "I was curious 'bout whatcha got going on."

I frowned. "Going on?"

"Back there at Whitefork Lodge. What's with the closed sign I seen drivin' out here tonight?" His eyes were so tiny that, as always, I had a hard time telling who he was looking at.

"We aren't quite ready to open yet," I said.

"How come?" he said.

"Max is putting in four new rooms upstairs," Bendel said. "Everyone knows that."

"That's strange. I heard Lyle and his boys was done at your place."

"We're waiting on furniture," Bendel said quickly with one of his best smiles. "You can't put paying guests on the floor, can you?"

Billy gestured to Ralph and Tommy. "Then who are these two?"

"Nephew," Tommy said and nodded his head at Ralph. "My friend Ralph and I stopped by to say hello to Uncle Bendel."

"And meet his new wife," I said.

"Tommy missed the wedding," Bendel added.

"Where is Stormy?" Billy said.

"With Merriam Martin."

Billy looked back at Tommy. "Where you from?"

"Rhode Island," Ralph said.

"Whatcha do there?"

Tommy shrugged. "Real estate."

"Where you two boys headed after here?"

"Home." Tommy shrugged. "Thought we'd go back the long way. Down the west side of the state. See the sights. The Bennington Battle Monument—that kind of thing."

Billy looked back at me. "So what's that padlocked chain for, Max?"

"A little added insurance." I said. "People don't respect signs, you know that."

He nodded thoughtfully. "Makes sense," he said. "Actually, Max, I was hopin' I could have a word with you." He glanced at the others. "In private?"

I sighed. "Sure," I said, standing. "C'mon. I'll go with you to the bar. You can buy me another beer."

I led him to the bar, where, probably because of the uniform, a space opened instantly. He ordered two Loon Lagers from Kate. "What's on your mind, Bill?" I said.

He cleared his throat. "You gonna be seein' Mayor Pearlman anytime soon?"

I shrugged. "I just saw her about an hour ago."

"She mention me?"

I shrugged again. "More or less."

"She mention about the state police?"

"Yeah."

"She gonna do it?"

"I don't know."

He looked around and lowered his voice. "I was the one who found Lyle, Max. By my count, that makes two murders since this thing started."

I nodded. He was obviously referring to the homeless man who was stabbed to death a month ago. "Well, it sounds to me like the mayor's right. You might need the help, Bill."

His face darkened. "Don't need any help." He squared his shoulders. "I don't need them staties around, you know? I'd kinda like to solve this crime problem we got myself. I can do it, too."

Kate brought the beers. Billy gave her a five as I picked up one. "I'm sure you can, Bill. But . . ."

"No buts." He grabbed the other beer and drained over half of it. "I already have leads nobody else knows about." He lowered his voice. "Found a couple of things at the bowling alley this morning I'm following up right now. I'm tellin' you, Max, I'm gonna solve this." He put his mouth by my ear. "Come November's election," he whispered, "Sheriff Ralston's gonna find himself with a bit of competition." He leaned away from me, his voice going up. "Know what I mean, Max?"

I nodded. "So, what do you want me to do, Bill?"

Kate returned with his change and he waved her away. "That's for you, honey." Then back to me, "You gotta tell the mayor we was talkin'. Tell her I only just started this job and I deserve a chance. She'll listen to you. Tell her to hold off on those staties. Tell her Billy Kendall's got this thing almost wrapped up."

"Why don't you tell her yourself?"

He blushed. "I still kinda get my words all garbled around her, you know? Be better comin' from you anyways."

"All right, Bill." I wanted to get back to the booth. "I'll tell her."

"Good." He smiled. "Tell her now that I'm in charge, things are gonna get done. And done fast." He put his hand on the gun at his hip. "No bullshit. I'm going to hunt those guys down."

I was already backing away.

"I mean it, Max."

I nodded and smiled again.

There were several people moving between us now and he had to move his head back and forth to maintain eye contact. "By the way," he said, putting out his hand like a traffic cop, "I never heard." Everyone stopped and looked at him. "She like that venison I sent her?"

"Didn't she send you a thank-you note?" I kept slowly backing up.

"Oh sure. Got a real nice card. I just wondered how it tasted."

"I'll ask her that when I talk to her," I said, and then I lost sight of him as the Johnson Boys began to play again and bouncing, jiggling bodies moved back out onto the dance floor between us.

When I got back to the booth, I gave the new beer to Bendel.

"Did I hear you right, Max?" he asked. "Young Mr. Kendall's acting sheriff?"

I nodded. "That's about the size of it." I looked at Tommy. "You're fast on your feet," I said.

He smiled. "I've been lying to cops since I was eight years old, Max. It's a reflex."

"Well," Bendel said, "I hope this one believed you."

Ralph glanced toward the bar. You could just see Billy's hat over the crowd dancing in the foreground. "Cops drink on duty up here?"

"He's not on duty," I said. "He just never takes that damn uniform off."

When the Johnson Boys took their next break, we ordered a large cheese pizza for Tommy, Bendel, and I. Ralph, who said he's lactose-intolerant, had a plain burger.

By ten o'clock I was ready to leave. Not only was Bendel on the dance floor more than at the table, but the young girl in the revealing green T-shirt followed him to the table after every dance calling him "Daddy." She was beautiful and very drunk. We were all getting a little high and the tone of the room had begun to change as an evening's worth of booze began to affect everyone. For my part, I had noticed a couple of very attractive single women I know and they had blatantly noticed me back. Ruth was having enough problems. I didn't need to add any more with the rumors I could create. So, when green T-shirt weaved to the ladies' room, I suggested the four of us take our little party back to the lodge porch.

Bendel, covered with sweat, looked longingly toward the ladies' room but said nothing.

Tommy paid the bill. "This one's on Kingfish," he said.

Ralph rode back with me. "That Thunderbird's like being in a boat," he claimed. "I'd puke this burger before we were out of the parking lot."

It was a lovely, soft spring evening. The moon wasn't up yet, but there were so many stars that in places in the blue-black bowl of sky out over the lake they almost seemed to run together, forming big areas of pulsing white. Bendel and I and Tommy and Ralph pulled the rockers to the porch rail, put our feet up, and looked out at the whole thing reflecting upside down in the still water. Spotter, who had been locked in my room while we were gone, now lay stretched out full length in the cooling air under our legs. Tommy had taken off his shoes and occasionally would put one stockinged foot on the dog and scratch him with his toes. Stormy had come back from Merriam's, said good night, and gone to the cabin. For a while the warm yellow light from the windows had illuminated the yard, but now only the porch light remained.

"What's all that cheeping noise coming from the lake?"

Tommy asked. The spring cacophony of peepers tonight was almost a wall of noise out in the dark.

"Peepers," Bendel said.

"Peepers?"

"Little froglike things about the size of your thumbnail out there in the mud."

"Noisy, aren't they?"

"They're horny." Bendel laughed and sipped his brandy.

We all had snifters of brandy except Ralph. Stormy had made him an Alka-Seltzer on ice before she went to bed and I could hear the cubes clink in the glass in the dark as he sipped it.

"On the way back here, Bendel told me how he became a part of Whitefork Lodge," Tommy said. "How did you end up here, Max?"

"A friend of mine and I bought it about ten years ago," I said. "He bailed out and Spotter and I stayed."

"What were you doing when you bought it? You in the hotel business?"

I laughed. "I was a copywriter in an advertising agency in New York City. They fired me and my wife filed for divorce all in the same week."

"That's pretty rough."

"Nah. Best thing that ever happened to me," I said. "I hated the job and the marriage was over. I think I'd always wanted to do this. I was just too chicken to take the chance."

For years my wife's parents owned a summer place up here, and for twenty of them I spent two weeks of my four-week vacation from Kempton and Kearsy Advertising fly-fishing the Whitefork and its tributaries. Then, like a lot of men my age and income bracket, I found myself divorced and, as the result of a major company cutback, unemployed.

Free of everything that held me to the New York metropolitan area, I decided to turn avocation into vocation, and with another fly fisherman I knew, purchased seventy-five-plus acres on seventeen miles of the Whitefork River, complete with the almost-two-hundred-year-old log "Riverbend Hunting and Fishing Lodge" on Sweet Lake. We renamed the lodge "Whitefork" and opened for business with what was, at that time, the new concept of catering only to fly fishermen like ourselves.

Business wasn't good and my partner sold me his share after the first year. He returned to civilization but left his dog, Spotter, promising to send for him when he got settled elsewhere. He never sent for the dog and Spotter and I hung on, with me resorting to a part-time job at an advertising agency in Montpelier three days a week in order to cover child support for my teenage daughter and help Stormy make ends meet at the lodge. I met Ruth Pearlman at that time. She was practicing law with a firm across the street from my office and she lived in Loon also, so we started commuting the sixty-eight miles each way together.

"How long's Stormy been here?" Ralph wanted to know.

"Long before I came along," I said. "She worked for the original owners and was only going to stay until I got my feet on the ground." I laughed. "Guess I never got my feet on the ground because she's still here." Stormy had been the housekeeper and cook at the lodge for six years by the time I bought it. Originally, she had agreed only to stay long enough to assist me in the transition, but one month led to two, which led to a year, and now, ten years later, I couldn't run the place without her. She knows it and is kind enough not to remind me more than once or twice a year. Her 1099 says she is over sixty, but her energy level is that of someone half her age. I have trouble keeping up. Rayleen and Bendel refuse to try.

"So," I said, "what can you guys tell us about Kingfish and his friend?"

"What'd'ya want to know?" Ralph asked. His head

had stuffed up from the pollen in the air as soon as we'd arrived back at the lodge and his voice had become very nasal.

"I don't know. Idiosyncracies. Likes. Dislikes." I looked at Bendel. "The more we know, the better we can serve, right?"

Bendel saluted. "Yes, sir," he said. "We're here to serve."

"We don't know Connie very well," Tommy said. "She's a new one. Only been around since last fall."

"What's to know?" Ralph grumbled.

"Ralph means she's a bit of a flirt."

"Flirt? Shit!" Ralph laughed derisively. "She's a cock-teaser, that's what she is."

"Ralph thinks Connie should be more loyal to the old man." Tommy shook his head. "Personally, I don't care. I just don't understand why he has to bring women on these fishing trips. They never like it."

"Nothing like a warm female body on these chilly mountain nights," Bendel said dreamily.

"Can't do that in separate rooms," Ralph sneered.

"They're going to want separate rooms?" I looked at both of them and they both nodded. I'd have to remember to tell Stormy. I knew she had only fixed up the big double in the front overlooking the lake.

"What's Connie do when she's not with Kingfish?" I asked.

"She's a dancer," Tommy said.

"Yeah." Ralph laughed. "At some crotch and titty joint in New York City. Her stage name is, get this," He spelled it, "M-E-R-R-Y L-Y-N-N M-O-N-R-O."

Bendel's eyebrows went up. "What's she look like?"

"Guess." Ralph laughed.

"Kingfish married?" Bendel asked.

Neither one of them answered. Finally Tommy looked at me and said, "Kingfish is no different than any of those old guys I was telling you about this morning, Max. It's the way. Even if they are married. They've all got chicks like Connie."

"Yeah," Ralph snorted. "Spend the poor old guy's money and fuck everybody else behind his back."

"Give it a rest, Ralph," Tommy said wearily.

"Aw, shit, Tommy." Ralph took his feet from the rail and leaned forward. "They're all the same." He looked over at me. "You'll see, Max. Fifty bucks says she starts hittin' on you out there in the woods before this weekend's over."

"Won't be me," I said, looking at Bendel and smiling. "Sounds like you've got your job cut out for you, though."

"Nothing new to me, Max." He drained the brandy snifter. "I've been fighting them off for years." He laughed. "Sort of."

I laughed and quickly explained to Tommy and Ralph what Bendel did periodically in New York City. They, of course, were instantly very interested and began asking whether he'd worked with this or that supermodel and what they were like. I'd heard much of it before so I excused myself, got up from my rocker, and went inside to call Ruth. It wasn't quite eleven and I wanted to see how she was. I was still worried about her.

After six rings I was about to hang up when she finally answered. "Hello?" I could tell I'd awakened her.

"I'm sorry," I said. "I thought you'd still be awake."

"I'm awake now. What time is it?"

I told her.

"You want to know what I did about the names, right?"

"No. I was worried about you."

"I haven't done anything with them. They're still in my computer."

"That's not why I called. Really. You looked beat. I was worried."

"I'm okay, Max. I'm sorry about screwing up our evening. You looked cute in the boots. Smelled good, too. What did you do instead?''

''Ate at the Starlight with Bendel and the bodyguards.''

''What time's d'Antella coming in?''

''Exactly? I'm not sure. Early, though. Probably just before sunrise.''

''I wish you were here,'' she said.

''I can be in twenty minutes.''

She sighed. ''I'll be asleep.''

''I'll wake you.''

''No, Max. I've got a big day tomorrow. So do you. We both need our sleep tonight.''

''We'll sleep.''

''No we won't. Maybe we can sneak away one night next week.''

''Promise?''

''Promise,'' she said. ''Now, good night, Max. Don't worry about me. And read the article.'' She hung up.

I went into the dining room, took the brandy bottle from the sideboard, and carried it back out onto the porch.

Bendel saw me. ''You can hit me again, Max.'' He held out his snifter. ''One shot, at least.''

Tommy held his glass out too. ''Just a splash for me.''

Ralph stood. ''I think I'll go to bed.'' He looked at Tommy. ''I'll set the VCR for you. Okay if I just put this glass in the kitchen, Max?''

''Stormy'll love you for it,'' I said and then we listened to him as he went into the lodge and down the hall. I looked at Tommy. ''Are you saying that every time that VCR starts recording tonight it's going to set off a buzzer in your room?''

He nodded. ''Every time anything bigger than Spotter here walks in front of one of those cameras.''

According to what they'd explained earlier, the video cameras not only had light-sensitive night lenses, but the VCR in the reading room had a special sensor that, once something walked in front of the camera and it began taping, a signal was sent to a small receiver in Tommy's or Ralph's room that would awaken one of them. Tonight it would be Tommy, and after the signal was received, he could then go down to the reading room, rewind the tape, and see what or who had walked by.

"You're going to be up a lot," Bendel said.

"Why's that?"

"I'll bet a couple dozen deer come through here every night on their way to the lake." Bendel looked at me and winked. "Not to mention old Festus."

"Who?" Tommy looked alarmed.

"A black bear," I said.

"What do you call him? Fester?"

"Festus," Bendel laughed. "You're too young to remember *Gunsmoke* on TV, aren't you?"

Tommy nodded.

"Well," I said, "you'll see him limping around on TV tonight."

Tommy sighed. "If you two are right, I might have to adjust the sensitivity on those cameras tomorrow. I hadn't thought about the big animals around here."

"We've probably got an animal for every calibration you've got on those cameras," I said.

"Mice to moose," Bendel made a toasting gesture with his snifter. He was getting a little drunk.

"Moose?" Tommy's eyes widened.

"That's right," Bendel said, a definite slur showing in his voice now. "Mice to moose. Deer to dogs. Possums to people." He chuckled to himself.

"Well, if that's the case"—Tommy drained his snifter and stood—"then I'm going to get to bed, too. You've got to be sharp around Mr. d'Antella."

"Kingfish," Bendel said.

"Right. Kingfish." Tommy went to the screen door. "Don't let what Ralph said color your thinking, Bendel. Connie's okay. She tries. She just seems a little bizarre at first."

"I'll treat her like a queen," Bendel mumbled into his brandy. "Just like a queen."

Bendel made no apologies for his love of wine and brandy and seldom held back, but I'd never seen him get quite as drunk as he had tonight. I was tempted to carry him but before I could get my hands on him, he staggered down the porch steps and, singing "I Feel Pretty" from *West Side Story*, stumbled across the lawn. As Spotter and I stood there watching him weave to the cabin and fumble at the doorknob, I wondered how Stormy handled something like this. She's a recovering alcoholic and, although it's been fifteen years since her last drink, I know for a fact that drunks still bother her. When the door closed behind him and the porch light went out, I put the rockers back in their places, picked up Bendel's overturned glass, and, shooing Spotter in front of me, went into the lodge and locked the door.

I wedged the snifters in the dishwasher and put what was left of the bottle of brandy back in the sideboard cabinet. Before I turned out the lights, I peeked into the dark reading room at the television monitor and VCR. Several tiny green and red LED lights stared back. Above them the monitor screen silently and automatically switched from camera view to camera view to camera view creating, because of the night lenses, an eerie greenish glow in the room.

Spotter was already sitting outside my bedroom door and I turned out the lights and joined him. "Haven't you had enough of this room?" I said as I opened the door.

Obviously he hadn't because he was up on the foot end of the bed, had done his turning-in-circles thing, and flopped down on the quilt before I'd kicked off the cowboy boots. He looked at me, yawned, and closed his eyes. If Spotter wasn't muddy or Ruth wasn't staying over, I let him sleep on the bed. Actually, he was the best bed partner I'd ever had. He didn't snore, barely moved, and didn't steal covers even on the coldest nights.

I wasn't the least bit tired, so I left the bedside light on, slid under the sheet, and, with the pillows propped up behind me and my reading glasses on my nose, finally took a look at the article Ruth had sent me.

Under the headline "ORGANIZED CRIME'S DYSFUNC-TIONAL FAMILY?" the article was almost a full page long. Ruth had highlighted several paragraphs with yellow marker and circled the black-and-white picture of d'Antella and two younger men who appeared to be ex-iting a restaurant when it was taken. The subhead read, "The Ozzie Nelson of Crime Bosses, Vincent d'Antella, Fights for 1950's-Style Crime Family Values."

I lit a cigarette and read the first highlighted paragraph.

". . . as the winds of change blow through the kitchen windows of organized crime, there's one family still eat-ing food made on a stove and not in a microwave. At the head of the table sits seventy-eight-year-old Vincent d'Antella. His brood is unique. Unchanged. It is truly the last of the old-time crime families. And not unlike families all over America today, it is feeling the effects of our rapidly changing modern life. Not only are drugs, terror-ism, and ecological disaster knocking on the door, but a tighter economy and new social pressures have . . ."

I skipped to another highlighted section. ". . . his sup-porters applaud his stand on family values and against child pornography. His critics decry his refusal to deal cocaine and heroin."

Farther down the page, Ruth had highlighted this line: "Vincent d'Antella is a dinosaur. And, unfortunately, like all dinosaurs, destined to extinction."

And a little farther, she had marked this assassination attempt: "Several attempts have been made on d'Antella's life, the most recent in a Mystic, Connecticut, seaport mu-seum in full view of scores of fourth-grade children on a school outing. Although the children were unharmed and Mr. d'Antella escaped without so much as a hair out of place in his trademark carrot-colored toupee, three of his bodyguards were killed in the burst of high-powered rifle fire. Police now estimate the shots came from a marksman in the restored sail-loft building several hundred yards away. Like all mob shootings and, especially attempts on d'Antella's life, suspects abound but no arrests have been made.''

I let the article fall to my chest and took off the glasses.

A high-powered rifle from several hundred yards? I thought. *How are three tiny video cameras and two bodyguards going to prevent something like that?* .

CHAPTER ✦ SEVEN

The next morning at five Tommy tapped on my bedroom door. It was dark. I clicked on the bedside light. "Kingfish is on his way, Max," he said.

I pulled on my robe and slippers and Spotter and I joined him in the hallway. He was wearing a dark green windbreaker over a black T-shirt, baggy olive drab canvas trousers with big thigh pockets, and black Converse Hi-Tops. A small white button was stuck in his left ear with a thin cord running from it down into the neck of his shirt. He held a cellular phone and I could plainly see his shoulder holster under the jacket. "Chopper pilot called about half an hour ago." He stuffed the phone in a thigh pocket and looked at his watch. "They should be here in forty-five minutes."

"I'll make some coffee," I said, opening the front door and letting Spotter out. "Then I'll wake Stormy and Bendel."

"I already made coffee. Hope you don't mind." He smiled. "Already woke them up, too."

We went into the dining room. The Bunn steamed on the sideboard. I dug a mug from the cabinet underneath. "Ralph up?"

Tommy nodded toward the reading room. "At the monitor, using the remote controls to adjust the sensitivity."

I poured myself some coffee.

"Hope I didn't make it too strong," Tommy said, taking the pot and pouring himself another cup.

I sipped. He did. It was like burnt rubber. "How many times did you have to get up last night?"

He shrugged. "Ten. Twelve. Finally just slept on the couch in there by the equipment."

"Anything interesting?"

"I saw Festus. Big, isn't he?"

I nodded.

"What's with the limp?"

"Stormy got tired of having him in our garbage cans. She shot him." I sipped the coffee and walked into the reading room. Ralph was in front of the monitor, a large bottle of Tums open beside his elbow. He was dressed exactly like Tommy, except his jacket was over the back of the chair. The wide, tan leather straps of his shoulder holster crisscrossed his bony back.

"How do you feel this morning?" I asked.

He didn't turn. "We'll see in about forty-five minutes."

Tommy stepped into the room beside me. "I'm sorry to push, Max, but we don't have much time."

"Sorry." I took my coffee and went back to my room. Stormy and Bendel were coming up across the lawn from the cabin just as I passed the front door. From what I could see, if he had a hangover, he didn't show it.

Fifteen minutes later we were all assembled in the dining room. Tommy sat on the edge of the table. Across his legs he held an obscene-looking blue-black automatic rifle with an elaborate laser sight. "Okay," he said, patting the rifle, "here's the drill. Ralph's stomach can't do canoes, so he's gonna stay here at the monitors. When they land, Max, you and Bendel go get Kingfish and Connie in that big green canoe. I'll follow in the little red one." He tapped the button in his ear. "Ralph and I will be in contact the whole time. Once Kingfish and Connie are safely ashore and in the lodge, I'll stay with them and you and Bendel can ferry in their gear. Okay?''

I looked at Bendel. He nodded.

''Once the chopper's gone,'' he added with a smile, ''we can all relax and have some fun.''

''I assume everybody's gonna want breakfast,'' Stormy said.

''Everyone except maybe Ralph,'' Tommy said and looked at Ralph. ''You're pretty particular about what you eat in the morning, aren't you?''

Ralph looked at Stormy. ''I think I could do a little oatmeal,'' he said sheepishly. ''And skim milk.''

After telling Stormy that we would be needing two rooms for Kingfish and Connie, I followed Bendel and Tommy down to the dock.

''It's gonna be another hot one, huh?'' Tommy said, putting on his sunglasses.

It was. There wasn't a breath of air and the lake was so still it looked like poured plastic that had set perfectly overnight.

Spotter trotted out on the dock, brushed by my leg, and stood on the end, his tail up, head cocked and nose working.

Tommy looked at Spotter, then at the distant horizon, then, at me. ''Can he hear it coming?''

''Nah.'' I shook my head. ''He's deaf.''

''What's he doing then?''

Bendel chuckled and drained his coffee cup. ''Telling us the helicopter's coming. Spotter can feel it.''

Tommy laughed. ''You're shittin' me, right?''

I shook my head and pointed out over the lake. There it was. Just a noiseless speck out over the hazy mountains, growing in size by the second. We'd be able to hear it in a minute.

Tommy squinted over the tops of his sunglasses. ''I'll be damned.''

And then we could see it clearly and the ''whomp-

whomp-whomp-whomp'' of its rotors got louder as d'Antella's helicopter sped toward the lake. As it flew into the final valley it disappeared and for the next few minutes we could only hear it. Then, like a scene out of some action movie, it reappeared and rose melodramatically over the trees on the far side. I could clearly see faces in the bubble window. Limbs beneath it whipped violently and a couple dozen mallards who had been snoozing in the morning sun exploded from the water with a frantic thunder of wings and frightened quacking.

The helicopter hung there just at the far treeline for half a minute like a giant dragonfly and then, dropping its nose, it thundered toward us.

"If that's one of the quieter ones," Bendel said as we climbed into the lodge's big nineteen-foot Old Town, "I wonder what the noisy ones sound like."

Tommy slid into the twelve-foot Coleman and side by side we set out toward the spot seventy-five feet offshore where the chopper was now hovering.

Paddling into the chopper's prop wash and the waves it kicked up as it descended was harder than I thought it would be and we had to hunch forward and really dig with the paddles to make any headway at all. We were still twenty feet away when the helicopter settled onto the water and the pilot cut the engine. Instantly, the waves subsided, the wind was gone, and there was silence. The rotor blades slowed and the chopper rocked in the water.

As we glided up to the starboard pontoon, the side door slid open and a sturdy-looking, extremely suntanned little man dressed all in safari khaki climbed out butt first. He turned, grabbed a strut for support, and waved. The wisps of carrot-red hair showing under his long-billed cap caught in the morning sunlight. "Hey, Tomaso," he said with a wave.

"Good morning, Kingfish," Tommy yelled back.

Kingfish frowned. "Where's Ralphie?"

"You know Ralph," Tommy said.

Kingfish rolled his eyes, stooped, and expertly fended our bow from the pontoon. Bendel tossed him a rope and he quickly tied it with a slipknot to a strut. The big canoe's forward motion swung it sideways and, although I tried to stop it, the gunwale banged loudly into the pontoon. "A real pain in the ass, isn't it?" Kingfish said to me, as I handed him the rope from my end. "This chopper thing was their idea." He nodded toward Tommy, who was back paddling, holding in the water ten feet away. "Me? I woulda come by car."

"Don't worry about it." I stuck out my hand. "I'm Max Addams, Kingfish. Welcome to Whitefork Lodge."

He shook my hand and smiled. "How soon do we start fooling trout?"

I shrugged. "Right after breakfast."

"Okay. How do you want to do this unloading, Max?"

I peered by him toward the door. "Tommy wants us to take your lady friend and yourself first," I said. "Once you're both on the dock, Bendel and I can off-load your gear."

He nodded and grunted as he pulled himself to a standing position. "Connie?" he yelled into the chopper. "Let's go. They want to take us in first."

We have a couple of plastic surgeons from Boston who regularly fly-fish at Whitefork Lodge and they've told me how patients come to them with photographs of models' and movie stars' noses, jawlines, legs, breasts, and buttocks . . . how these pictures are used for the actual "improvements" they make. However, even knowing this, when I looked up and saw Constance Roth step into the half-light of the chopper doorway, I was stunned. Although no updraft of air caught her skirt and lifted it around her waist, it was Marilyn Monroe smiling down at me. The porcelain skin, bright red lips, plunging neckline, and platinum hair carefully covering one big blue eye were all Marilyn. And then some. Her low-cut bright red sweater and short red leather skirt looked sprayed on. And when she lifted one bare leg and slipped off one of her candy apple–red six-inch stiletto-heeled pumps, I couldn't help but think, *Oh Jesus. Poor Bendel.*

She was holding a pair of canvas-and-leather hiking boots in her other hand. "Do I have to put these stupid things on, Fishy?" she whined, pointing her red toenails at Kingfish. "I just did my feet last night, remember?" Her voice even had that breathy Monroe sound to it.

"Jesus Christ, Connie," Kingfish growled. "Do what you want. Just get the hell out here. Our ride's waitin'." He held out his hand. "But take those heels off. You wanna poke holes in the canoe?"

I felt the canoe lurch as Bendel quickly climbed out onto the pontoon. "Here," he said, stepping around Kingfish, "let me help." He took Connie's elbow and helped her down onto the pontoon. Her panties were red too. Then, with a little bow, Bendel introduced himself to both of them. "I'm Bendel Domini," he said. "If there is anything I can do for you, don't hesitate to ask."

"You can help me into this boat," Connie cooed, taking his hand with both of hers and cautiously placing her now-bare feet into the center of the canoe. It rocked and she quickly sat on her knees. "Oh! Ick! It's wet in here, Fishy."

Kingfish climbed in. Once he was seated behind her and Bendel was back in his seat in the bow, we jerked the slipknots free.

"Those things you're sitting on are life preservers," I said, pushing us off.

"This boat is so wobbly." Connie's knuckles were quickly turning white on the gunwales.

"Canoes wobble, for Chrissakes," Kingfish said.

A couple of deep strokes with the paddles in the now-glassy water and we pulled smoothly away. I feathered my paddle and aimed us at Spotter, who was still standing on the dock. Tommy had turned his canoe and, staying five feet behind us, paddled slowly, carefully scanning the lakeshore from behind his sunglasses and mumbling occasionally into the microphone on his wrist. The chopper pilot was now out on the pontoon and, over my shoulder, I watched him open the cargo hatch and begin to unload what looked like several canoe trips' worth of expensive embroidered luggage, equally expensive waxed canvas duffles and fly-rod tubes, and set them out on the pontoon.

"Milton?" Connie yelled back at the chopper without turning. "Milton? I want Quincy the next trip. I won't leave the dock until he's in my arms."

I assumed Milton to be the pilot and he nodded broadly and waved. "Yes, ma'am," he yelled back.

"Who's Quincy?" I asked.

"Goddamn dog," Kingfish said. "She don't go anywhere without it. Thing's asleep in a dog crate."

"Asleep? The hell he is." Connie turned carefully and frowned at both of us. "They gave him a shot is what they did, Max. Poor Quincy. He probably thinks he died." She glared at Kingfish. "If he's dead, Fishy, I don't know what I'm going to do."

"He's fine." Kingfish patted her back. "Just hold on. Quincy will be just fine." When she'd resumed her position, he looked back at me and sighed. "Thing's real small, Max. Hope you don't mind."

I shook my head. What difference did it make? It was too late now to worry about it. "I'm sure my dog will appreciate the company."

"That your dog there on the dock?" Connie asked.

"Yep. Name's Spotter."

"Does he like little dogs?"

"I don't think he's ever met one."

"He slobber?"

"When he's hot. Why?"

"Quincy hates it when big dogs slobber on him."

It took Bendel and me five trips to get all the luggage to the dock. Piled on top of the first load, of course, was the dog crate holding a comatose Quincy. From what I could see through the slits in the door of the cage, he looked like one of Stormy's string mops when she's just about to throw it out. I hoped for Kingfish's sake the little thing wasn't as dead as he looked.

Spotter was almost as interested in Quincy's condition as Connie was, and when she lifted the limp little form from the crate, he sniffed at it before she could fold the little dog into her arms. "Oh, look, Fishy." She beamed. "This big old dog likes my Quincy."

Kingfish wasn't interested. Like just about every fly-fishing guest we've had before him, he was already thinking about trout. Hands on his hips, he stood squinting out at the lake. "I think I see something hatching, Max," he said and pointed. "What are they? Hendricksons?"

I was still in the canoe, holding onto the dock. "Could be." I looked at the lake but didn't see anything. "This early in the morning, though, they're most likely midges."

Connie was trying to stroke some life into Quincy. The Marilyn Monroe from the chopper doorway had faded to a sort of burlesque caricature now that she was out in the bright morning light. It was still a stunning impersonation, but, obviously, the illusion was at its best in the softer, more flattering glow of jelled stage lights. "I can't get Quincy to wake up," she said, kissing the little dog, "and you're looking at bugs?"

"I told you," Kingfish growled, "the damn dog'll be fine. Unless you pet him to death."

Bendel, who had climbed up onto the dock to help them from the canoe, lifted the little head from her breast. "He'll be all right, Miss Roth," he said. "Don't worry."

She peeked innocently around the platinum hair, slowly ran her tongue over her smile, and, in a perfect imitation of Marilyn, breathed, "I hope you intend to call me Connie."

Tommy, who was out of the canoe and visibly nervous, stepped between Bendel and Connie and took Kingfish by the arm. "I'd feel better, sir," he said, beginning to herd them off the dock, "if we were up in the lodge for now." He quickly scanned the lake. "At least, until the helicopter has gone."

Back out on the lake for trip number two, Bendel put the paddle across his knees and lit a cigarette. "Max," he said over his shoulder, "are you thinking the same thing I'm thinking?"

"Could be."

"It's going to be an interesting week, isn't it?"

I laughed. "Probably more interesting for you than me."

By the time the chopper lifted off and roared back where it came from, Tommy had carried all the luggage to the lodge, and when Bendel and I got there, Stormy was already upstairs getting Kingfish and Connie settled into their separate rooms. The smoky aroma of ham mingled with yeasty baking bread filled the hallway. Spotter was sitting by the banister newel post at the bottom of the stairs, staring up at the second floor. As we went into the dining room to set the table for breakfast, I heard a squeaky "yip yip yip." Quincy was alive.

I'm pretty certain that Whitefork Lodge is fast becoming as famous for Stormy's cooking as we are for our big, feisty wild brook trout. Seldom does a guest angler leave without asking for—and receiving—the recipe of something he or she ate while at the lodge. We've even had guests request certain dishes when making reservations. And I've lost count of the times Stormy has been told she should write a cookbook.

There is a simple, hearty elegance to the things she makes and serves. At its core, it's just plain food. But it's the unique little things she does that seem to make it so special.

The breakfast she set out on the long, wide planks of the dining room table this morning was a good example.

Besides the ham I'd smelled in the hallway, there was a platter of her own maple-cured venison link sausage. A soft mountain of buttery scrambled eggs laced with soured cream and snippets of chives from the bunch always growing on the kitchen windowsill sat beside a big blue bowl of steaming, crispy-brown-edged home-fried potatoes mixed with roasted garlic and sautéed yellow onions from the Whitefork garden. Stormy makes all her own bread, and this morning she had sliced a yeasty loaf of cinnamon raisin, toasted it, and served the hot, thin slices with soft butter and homemade wild blueberry jam. For a beverage she served big glass mugs of hot cider. An apple wedge was perched on the rim of each and inside was a stick of cinnamon bark to stir it with. On the sideboard next to a fresh pot of coffee, there was a warm bourbon-and-maple-syrup apple pie "just in case."

"My goodness!" Kingfish said, as he and Connie walked into the dining room. "Look at this food."

"Remember your diet, Fishy." Connie had changed into a long, red silk robe. The red stilettos had been replaced by clear-plastic-heeled backless pumps with black fur on the toes. Quincy wasn't with her. "He's still recovering," she answered when I asked how he was. "The poor dear."

"Do you always eat a breakfast like this?" Kingfish took a piece of sausage and popped it in his mouth.

"Most days." I gestured for them to sit down. "Usually the fishing's too good to come back for lunch."

"Awww, Fishy," Connie said, sitting in a chair facing the windows. The robe front yawned open. "I won't see you at lunchtime?" She patted the captain's chair seat next to her.

Kingfish sat and took her hand. "You're going to be busy too, baby," he said, taking a sip of his cider. "I told you. You're going to learn how to cast a fly rod."

Connie looked at me from under the curtain of platinum hair. "Are you going to teach me, Max?"

I shook my head and pointed to Bendel, who had just entered the room with Stormy. He was carrying a second bowl of scrambled eggs. "Bendel's the teacher this week," I said.

Her eyes followed Bendel as he put the bowl on the table and took the seat across from her. "Oh, yes." She smiled at him. "The man who said he'll do anything I want."

He returned the smile. "We can start this morning, if you'd like."

Stormy, an uncharacteristic scowl building on her face, sat at the end opposite me. Tommy sat beside Bendel, his back to the windows.

"Isn't Ralph joining us?" I asked Tommy.

Stormy answered for him. "Already took Ralph his oatmeal in the reading room."

Kingfish turned and yelled over his shoulder. "Ralph! Get in here. You don't hafta eat this stuff, but long as I'm here, you're gonna sit with us."

"I can't, sir," he yelled back. "Someone has to watch the monitor."

"Screw that monitor crap. Get in here."

"Sir." Tommy smiled at Kingfish. "Ralph's right. Mr. Collingwood left explicit instructions about the security."

Kingfish sighed and shook his head wearily. "All right. All right." He waved his hand as if to clear the subject from the air and looked at Bendel. "Pass me those eggs."

"Just a little, Fishy. Remember your arteries."

"Screw my arteries," he said, taking the bowl of scrambled eggs. "I bet I got the best plumbing in this room." He scooped three big, steaming spoonfuls onto his plate.

"Kingfish had a quadruple bypass two years ago," Tommy explained, taking a slice of ham and passing me the plate.

Kingfish looked up. "Used a nice clean vein from my leg too," he said, now with a mouthful of eggs. "Doctors said to watch what I eat. No smoking. Crap like that."

He took another forkful. "I said, why the hell do I gotta do that now? I'm fixed, right?" He washed it all down with cider. "Doctor says to me, Mr. d'Antella, you don't want to have this problem all over again, now do you? And I says, 'How long did it take me to clog up my arteries the last time?' And he says, 'Thirty, forty years.' And I says, 'Then screw the diet. I ain't gonna be around no thirty, forty years, so I'm eatin' what I want. Period.' " He looked at Tommy. "Pass me that cinnamon bread. And that thing full of butter."

Unlike most fishing lodges I know about, at Whitefork we eat every meal with our guests. I find that most of them not only like our company, but love having the opportunity to discuss fishing strategies, equipment, and tactics with those of us who are supposed to be the "pros." Kingfish was no different, and as soon as he had his plate heaped with eggs, sausage, and cinnamon toast, he launched into questions about the Whitefork River, Sweet Lake, our famous trophy brook trout. Meanwhile, behind him, Connie and Bendel were having a separate conversation about New York City, the fashion industry, and from the snatches I heard when Kingfish paused to take a bite or swallow, photographers she'd posed for. Tommy didn't join in either conversation, but his eyes roamed the table as he ate, occasionally smiling and nodding politely, even though no one was specifically conversing with him. Stormy, normally the one to monopolize table conversation, was quiet. Her plate was full of food but, as far I could tell, untouched. Instead, she glared at Bendel over the rim of the coffee cup gripped tightly in her hands.

Kingfish wiped the last of his eggs up with a scrap of toast, stuffed it in his mouth, and, with a sigh, pushed his plate toward the center of the table. "Damn fine breakfast, Stormy." He leaned back in the chair and patted his stomach. "Best cinnamon bread I've ever tasted."

She gave him a weak smile. "My pleasure," she said.

He looked at Tommy. "I want our cook to have that

recipe,'' he said. ''Get it before we leave, huh?''

Tommy nodded.

Kingfish looked at me and made a casting gesture. ''Whenever you're ready, Max. Let's go fool the trout.''

Tommy put down his fork and wiped his mouth. ''This might be a good time to lay down a few rules,'' he said.

Kingfish narrowed his eyes. ''Rules, huh?''

''Yes, sir.'' He blushed slightly. ''I'm in charge of security this trip. And the way I'd like things done will be very simple.''

Kingfish shook his head in disgust. ''Nothing's simple with these guys,'' he said to me.

''I want you to enjoy yourself, sir. But I've got my job to do.''

''Yeah. Yeah.'' Kingfish pulled large cigar from the inside pocket of his safari shirt. ''Go ahead, then. Tell us how simple this is going to be.'' He bit off the end and spit it in his napkin.

''Well''—Tommy took a deep breath—''I've looked over things here at Max's place and, unlike the place in Montana, we're more closed in. There's a lot of cover . . .''

Kingfish pointed to the end of the cigar. ''You gotta match, Tommy?''

''I do.'' I held a match under the cigar while Tommy continued. ''Like I said, there's a lot of cover. The woods are thick. But we've got three cameras looking at most of the possible ways in. They'll be on all the time and either Ralph or myself will be sitting in that room in there monitoring them.''

''Good. Good.'' Kingfish exhaled a thick cloud of smoke.

''Although we'll be in constant radio contact''— Tommy pointed to the little button still in his ear—''only one of us will be able to be with you at all times during the day. So, I'd appreciate it if you don't go anywhere outdoors without either me or Ralph with you.'' He smiled. ''Or, without a Kevlar vest.''

''Definitely not.'' Kingfish shook his head. ''I'm not wearing one of those things. I sweat like a pig in them.''

''But, sir . . .''

Kingfish pointed the lit end of the cigar at him. ''Look, Tomaso. I know what you're tryin' to do. And I also know what a royal pain in the butt Collingwood can be about this stuff. But I ain't wearin' a bulletproof vest. Like I told you last year in Montana when I wouldn't wear one, I need the freedom to cast.'' He looked around the table at each of us. ''You want to be sure someone's dead, it's not the body, it's the head you shoot. Right?''

None of us answered.

Tommy sighed. ''All right,'' he said.

''Damn right it's all right.'' Kingfish jammed the cigar in his mouth. ''And, long as we're talking about what is and isn't all right''—he let a big wad of smoke drift from his mouth—''it's not going to be all right for you to be in the water when I'm fishing.'' Smoke came out with the words. ''So, stay outta the water. If I'm fishing, you be sitting on a rock.'' He looked at me. ''Last year in Montana, Max, these knotheads scared away more fish wadin' around, slippin' on rocks than I've caught in my whole life.'' He looked back at Tommy. ''Protectin' me's one thing, kid. Pissin' me off's another thing entirely.'' He knocked an ash in his coffee cup. ''So, I'll only say this once more.'' He leaned forward and pointed the cigar at Tommy. ''You and Mister Sickness stay outta the water when I'm fishin'.''

Tommy nodded thoughtfully. ''That's fair.''

''Good.'' Kingfish jammed the cigar in his mouth, stood, and looked down at me. ''So, let's go fool some trout, Max.''

CHAPTER ✦ EIGHT

Connie, deciding she wanted to spend time with Quincy after his harrowing "near-death experience" and maybe take a nap, opted to start her casting and fishing lessons after lunch. Bendel, now having nothing to do and wanting to get on the water as much as we all did after the long winter, asked to join us. Kingfish was elated. Stormy, however, still seemed angry, and hoping for a chance to find out what it was, I carried a pile of dishes into the kitchen. She was at the sink, the sleeves of her caftan rolled to her elbows.

"You okay?" I asked, setting the dishes on the island.

She nodded.

"You mad about all the drinking last night?"

She shook her head. "I'll be fine."

"I know this security stuff's a pain and, well, I wish it didn't have to be Bendel teaching Connie but . . ."

"I said, I'll be fine, Max," she snapped.

One thing you don't do is push Stormy. I sensed I was getting close, so I reluctantly left her standing there, shoulders hunched, looking into the sink full of dirty pots.

Although the workshop stands only about ten yards from the main lodge and is made of logs also, it somehow was spared by the fire. It had originally been a stable and boathouse. The left two-thirds now garage the lodge's old workhorse Jeep, snowplow, and the Harley-Davidson Sportster that Rayleen rebuilt for me in his spare time but I seldom have the time to ride. Along the back wall is the workbench, the wader drying rack, tubes of fly rods, paint cans, extra fishing gear, and all the tools necessary to perform emergency maintenance at Whitefork. Next to the Harley is a door that leads to a ten-by-eighteen-foot room with two shoulder-high windows that look back at the lodge. In Thornton Webster's time it had been used for tack and hay storage, but now it contains a small closet, kerosene space heater, stuffed chair, and a twin bed, which makes it adequate extra guest quarters in a pinch. Ruth thinks it's the most romantic room at the lodge.

I found Bendel at the workbench, already dressed in chest waders, felt-soled boots, and a vest, sorting through fly boxes. "I assume," he said without looking up, "that nymphs and streamers are the order for the day."

I nodded. "This morning, at least." I went to the workbench and stood beside him. "What's up with Stormy?"

"You noticed, huh?"

"Kind of hard not to."

He sighed. "She's jealous."

"Of what? Connie?"

"I guess," he said. "Among other things."

"Because you were talking to her at breakfast?"

"I suppose that didn't help. But, no. This happened just after they arrived."

"Yes . . . ?"

"Oh, hell, it was nothing." He sighed. "The toilet in the middle bathroom stuck again. The water wouldn't stop running and Connie thought she'd broken it," He shrugged. "I went in there with her and, you know what you have to do. I lifted off the tank lid, started fiddling with the intake valve, and . . ." He rolled his eyes. ". . . Stormy thinks it took longer than was necessary and she . . ."

The loud crack of a rifle shot made us jump. Bendel

dropped the box of tiny nymphs he was holding on the floor and before either of us could say anything, there was another shot. It came from just outside.

"Jesus," I said, running to the workshop door and out into the yard. "What the hell . . . ?" Bendel was right behind me.

A third shot boomed from the kitchen side of the lodge.

I looked. There was Stormy, like a poster of Annie Oakley, standing on the stoop outside the door, a faint haze of smoke curling from the long barrel of the Winchester in her hands. She saw us. "Got one of 'em," she yelled. "Nailed the overgrown rat mid-munch." She worked the lever and a spent brass shell spun out into the sunshine, clinked on the step at her feet, and rolled into the grass. She stomped down the steps and strode to the far side of the garden where she stooped and picked up a large dead woodchuck by the hind leg and held him out for us to see. He was about twice the size of Quincy. "Right in the head," she said, and then, with Spotter frantically sniffing at it, she unceremoniously carried the rodent to the garbage shed.

Tommy and Ralph, armed for battle, came running. Stormy saw them. "Too late boys. I got him," she said and held the big animal up for them to see. A long red string of blood swayed from its head. "Right behind the ear." She tossed the big rodent in a garbage can and closed the lid.

Even from my distance, I saw the color drain from Ralph. He dropped his gun and ran the short distance into the trees behind the lodge, where he fell to his knees behind the trunk of a big hemlock and threw up.

Tommy looked at Bendel and me. I don't think he knew what to say.

I didn't either, so I just shrugged.

"If I was you, Tommy," Bendel said with a laugh, "I'd work on your response time."

He blushed.

An upstairs window opened and Connie's head, shoulders, and 90 percent of her naked breasts leaned out. "You all right, Bendel?"

He gave her a little wave.

"Response time? Hell." Kingfish staggered out onto the porch, a freshly lit cigar barely clearing the top of all the fishing gear he was carrying. "A shot like that, maybe Stormy oughta be the one guarding me." He dumped everything on the porch floor. "Where's Ralph? I want him to help me sort this crap out."

Ralph didn't move from his place behind the tree.

"Ralph's busy right now, sir," Tommy said, slinging the rifle over his shoulder and walking to the porch. "I'll help."

Stormy leaned the Winchester against the porch rail and went to help Ralph. Bendel and I went back into the workshop. While he got down on his knees and picked up the spilled flies, I put on high bib-style neoprene waders, felt-soled wading boots, and chose my six-weight nine-foot three-piece Winston and a matching reel loaded with weight-forward, floating line.

Every fly fisherman has his preferences when it comes to a rod and reel. Where we're all very much alike is the vest. Everything a spincast or bait fisherman carries in his tackle box, a fly fisherman carries in his vest. And then some. My vest has thirty-two pockets. Front, back, and inside, and it looks like a Mae West life preserver when it's loaded. As usual, the outside front twenty pockets bulged with five fly boxes, packages of leader in a leather wallet, spools of tippet, fly floatant, a box of split shot, two kinds of bug repellant, a pocketknife, a pipe I seldom smoked, stale pipe tobacco, and an aquarium net. There was a wool drying patch pinned to a pocket flap and an embroidered Whitefork Lodge patch sewn on another. Forceps for removing hooks from fish mouths, nail clippers for cutting leader, a thermometer, and small scissors all swung from "D" rings. Inside, I carried line cleaner, a small book on entomology, adhesive bandages, tweezers, a flashlight, two pairs of reading glasses, cigarettes, matches, a lighter, line lubricant, sunglasses, strike detectors, and a coil of sinking tips. My plastic poncho, sunscreen, mosquito-proof head net, tape measure, an extra reel and reel spool filled with sinking line were in the large pockets on my back. I always feel a bit like the Michelin Man when I first put it on and have, more than once, heard chuckles as I waded into a river with a bunch of neophytes wearing brand-new vests.

But funny as I might have looked, Bendel and I couldn't help laughing out loud when we came out of the workshop and saw Kingfish on the porch. Bendel began taking pictures immediately.

Jumping up and down on the steps in the morning sun, Kingfish was struggling to force his blocky body down into a pair of tight green waders. His orange toupee was slightly askew, his face beet red, and he was breathing hard around the cigar. "Gimme a hand here, huh?" he said when he saw us coming up the lawn. "Food and cigars might not kill me, but, damn, this sure will. And knock off the laughing."

He was right. As far as I'm concerned, donning neoprene waders is the only facet of the gentle sport of fly fishing that's violent. No matter how you approach the task of putting them on or removing them, it's a fight you never really win.

Bendel and I each got a grip on the top of the waders and yanked upward while Kingfish, like a small child in one of those baby jumper things, bounced up and down between us.

When he was finally down into the waders, he sat on the steps, laced on his wading boots, and asked our opinion of the flies he might need to bring with him. "I got flies comin' outta my ass." He pointed at the small tower of stacked fly boxes beside his vest on the porch floor. "Look through those and tell me what I'll need."

Kingfish had easily a couple of thousand dollars' worth of high-end, name-brand gear lying around him. The Egyptian cotton vest alone must have cost four hundred dollars. His rod was a custom-made two-piece split bamboo and the reel attached to it was a Hardy from England. The green neoprene waders he was now trying to put on looked like they had just come out of the box.

I opened each box of flies, set aside the ones containing dry flies and terrestrials and handed him four boxes of nymphs, streamers, and beadheads. "These'll do for this morning," I said. "This afternoon, if we get a good hatch, we can all use dries."

Ordinarily, the first place on the river we take a sport new to Whitefork Lodge is a wide, easy-to-fish section of classic riffle water we call the "the Cobble." Today, however, the Cobble was like a lot of the Whitefork River running through our property. It was too deep, the current was dangerously fast, and it was still milky from runoff.

Instead, Bendel, Spotter, and I took Kingfish, with Tommy tagging along carrying the ugly little Uzi, upstream to a complex piece of pocket water about a hundred yards above the lodge Rayleen had named "God's Dump." "Looks to me like it might be the place," he had said when he first saw it, "where God got rid of everythin' he didn't need when he was creatin' the earth."

It's actually a good description. There are compact car-size granite boulders of disparate origin, wind-felled dead trees of several species jammed at tangled angles, waterfalls, deep pools, and roller-coaster chutes. The resulting labyrinth of currents, overhanging limbs, and steep, thickly overgrown, rock-encrusted embankment make basic overhead casting practically impossible. God's Dump is a great place if you know what you're doing, because in this hodgepodge of terrain and complex water, some of the Whitefork's biggest trout hide out and just keep getting bigger.

True to his nickname, Kingfish loved it. He stood at the

water's edge, his face slick and cap bill dripping from the fine waterfall mist in the air, and chuckled with delight. "This is a fantastic piece of water, Max. I don't know where to start."

"You might want to try over there." I pointed. "Where Spotter's pointing." Spotter had bounded ahead and now stood midstream on a giant weathered chunk of marble-veined, greenish granite. He was in his pose: tail straight out, graying muzzle pointing to a plunge pool at the tailout of a surging fifteen-foot chute of whitewater ten feet in front of him.

Kingfish frowned at the dog. "What the hell's he doing?"

"Showing you where the fish are," Bendel said, putting his eye to the Nikon's eyepiece and focusing.

"Bullshit."

"Really," I said. "That's why we call him Spotter."

"A fishing dog?" Kingfish threaded his line through the rod guides. "I don't believe it."

"Why don't you tie on a #14 gold-ribbed hare's ear and wade in here," I said, pointing to the swirling, thigh-deep water closest to us. "Cast it up into that chute." I smiled and began to string up my rod. "See what happens when your fly plunges back down into that pool Spotter's pointing at."

"Hell, why not," he said, digging the nymph I'd suggested from a fly box. "Gotta start somewhere." He began tying it onto his leader.

"I'd shorten your tippet a couple feet too," I said, looking at the length of the leader he was using. "You'll never feel the take with all that."

He paused with the knot, raised a bushy eyebrow, and gave me a sideways look. "I'll let you know when I want advice on my rig, all right?"

I shrugged and watched him bite the tag end from the knot and step into the water. I looked at Spotter. He hadn't changed his point.

Spotter can locate trout from the bank of the Whitefork that I can't see from midstream wearing expensive Polarized sunglasses. Since I insist on catch and release, part of his secret is, of course, he remembers. Once he's seen one caught and returned to the water he knows where they are. And 99 percent of the time they are. But it's when I've taken him to a new river or lake that his talent approaches a kind of doggy mysticism. It only takes him a minute or two; he stops, sniffs the air, and looks at the piece of water. Then, with his tail wagging slowly, he walks to the lip of the bank, takes a stance, and points his nose at the place where the fish are. I've tried him on warm-water farm ponds where I've been fishing for bass and big bluegills and he can't do it. He can only do it for members of the salmon family—and, especially, trout. But he is infallible. In fact, there are times he's just plain embarrassing. More than once I've positioned a sport in what I thought was a good place, only to look over at the riverbank and see Spotter sitting on his haunches watching us. I am positive that if he doesn't like the place I've picked, he slowly shakes his head "No" and then points with his nose to the spot in the river where he knows the fish really are.

The current was strong and for a couple seconds I thought Tommy was going in after Kingfish as the old man waded in, struggling to find firm footing on the slippery rocks below the fast-moving surface. Finally his felt soles got purchase and he faced upstream and began false casting, the loop in his pale green fly line building beautifully in the misty streamers of sunlight behind him. Tommy sat on a rock and, as is our custom, Bendel and I stayed where we were and let our client try for the first fish of the day.

Kingfish's short, thick torso put him low to the water and, as a result, his backcast whistled smoothly beneath the line-fouling overhanging branches that would surely have snared the rest of us.

I still thought his leader was too long, but when he finally shot the cast upstream, it unrolled beautifully, dropping the hare's ear nymph perfectly at the top end of the chute. Instantly the fly disappeared in the froth and Kingfish's leader and line were swept down the chute toward him, being pushed by tons of water deep into the plunge pool. He stripped the line back as fast as his stumpy little arms could work, a curling tangle of it stretching out in the current behind him.

Everything in fly-fishing boils down to microseconds, and it wasn't more than a heartbeat when Kingfish's line, leader, and fly were spit out of the pool and floated, untouched, toward him. He quickly and expertly rolled the line from the water, false cast twice, and shot the fly back up into the chute, this time flicking an expert little series of "S" curves in the line just as it settled on the water. His strategy was sound. The curves in the line would allow the fly to remain in the pool, perhaps, two seconds longer.

Two seconds was all it took and this time, instead of coming back down toward him, his fly line tightened and trembled and the polished bamboo rod arched as the hare's ear nymph was snatched by a hungry trout.

"All right, Kingfish," Tommy yelled and then mumbled into the microphone on his wrist. "Yeah. The old man's got one, Ralphie."

An excited Spotter, his tail almost wagging him off the rock, was barking as the fish jumped into the morning sunlight. It was a brookie. Still winter pale, I guessed it to be maybe sixteen inches long. By now Kingfish had all the loose line on his reel and as the trout dove back into the water and went deep, the expensive Hardy buzzed. He let the fish have its way for a couple seconds and then, holding the tip of the rod close to the water, expertly began to work the fish downstream toward himself.

"Watch that submerged branch," Bendel yelled.

It only took another minute and I stepped into the water

with my net and scooped up the pretty fish. Gills pulsing, one of its golden eyes glared at me. I carefully removed the hare's ear nymph from its lower lip and held the heavy, sagging net out to Kingfish. "You want to do the honors and release him?"

Reeling in his line, Kingfish waded over to where I stood. "Release him?" He tucked his rod under his arm, reached into the net and lifted the trout out. "Well . . ." He hefted the fish, turning it in his hand in a streamer of sunlight. "No," he said. "I think I'll keep this one. First trout of the year and all that."

I looked at Bendel for help. He was clicking pictures.

"Whitefork Lodge is catch and release only," I said to Kingfish. "I'm sorry but we don't kill fish here." I took the trout from his hand, stooped, and, holding it by the tail, slid it back into the water where I moved it back and forth in the current. "I thought you knew that." I let go when the fish had revived from its ordeal, and after a pause it darted away and dissolved into the deeper water. "It says clearly in our brochure that . . ."

"I read it," Kingfish said. "C.P.R. Catch, Photograph, and Release. But I also told Collingwood to tell you that I was gonna keep a few. I always do."

I rinsed my hands and stood. "Not here you don't." I gave him my most gracious smile.

He looked up at Tommy. "You know about this, Tomaso?"

Tommy nodded. "Max mentioned it." He shrugged. "I figured you'd work it out."

Kingfish looked back at me. I was still trying to smile but I could feel the tension growing like the mist in the air. "Catch and release, huh?" he said.

I nodded.

"You put 'em all back?"

I nodded again.

"No exceptions?"

"None." There were exceptions like accidently foul-hooking an artery or a fish too exhausted to be revived. Stormy had a bunch of delicious recipes she could implement at a moment's notice if a trout was accidentally killed, but I wasn't going to mention that now. "No exceptions," I said.

He looked at Bendel. "You too?"

"It's the right thing to do," Bendel said. "*Le trote sono troppo belle pescare soltanto una volta.*"

Kingfish looked upstream and didn't say anything. None of us said anything. A pair of chickadees flitted over us and chattered into the trees on the other side of the river. Finally Kingfish said to me, "You ever catch the same one twice?"

"Hell, yes." I laughed and pointed to the place in the water where I'd just released the trout. "I'm reasonably sure Bendel caught that one last fall."

"Every time a trout is caught and released," Bendel said, "he's that much harder to catch for the next guy."

"Besides that, he gets bigger," I said.

He rubbed at the white stubble showing on his chin. "I'll follow your rules, Max." He looked at Bendel. "I think Signore Domini is correct. *Le trote sono troppo belle pescare soltanto una volta.*"

"*Sì. Molto bene,*" Bendel said. "*Molto bene.*"

Kingfish turned to me and shook my hand. "Now," he said with a smile, "let's catch another."

I gestured to Spotter, who was back to pointing at the pool. "Spotter says that there are still more where that first one came from."

"Of course he does." He laughed. "He saw them all caught there before."

As we stepped back out of the water to give Kingfish room for his next cast, I whispered to Bendel, "What the hell was that you said?"

"You mean the Italian?"

"Yeah."

He smiled. "I told him, trout are too beautiful to catch only once."

CHAPTER ♦ NINE

Although Kingfish caught several more brook trout in the next fifteen minutes or so, each larger and prettier than that first one, nothing more was said about keeping any.

He certainly didn't need my suggestions this morning. His expertise with the fly rod and ability to read the God's Dump water made guiding unnecessary. And as far as his safety, he had Tommy glued to his hip. So Bendel and I held back and let him work his way upstream with Tommy and Spotter. When they were out of sight, we waded into the river. It had been an unusually long winter and neither of us could wait to wet our lines. We chose yellow-tailed #12 maribou muddlers and, casting them downstream, stripped the flashy flies back up toward us through the pockets and eddies, imitating wounded minnows. We each had splashy strikes at the downstream side of just about every rock but, whether it was ineptness, the barbless hooks on the muddlers, or just our early-season eagerness, we managed to lose every trout seconds after it was on.

It didn't make any difference really. It was great to finally be back out in the river and each time I had a trout on, no matter how brief, his intense, wild energy seemed to run right up my line into me like an electrical charge.

After about a half an hour and several more hits and misses for each of us, we reeled in and, following the sound of Spotter's barking, hiked up the tangled, rocky bank to where Tommy, sitting on a rotting birch log, was watching Kingfish. The old man was almost to his armpits below him in the center of the river and reeling in what, from our distance, looked like a large brown trout. Kingfish looked up and saw us. "Didn't know there were browns in the Whitefork," he yelled, maneuvering the big fish toward the net in his outstretched hand.

"We have a few," I yelled back. As a result of a stocking program long before I bought Whitefork Lodge, maybe two hundred very large, very elusive brown trout live under the cuts in the banks and the deeper holes in sections of the river like God's Dump. Every year one or two sports accidentally hook up with one of these leviathans but, because of delicate tippets and strong current, it's very seldom anyone ever gets their hands on one.

Kingfish, however, knew how to play a big fish in big water and the fat brown slid exhausted into his net. He tucked his rod under his arm, carefully removed the fly, and lifted the fish with two hands. "Bendel. Get a picture." He beamed. "He must be four pounds."

It was a beautiful fish with a red-and-black-spotted bronze back and a deep, butter-colored belly.

"What did you have on?" Bendel yelled, focusing his camera and clicking off two shots of the smiling old man and his fish.

"Same fly," Kingfish yelled back. Then he leaned and held the fish under water and when he was satisfied it was revived, let it go. He looked back up at us and, smiling broadly, began wading in. "It was Spotter that did it," he shouted. "I knew it was big fish. The dog was pointing differently." He climbed out of the water and, for a second, teetered on a rock. "The fur on his neck was standing on end." Kingfish climbed up the short hill through the trees toward where we stood. "I swear that dog was growling at the thing."

"I don't blame him for growling," Tommy said, extending his hand and pulling Kingfish up the final three feet. "That fish was almost bigger than Quincy." Tommy took Kingfish's rod and the old man sat heavily on the log. "Good job, sir." He patted Kingfish on the back.

"You think that's something," Bendel said. "Wait until you accidentally hook up with one of the landlocks we have coming up the river this month."

"Salmon?" Kingfish's eyes lit up.

"They come from Lake Champlain," I said. "Come up the Whitefork to spawn. They usually seem to go through at night, but every now and then we get lucky."

Spotter came running up through the trees with his tongue flapping at his cheek and a smile on his face, and after sniffing each of us, sat at Kingfish's feet.

"This is a great piece of water," Kingfish said, scratching Spotter's wet ears. "If every day up here is like this morning, Max, I might just stay here fooling big trout forever."

I smiled. "The Whitefork River is a great piece of water," I said. "Maybe, one of the last in Vermont." It begins in a series of small beaver ponds about twenty miles across the Vermont border in Canada. Once it crosses into the state of Vermont it is a gin-clear, twisting ribbon that snakes west through some of the most beautiful rolling forest country in New England, threading together fifty or so mere dots of towns with names like, "Moosenose," "Birch," "Stoneboat," "Graniteville," and, of course, "Loon." Just southwest of Loon it curves by the lodge, creates Sweet Lake, and eventually, dumps into Lake Champlain.

Bendel had taken off his vest and was squatting over it, digging through the big zippered back pocket. "Here it is," he said, pulling out a pint-size chromium flask, holding it up, and shaking it. The contents sloshed. "Bourbon, anyone?" He smiled and pulled out a chipped and dented blue tin cup.

Tommy declined and, telling Ralph what was going on, took the ugly, scoped rifle and worked his way down the steep, rocky embankment, across the boulders to the other side of the river, where, I guess, he thought he had a better view. We, however, could barely see him through the thickly budded birch, maple, and slippery elm.

Bendel, Kingfish, and I sat on the rotting log in the dappled, warming sunshine and passed the tin cup full of warm bourbon. I'm not much of a drinker and certainly don't care for hard liquor in the morning, and I try to discourage sports from drinking while fishing, but there is something about bourbon from a tin cup on the bank of a beautiful river deep in the forest that just seems right anytime of the day. Ruth, if she could see us, would laugh and call it "Male bonding," but it felt more primitive than that. It was almost ceremonial. As though, instead of the cup, it was a red clay pipe being passed between the three of us as we silently confirmed a mutual love for the outdoors and the sport we used to access it.

I lit a cigarette and looked at Kingfish. His cap was pushed back on his head and still damp from the earlier mist. The lines around his eyes behind the sunglasses were deep. "You look tired," I said. "How about we go back to the lodge, rest up, and then we can try the lake?"

"I could actually fall asleep right here," he said, closing his eyes.

"I'd go for that," Bendel said, sliding from the log to the ground in front of it and leaning his head back.

Kingfish put his hand on Bendel's shoulder. "It's a bitch gettin' old, isn't it?"

"Well, I don't know about you," Bendel said, taking another sip from the tin cup and handing it up to Kingfish, "but I asked for it. When I was a boy I couldn't wait for my birthday. And then when we moved to America, I couldn't wait until I was old enough to drive. Then it was old enough to drink. And when I became a photographer, I counted the years until I was no longer an apprentice." He laughed. "It seems like I've spent my life wanting to be old."

"It was the same for me," Kingfish said. "I was a barber. Years ago. A little four-chair place in Providence. My English still wasn't so good then, but the shop was owned by my cousin and most of our customers were Italian so it didn't matter. Like everyone did then, we paid protection." He smiled. "If you didn't, you got your place busted up. They were just punks. But they were connected." He sipped from the cup and handed it to me. "My cousin was a gambler. Horses mostly. He got into the punks for a lot of money and couldn't pay. They shot him." He shrugged. "Suddenly the barbershop was mine and I decided I wasn't gonna pay protection anymore. I figured, we'd given a life and that was enough. So I fought the punks and one day they came around in this big car and three of them got out and I knew they were going to kill me. So I took my cousin's gun and shot two of them before they even got to the first chair. I made the other take me to his boss." He smiled. "Nobody had ever done that before and the boss—his name was Nuncio Ragazzi—put me in the organization. At the bottom. I couldn't go back to the barbershop"—he looked at Bendel—"so, like you, I counted the years, dreaming to get to the top. From soldato to capo to underboss. And now here I am. Capo di capi." He sighed. "And there are new Vincent d'Antellas out there. Only today, they don't want to count years. They don't want to earn it by getting old. They want it now."

When we'd finished the cup of bourbon, Bendel repacked it in his vest and looked at his watch. "It's almost noon," he said, standing and putting the vest back on. "I should probably get back to the lodge and get things ready for Connie's first lesson."

Kingfish looked up at him and shielded his eyes with his hand. "Don't let that woman get to you, huh?"

Bendel smiled.

"I mean it. I'm sure you know that expression, 'All the world's a stage,' right?"

Bendel nodded. "Shakespeare."

"No. It's not Shakespeare," he said. "It's Connie. She lives it. Sometimes, I swear, she actually thinks she *is* Marilyn Monroe."

"It won't bother me." Bendel smiled and picked up his fly rod. "Although, when I was a young man, Marilyn Monroe was my fantasy woman."

"You're not alone." Kingfish laughed. "She can really pack them in. You know The Crazy Mule?"

"In New York City?"

"Yeah. Forty-fourth and Eighth."

Bendel shook his head. "I used to have a studio up in the Seventies on the West Side but I never got down into that neighborhood."

"When were you there?"

"Until a couple years ago when Stormy and I were married."

Kingfish shrugged. "Too bad. You should see Connie when she dances at The Mule." He smiled. "What a body. And those legs! Wrap yourself in those and you're Joe DiMaggio."

As it turned out, we all went back to the lodge together. Kingfish decided a nap wouldn't be a bad idea. "They had me up at three this morning to get here, Max," he said. "Then all the way up in the chopper Connie's yakking about that damn dog." He smiled. "An hour or so of lie down'll do me good."

I was just as happy to be going back. I wanted to call Ruth and find out what she had decided to do with the names in the computer.

As we pushed our way out of the trees from the river

we could see Connie, in a bright red bikini, sitting in the hot sunshine in the middle of the lawn in front of the lodge. Her skin looked startlingly white against the rich green grass and shone with suntan oil. I could faintly smell its coconut fragrance even from where we stood. Quincy, contorted in the grass beside her, was licking his ass. There was a leash from his sequined collar to a metal stake in the ground. When he saw Spotter, he jumped to his feet and, yipping insanely, sped toward us only to be yanked to an abrupt, almost neck-breaking halt at the end of the leash. His little eyes bulged as, still yipping frantically on his hind legs, he lunged repeatedly at the leash.

Spotter ignored him and continued around the lodge, probably to check on the dead woodchuck.

"Quincy, baby," Connie cooed, pulling on the leash, "you stop that or Momma will be mad."

"Momma's gonna burn, baby," Kingfish said, as we crossed the yard to the porch.

She looked over her big sunglasses. "I want a little color, Fishy," she said, running a finger down her long, greasy thigh. "Besides, this is a fifteen."

"Don't forget what happened in Grand Cayman," he said, as we climbed the steps up into the shade. "You said that was fifteen too." He looked at me and whispered, "Burned her tits so bad I couldn't touch 'em for three days."

"In case you haven't noticed, Fishy"—she adjusted her bra straps—"they're covered today." Her eyes moved to Bendel and she smiled.

We took off our waders, hung up our vests, and broke down our rods. Bendel went out into the yard to talk to Connie about a time for her casting lessons. Kingfish, Tommy, and I went into the lodge, where we split up in the hallway; Kingfish up the stairs and Tommy to the reading room to relieve Ralph at the monitor. I went to the kitchen to look for Stormy. She would need to know that we were all back and everyone would eventually be wanting lunch.

The kitchen was empty and I found her outside the back door in a straw hat with a wide, tattered brim, hoeing in the garden. Behind her, Spotter was sniffing around where the woodchuck had been shot. Stormy had safety-pinned the hem of her caftan up above her knees and her Bean boots and pale calves were covered with wet dirt. The ubiquitous Camel smoldered from the corner of her mouth. She looked up as I came out the door. "Through already? What's the matter? Water too high?"

"No, Kingfish is tired," I said. "And Bendel has to get ready to give lessons. So we knocked off for the morning." I went down the steps and stood at the edge of the rich-smelling, freshly tilled earth.

She gestured to the two rows of foot-high pea shoots just beginning to show curls of climbing tentacles. "Need to put in the trellis for these. Maybe you could do that while I'm fixin' lunch."

"Sure." Rayleen had built a bunch of two-by-eight-foot sections of lattice fencing that we used every spring as trellis for Stormy's peas and then again, when they were gone, for the tomatoes. The trellis had sharpened stakes on each end and hammered easily into the ground. We keep them in the rafters of the workshop.

She picked up a small clump of sod, shook the dirt loose from its root system, and tossed it out of the garden. "See our bathing beauty?"

I nodded. "Hard not to."

She shook her head in obvious disgust. "Some plastic surgeon made enough college tuition off that one for ten kids." She chopped the ground with her hoe.

Ruth was the same way. Why reconstructive cosmetic surgery was any different than dying hair, waxing legs, false eyelashes, fake fingernails, straightening teeth, or wearing padded bras, I'll never know. I did, however, know enough to say nothing and instead walked down to the workshop to get the lattice fencing out of the rafters.

Over in the yard, Quincy, still on his leash, was lying in the grass chewing on a tennis ball. Connie was gone.

Not surprisingly, I found her with Bendel in the workshop. She had slipped a denim shirt over the bikini bra and backless pumps on her feet and was sitting, legs crossed provocatively, up on the workbench while he hovered before her, his eye glued to the Nikon.

Neither of them saw me at first and, although I probably shouldn't have, I stopped just inside the doorway and watched. I have to admit, from my distance and in the half light of the room, Connie looked very sexy as she sat there in her cliché, classic cheesecake pose.

"Pout," he said, his ponytail bobbing and his camera clicking. "That's it. More. More. More. Beautiful!" He dropped to one knee. "Arch that long neck. That's it. Great." He climbed up onto the workbench and aimed down at her. "Open the shirt more. No. More cleavage. No. Like this." He reached down and arranged her collar and she grabbed his hand. They looked at each other and, although I couldn't see his face, she peered around the wave of blond hair and stuck out her lower lip like a little child. As his hand began to move toward her breasts, I cleared my throat and, rubbing my eyes as if I'd just entered, started across the room.

He straightened. "Oh, hi, Max," he said. It was too dim to see his reaction, but the window light was strong on her face and she looked perturbed.

"Which month is this you're shooting?" I laughed, referring to next year's Whitefork Lodge calendar, which he had already started to work on.

Bendel laughed too and climbed down from the workbench. "Just doing my thing," he said, helping her from her perch. "Guess we got carried away." He began picking through the bin full of fly rods we use for casting instruction. "Don't we have an eight-footer in this bunch?"

"Yeah," I said, digging into the bin. "There should be two of them."

As Bendel and I picked through the rod tubes, Connie wandered around the perimeter of the room, touching this and lifting that. I could feel her looking at us. It was obvious to me that she was waiting for me to go about my business and leave them alone. After what I'd seen, I wasn't about to accommodate her, so not only did I stay with them until Bendel had put together a small pile of gear he would use for her lessons, but I had him help me get the trellis down from the rafters and carry it all up to the garden. By then Connie had tired of the whole thing and went back out into the yard where she snatched up Quincy and, with her shirttails flying, disappeared into the lodge.

Bendel helped me put the trellis in and we were just hammering the last one in place when Stormy announced lunch was on the table.

The meal was buffet style with plates, utensils, and food spread out on the dining room table. Loon Lager, iced tea, and bottles of spring water were on the sideboard. Stormy was apologetic about the food, but I thought it was great considering the short notice. Three kinds of sliced bread, a platter of cold meats, two cheeses, and sandwich fixings were spread out beside three matching big blue bowls containing, left to right, potato salad, green salad, and her famous kidney-bean-and-onion salad. The apple pie we hadn't touched at breakfast sat at the end with a stack of paper plates, dessert forks, and a tub of Cool Whip.

Except for Tommy, who was taking his turn at the monitor, and Stormy, who said she wanted to tie up strings for the peas in the garden, we all filled our plates, grabbed something to drink, and went out onto the porch to eat.

Connie had changed into a pair of tight dungarees and a white cotton sweater so tight it would have revealed every stitch on a bra had she been wearing one. She had

pulled her hair back in a ponytail and, as she carefully
eased into the rocker next to mine with her food, I noticed
what might have been a faint vertical facelift scar in her
hair just above her ears. Bendel sat on her left. Kingfish
sat on my right. Ralph, with only a sandwich on his plate,
sat with one cheek up on the railing in front of us. He
balanced a bottle of spring water beside his hip.

"Maybe you'd feel better," Connie said to him, "if you
ate a little more balanced diet."

"I eat what sounds good," he said, taking a small bite
of his sandwich.

"That's the way they say you should feed small children," Bendel said, stabbing several leaves of olive-oily
radicchio with his fork. "Let them eat what they want.
Their body knows. And eventually they get everything
they need."

"Leave the kid alone, Connie," Kingfish said. "He
wants to miss out on this good food, that's his problem."

"He'd probably just throw it up anyway," she mumbled.

Ralph blushed, stopped chewing, and glared at her.

Kingfish saw the look also. "Hey, you two!" He narrowed his eyes and looked from Ralph to Connie and back
again. "Don't start."

They continued to stare daggers at each other but said
nothing.

"I thought we might try fishing at the mouth of the
river this afternoon," I said quickly, hoping I could get
the conversation going in another direction.

It did. "What about out in the lake?" Kingfish asked.
"I thought that was the plan for this afternoon."

I shook my head. "Save that for this evening," I said.
"Right now, my bet is that the big ones are all holding
in the fast water where the river runs into it. It's downstream casting with streamers. Take my word for it, you'll
enjoy it. And, who knows, you might even luck into a

landlocked.'' I looked at Ralph. ''Are you going to join us this afternoon?''

''Nah,'' he said. ''I'm really allergic to pollen. It's bad enough up here inside the lodge.''

Connie helped Stormy and I lug everything that wasn't eaten back to the kitchen. ''Why isn't the kitchen up here in the front of the lodge where your room is, Max?'' Connie asked as she started back toward the kitchen the second time with a salad bowl in each hand. ''Wouldn't it be easier?''

When she was gone, Stormy whispered, ''See? Even bimbos agree with me.''

Connie staked Quincy in the yard again and then joined Bendel out on the dock for her first lesson. Ralph joined me on the porch steps as I waited for Kingfish and Tommy, who had gone upstairs to change into some cooler clothes. The thermometer outside the kitchen window read seventy-eight degrees.

''Look at her out there, Max,'' he said, sitting on the upwind side of my cigarette. ''You gonna tell me that woman's no cock-teaser.''

I looked out at Connie and Bendel. He was standing behind her, arms around her, his hands on hers as he helped her wave the fly rod in the classic ten o'clock–to-two o'clock position. ''If it is,'' I said, laughing, ''then just about every student we get up here is guilty of it.''

He frowned.

''That's the way people learn to swing a golf club too,'' I said. ''Put your hands on theirs so they can feel the right way to do it.''

''There's feeling all right.'' He pointed. ''But I think Bendel's the one getting it.''

I looked back out at the dock. Connie had arched her back in such a way that, at least from our point of view, it appeared her buttocks were pushing suggestively at Bendel's groin.

''She doesn't care who sees her,'' Ralph said. ''Long

as she's having fun, the hell with everyone."

I sighed. It also appeared, from where I sat, that Bendel
didn't care much either.

Typical of spring runoff, several pods of feeding brook
trout hung in the still-cloudy tail-out water of the "Inlet
Pool." I could even see what looked like the big silver
torpedo shapes of a landlocked or two. Unfortunately,
hard as I tried, I could not decipher what it was they were
eating. As a result, no matter what fly pattern I suggested
Kingfish cast to them, it didn't work. It was almost embarrassing. The only explanation I could offer was the
possibility that the unseasonably warm weather combined
with the extremely cold, turbid water had confused the
trout.

Kingfish reeled in and looked over at Tommy, who was
leaning against a beech tree on the far bank. "Stay there,
Tomaso," he yelled. "I want to talk to Max. In private."

Tommy gave a nod.

"Don't worry about the fish, Max," Kingfish said, as
we waded out of the water onto the gravel bar that splits
the river at its mouth. He pulled a cigar from a vest pocket.
"What I'd worry about, I was you, is Bendel."

"Bendel?"

"Yeah, Bendel." He bit off the end of a cigar and spit
it at his boots. "He'd better watch his ass with Connie."

"I don't know how to say this, but," I said, "I've seen
it. She's the one flirting, not him."

He studied me with one eye while he cupped a match
and lit the cigar. A thunderhead of thick smoke rose above
him in the still air. When he was satisfied with the way it
was lit, he shook out the match and dropped it. "I'm not
criticizing Bendel," he said. "I'm saying he should watch
out. You can make a real fool of yourself with a woman
like that."

"Then why don't you tell her . . . ?"

He slowly shook his head. "There are some things I

can't do for her. You know what I'm saying, Max? She has needs.'' He shrugged. ''I understand that. I don't own her. And it's her vacation too.''

''Bendel's married. He has more sense than . . .''

''That woman's the best stripper I've ever seen, Max. Packs 'em in. You know why?'' He didn't wait for an answer. ''It's not that Marilyn Monroe look. Or even that body. Although that don't hurt.'' He smiled. ''What gets her hundred-dollar bills stuck in her G-string is, she knows how to work an audience. She picks out one guy. Maybe two. And she plays to them. Like every move she makes is just for them.'' He took the cigar from his mouth and blew on the ash. ''Trouble is, Connie don't know how to stop when the show's over. And now she's working Bendel.''

I smiled. ''I think he can handle himself.''

He smiled back. ''If he does, he'll be the first.''

CHAPTER ✦ TEN

During the next three days the temperature not only went up but you had to be blind not to see Connie pouring on the heat as far as Bendel was concerned. Whether they were out on the dock, at the dining room table, or on the porch in the evening as we all watched the sun set over the lake, her coquetry was blatant.

I had pulled Bendel aside after my talk with Kingfish, but he had only laughed and dismissed any suggestion that he might be vulnerable to Connie's advances. "The woman flirts, Max," he said with a laugh. "I respond. But there's nothing to it. It's part of the job. Stop worrying."

It was Stormy I was worried about. I've known her a long time and I know when something's bothering her. Normally she comes on twice her size. Her voice is big. Her gestures bigger. Generally there's nothing she can't handle or at least get someone else to handle for her. But now she was quiet. And other than cooking and cleaning, she spent her time on her knees in the vegetable garden. She didn't join us at meals or on the porch in the evening, preferring to eat alone in the kitchen or retire early to the cabin to read. And her color seemed to be fading, her eyes had lost the sparkle, and her hair, usually plaited in that long, tight, precise braid, appeared almost unkempt.

Of course, like Bendel, she denied everything when I confronted her. "Told you, Max," she said, "I don't get jealous. It's just a touch of the flu. Probably caught somethin' from that Ralph, is all. It'll be gone in a day or two."

"But you and Bendel hardly say a word to each other," I said.

"Nothin' to talk about." She shrugged, jammed her straw hat on her head, and went outside to the garden.

As I stood at the kitchen window watching her attack the weeds around the roots of the peas with a hoe, I heard voices coming from the front porch. Not wanting to eavesdrop, I headed for the garden myself. As I got to the back door, the voices turned angry.

One of them was Connie. "You don't own me," I heard her whisper.

The voice that answered her was Ralph's. "You don't even see what you're doing, do you?" he whispered back. "You think you can just . . ."

She interrupted, "Deal with it." Then I heard the screen door slam, feet going up the front stairs, and it was quiet.

I went out the back door and sat on the stoop and lit a cigarette. Stormy didn't look up.

Ruth's problems had been growing too. Although, on Monday, she had the Vermont State Police begin patroling through town, the incidents of crime, although mostly late-night petty robberies, began again with alarming regularity. As Gordon Miller observed in an editorial in the Tuesday morning *Sentinel*'s "UpCountry Insider" column, ". . . Whoever these felons are," it read, "they obviously know what the police are doing, when they're doing it, and where. If Acting Sheriff Kendall wants some advice, this Insider suggests maybe looking closer to home."

Lyle Martin's funeral was on Monday afternoon and Stormy, Bendel, and I left the lodge for a couple hours to attend the services with thirty or forty other friends, co-workers, and family members. Those of us who knew of

Lyle's carving skills looked at each other when we first saw his casket. Stained to look like solid cherry but made from some sort of molded wood composite, its sides and top were laced with leaves and vines embossed to look like carvings. John Quinn, who sat next to me in the church pew and for whom Lyle had done lots of fancy, carved cabinetry work when the Loon Hotel was remodeled, leaned over and whispered, "Good God, Max. Lyle must be rolling over in that thing right now." Seeing Lyle's three little strawberry-blond daughters sitting there in the church in matching dark blue dresses all fluffed out with crinolines and then again lined up at the gravesite like little porcelain dolls was more than any of us in attendance could take and all of us wept freely as first one then the other dropped tiny handfuls of dirt into the hole onto their daddy's coffin.

Rayleen returned Tuesday morning with his cap on backward, a cross finger-painted in red on his forehead, and a vial of "tears" on a leather thong around his neck. I had thought that I might solve my Bendel/Connie/ Stormy problem by putting him in charge of Connie's fly-fishing instruction for the remainder of the week. But no. As soon as he heard about Lyle's murder and the trashing of the bowling alley, he was off to town not only to see Merriam and the girls, but to check on the condition of his apartment above the alleys. "Be back tomorrow, Max," he said as he climbed back into his truck. "Them folks need me right now more'n you do."

The fishing continued to be frustrating. Sweet Lake, which usually is like trout soup in the evenings this time of year, wasn't cooperating. Ordinarily, it wouldn't have bothered me. Fly-fishing's like that. Sometimes you can go a week and not catch anything even though you can look into the water and see them looking back. Spotter was no help either. His job was finding them, not catching them. But with Kingfish I felt antsy. He had paid so much money up front that I felt an unusual obligation to put him onto fish. "Stop worrying about it, Max," he said after Rayleen had left for town. "It'll get better. Meanwhile take me back to that place where I caught the brown. I told you I could fish there forever."

So Spotter and I took him back to God's Dump.

This time Tommy stayed on the lodge side of the river while Kingfish and I continued with Spotter down the steep embankment and across to the other side where the sun was at our backs and we had better wading access to the more-promising-looking pools and runs.

Kingfish was digging through a box of nymphs when Spotter went on "point" right where we were standing. "That was quick," he said to the dog. "If only you could tell me what fly to use."

"When in doubt," I said, "tie on an olive woolly bugger."

He did and, in an almost carbon copy of that first morning at God's Dump, Kingfish began catching big, hungry brook trout almost immediately. This time, however, I didn't stand by and watch. I waded in and started catching them too.

We split the river, Kingfish taking the left half and me, the right, and we slowly worked upstream, casting as we went. It was fun. The casts were short, the strikes were hard, and the trout jumped into the shafts of sunlight with sprays of diamonds when hooked. Once we even had fish on at the same time and, for a few seconds, the two beautiful brook trout leapt and tail-walked side by side like escapees from a freshwater SeaWorld until finally, with our lines hopelessly tangled together, Kingfish and I collapsed in laughter on a couple of boulders.

It went on like this for a couple of hours as we moved farther upstream, crawling over tangles of downed trees and boulders, casting, catching, and releasing trout as we went. I had completely forgotten Tommy as he moved along silently above us and was startled when I heard him shouting down at us over the roar of the water. "Kingfish? Kingfish!" he yelled.

We stopped in a waist-deep pool and peered up through the trees. Tommy was waving with the rifle. "Ralph says cops are here. Get up here on my side of the river, please."

"What the hell?" Kingfish frowned at me. "Cops?"

By the time we'd climbed up the steep hill to Tommy, he was arguing over the two-way radio with Ralph. "What'd'ya mean, they want to see Max at the lodge? Fuck them. We're fishing. Tell them we're miles away." He pressed the button tighter to his ear and listened. Finally he looked at Kingfish. "They know you're here, sir." He looked at me. "Ralph says it's that redneck deputy from the restaurant last Friday night." Tommy listened again and smiled. "Ralph says Stormy's really chewing the guy out about wasting time out here at the lodge instead of finding out who killed your friend Lyle." He listened and laughed. "Says she chased them out of the lodge with a mop."

"He's not alone?" I asked, picturing the entire Loon County Sheriff's Department milling around inside the lodge, poking through drawers and breaking things. I didn't want Stormy any more upset than she already was.

"Is the redneck alone?" Tommy asked Ralph. He pressed the earpiece, listened, and then looked up at me. "Ralph says it's just the deputy and some big guy in a suit." He returned to the microphone on his wrist. "What's his name? Repeat that." He listened, nodded, and looked back at me. "Somebody named, McMiller?"

"Jesus," I said. "It's Earl MacMillan."

I tried to convince Kingfish to stay at the river with Tommy and fish, but he wouldn't listen. And as we climbed the embankment up out of the trees to the access road, he said, "Only reason they're here is because of me, Max. They're curious. And the only way to keep them from coming back over and over again, is to go to the lodge, introduce myself, and show them I'm no bogeyman." He patted me on the back. "It's happened before."

"I'm just sorry it had to happen here," I said.

"It's not cops we worry about," Tommy said.

The three of us came out of the woods on the access road about fifty feet below where it connects with Route 16. A Loon County Sheriff's Department squad car was parked on the far side of the chain. The driver's side door was open and the car's radio was blaring unintelligible static and cop jargon. Inside, I could see a scoped deer rifle clamped to the dashboard where usually a shotgun is kept. It was Billy Kendall's car.

Spotter bounded ahead and was on the porch sniffing crotches by the time Kingfish, Tommy, and I got there.

Billy Kendall, hands on his hips, was standing in the sun at the top of the porch steps. Flashes of light reflected from his badge, belts, and the sunglasses he slowly removed as we walked up. Earl MacMillan, in a wrinkled dark gray suit, was back in the shade in one of the rockers. He had a glass of water in his hand. Ralph and Stormy stood just inside the screen door. She had her big forearms crossed over her bosom. I didn't see Connie or Bendel, but I could hear Quincy yipping excitedly from somewhere inside.

Billy looked at Tommy and sneered. "Nephew, huh?"

MacMillan stood, set the water glass on the porch rail, and came down the steps, buttoning his suit jacket. His tie was a tartan plaid. "Heard you had a famous guest, Max," he said. "Since I assume Mayor Pearlman's met him, I thought acting Sheriff Kendall and I might just as well come out and say hello too."

"You did, huh?"

MacMillan went straight to Kingfish. "Mr. d'Antella," he said, extending his big hand, "I'm Earl MacMillan, Loon City Council president." They shook. MacMillan was as big as Kingfish was small. "What brings you to Loon?"

"Trout, of course." Kingfish smiled.

Billy laughed, lumbered down the steps and up to Tommy. "What are you doin', nephew? Shootin' them?" He touched the laser sight almost reverently. "This baby make aimin' as easy as they say?"

Tommy nodded.

"Ever hunt with it?"

"Lay off, Billy," MacMillan snapped.

Billy frowned and put his sunglasses back on.

"We aren't here to hassle anyone," MacMillan said to Kingfish.

Kingfish smiled tolerantly. "I understand."

"Then why are you here?" I asked.

"Told you, Max." He turned and put a hand on Kingfish's upper arm. "We're just being neighborly." He smiled and looked back down at Kingfish. "And, of course, curious. Isn't often we get someone of Mr. d'Antella's, ah . . . stature up here."

"Well," I said, "now you've met him. Quite frankly, Earl, Mr. d'Antella's here to fish and we've got things planned." I turned to Tommy. "Why don't you two go inside. I'll join you in a minute."

Tommy nodded and after Kingfish and MacMillan shook hands again, Tommy ushered Kingfish to the porch, where the old man leaned his fly rod against the log wall and began taking off his waders.

"Don't worry about them waders," Stormy said, holding the door. "Just come on inside for now."

When they were inside, MacMillan narrowed his eyes, put his hands in his pockets, and we walked a few paces out into the yard. Billy followed. "Okay, Earl," I said. "You've seen him. Now what?"

He raised his eyebrows. "I've no agenda, Max." He smiled. "But Deputy Kendall might."

I looked at Billy. He nodded. "I'm going before Judge

Emery tomorrow, Max. Going to ask him for a search warrant. I think I got probable cause to be suspicious of your guests here.''

''Suspicious of what?''

''Kinda hard not to wonder about the coincidence, ain't it?''

''Coincidence?''

''Yeah, coincidence. We got ourselves a bona fide crime wave and Mr. Vincent d'Antella just happens to set up shop here at Whitefork Lodge?''

''Set up shop?''

Billy nodded, a smile of self-satisfaction spreading beneath the sunglasses. ''I don't miss much, Max. I saw that equipment in there''—he gestured to the lodge—''before Stormy threw us out. Looks like headquarters for somethin' to me.''

''You watch too much TV, Bill.''

Billy creaked as he put his hands on his hips again. ''You might wanta show a little more respect there, Max.''

''I'll show you respect, Bill,'' I said, ''when you've earned it.''

''Hey.'' MacMillan held up his hands. ''We didn't come out here to argue.''

I was still glaring at Billy. ''All of a sudden you know big cop words like 'probable cause,' Bill?'' I said. ''Then do you understand the words 'harassment' and 'trespassing'?''

Billy looked to MacMillan for help.

''I don't see where anyone's harassing anyone, Max,'' MacMillan said.

''You don't?'' I could feel the muscles in my jaw working. ''Well, I do. And I'd like you to leave.'' I looked back at Billy. ''Get your damn search warrant, if you can. Just don't come back until you've got it.'' I pushed by them and went up onto the porch. ''Meanwhile,'' I said, imitating, if not Earl's exact smile, at least the insincerity of it, "there's one thing I know for sure. These people are my guests. They paid for a week's fly-fishing and they're not going anywhere until they get their money's worth." I slipped off my vest, sat on the steps, and began untying my wading boots.

"Don't say we didn't warn you, Max," MacMillan said, starting toward the access road. "C'mon, Billy."

"And, Max," Billy said, adjusting his hat, "tell that *nephew* of Bendel's that I don't forget liars."

"I said, c'mon, Billy." MacMillan crooked his finger. "My guess is, we've got people waiting for us up at the top of this driveway."

I stepped out of the boots and stripped off the waders while, out of the corner of my eye, I watched them walk across the gravel turnaround and then up the access road until they disappeared into the trees. I hung the waders, feet up, on one of the pegs by the door and went inside.

Quincy came galloping out of the dining room with his toenails *clickety-click*ing on the wood floor and yipping like a squeeze toy, and before I could sidestep the little monster, he attacked my trouser legs. Connie, dangerously close to bouncing out of a tight, low-cut black tanktop was right behind him. "Quincy? Quincy! No! Come! Come, Quincy. Come!" She snatched the little dog from the floor, buried him back first in her cleavage, and wrapped her arms around him. He didn't stop yipping and the legs that were free kept right on running. "Sorry, Max," she said, straightening the blue bow tied between Quincy's ears. "I think the poor baby can sense the excitement."

I sighed. "Where's Kingfish?"

"In there at the TV with Ralph and Tommy." She peered out the door behind me. "Are those men gone?"

I nodded.

"Oh good. Quincy needs to go out." She kissed his wet nose. "Don't you, baby?" As she sidled by me to the door, Quincy lunged with a squeaky snarl and snapped at me.

I went to the phone and dialed Ruth's private number. As I waited for it to ring, I thought I could hear Stormy and Bendel's voices coming from the kitchen. At least they're talking again, I thought.

Ruth answered on the third ring. "Mayor Pearlman."

"I just had a not very social social call from Billy Kendall and you-know-who," I said.

"MacMillan was at Whitefork Lodge? How did he find out d'Antella's there?"

"That's why I'm calling you."

"I didn't do anything with the names. They're still right where they were last Friday."

"Someone saw them."

"Not a chance. Only Pauline knows the password to my computer."

"Then, dammit, how the hell did he find out? D'Antella's only been here three and a half days. We've never set foot off this property."

"Why are you angry with me?" she asked. "I should be the one angry. This is what I was most afraid would happen."

"I'm not angry," I said. "I'm pissed off. There's a difference." Ruth didn't reply and we both were quiet for a half minute or so. I lit a cigarette.

Finally she said, "I suppose the newspaper was there, too."

"No. Just them."

"Then I wonder why Earl didn't just call you on the telephone? He's not the kind to make a personal appearance without an audience."

"I don't know, Ruth," I said. "I've given up trying to understand this political crap you guys pull on each other."

She ignored my comment. "I think you'd better tell d'Antella what's going on as soon as you can."

"I intend to. Billy said he was coming back with a search warrant."

"What?"

"That's what he said. He's going to Judge Emery tomorrow."

"The hell he is," she said. "I'll stop that."

"He claims he has probable cause."

She sighed. "He's got no more cause searching Whitefork Lodge than he does any other business in Loon. Don't worry about it, Max. I'll take care of it."

We were silent again. My cigarette had a one-inch ash and since I couldn't find an ashtray on the table or in the drawer, I pulled the phone cord to its maximum and opened the screen door with my stockinged foot. As I flicked the ash out onto the porch I caught a glimpse of Connie and Bendel out on the dock. She was lying on her back on the dock's weathered planks and he was moving around above her, his Nikon to his eye, shooting pictures. As I let the door close and moved back to the table, Ruth said, "If only you'd listened to me."

"I thought we were past that."

"How can I get past it when it keeps getting shoved in my face?"

I didn't answer.

"Max?"

"I'm here."

"This is getting us nowhere," she said. "I've got a busy day that I'm sure will get busier as more people find out about d'Antella." She was all business now. "I'll take care of Judge Emery, but I'm going to have to take a public stand on this, Max."

"So?"

"So, you should know what it is."

Suddenly I was tired of the whole thing. I didn't care. "Sure. Why not?" I said.

"I intend to let the people of Loon know that I have advised you against having someone with Mr. d'Antella's reputation as a guest since the very beginning. That said, I will make it clear that Mr. d'Antella has every right to stay at your lodge, just as you have every right to have him there. If he and the people with him obey the laws of Loon Township and the state of Vermont he should be free to do what he wants." She paused, as if waiting for a comment from me. When I didn't give her one, she continued. "I'm also going to state that, until Mr. d'Antella leaves Whitefork Lodge, you and I have severed our relationship."

"First rat off the ship," I mumbled.

"I'm not deserting you, Max, but think what you want. I have my job to protect and no matter what happens in the next three and a half days, I don't want anyone capable of suggesting that my judgment is anything but objective."

She paused and, I think, thought I was going to say something. I didn't.

"I'm going to hang up now, Max."

"Fine."

"I don't think we should see or talk to each other until your guests of the moment have left."

I hung up on her this time.

Tommy stuck his head through the dining-room door. "Good. You're off the phone," he said. "You've got to see what's going on up at the chain by the highway, Max. Come to the reading room. Hurry."

As I followed Tommy back to the reading room, I peeked out the front windows at the lake. I couldn't see Bendel, Connie, or the dog. "Look," Tommy said, as soon as we were inside. "Look what's going on." He was pointing to the monitor. Ralph and Kingfish moved away so as to not block my view.

"It looks like there's a newspaper or magazine interviewing that MacMillan guy," Ralph said. "Too bad we don't have sound."

Ruth had been right about MacMillan not going anywhere without the press. "It's a newspaper," I said, squinting at the image on the screen. "Our own *Loon Sentinel*." From the area covered by the camera, we could see the squad car, MacMillan, and Billy. Parked to the right of the screen was the *Loon Sentinel*'s big black Jeep Cherokee. Looking down into the ground-glass lens of a big twin-lens reflex, *Sentinel* photographer Rusty Granger was kneeling on the blacktop. The periodic white flashes from his flashgun made the TV picture roll. Right in the middle of everyone was Gordon Miller, Jr. He was facing MacMillan and Billy, his hand outstretched toward them.

"Zoom in, Ralph," Tommy said. "What's in that guy's hand?"

"Probably a little tape recorder." Ralph zoomed in and Gordon Miller filled the screen, the moustache he'd recently grown to make himself look older simply making him look like a little boy with a fake moustache.

"Yeah," Tommy said. "It's a tape recorder."

"Too bad we can't read lips," Ralph said, zooming all the way in until Gordon's moustache and lips filled the screen. "Angle's wrong, though."

I didn't have to read Gordon's lips. Or MacMillan's. I knew the kind of rhetoric Earl was capable of. And I knew the sensational spin Gordon could and would put on it. I looked at Kingfish. "This is could become a bigger deal than you think," I said.

They all looked at me. "What do you mean by that?" he said.

I lit a cigarette and told him everything. I told him about the crime in Loon. The robberies, muggings, vandalism, and now Lyle's murder. I told him about Ruth, her problems with MacMillan, our relationship, and her initial reaction when Collingwood had called that first night. And I told him about the names in the computer, what Billy Kendall had said about the search warrant, and the conversation I just had with Ruth a few minutes ago.

While I talked, Kingfish had taken a cigar from his

pocket and he was still turning it slowly in his fingers when I finished. He looked at it for a long minute before he finally looked up at me and spoke. "I wish you'd said something to me sooner, Max."

"I know," I said a little sheepishly. "But I wanted the rooms finished."

He chuckled. "I'm not talking about that. Nothing you coulda said would've kept me from coming here. Right, Ralphie?"

"That's for sure," Ralph said.

Kingfish continued, "How old was this Lyle Martin?"

"Early forties."

"He have a family?"

I nodded. "Wife. Three little girls."

"And this so-called crime in your girlfriend's town. How long has it been going on?"

I shrugged. "Pretty much since she got back from running for governor last November."

He studied the activity on the monitor for another minute. Finally, he said, "It would've been nice to know about it a few days ago, but I think we can still do something." He looked at Tommy. "What do you think, Tomaso? Maybe we have Collingwood call Martino?"

Tommy nodded. "Marty could do it."

"You take care of it, huh? And tell Collingwood about this deputy and his warrant. Martino should know he has to hurry. Get anybody he wants to help. I don't care what it costs. You tell him, I wanna know who these assholes are who killed this young father, Lyle Martin, and who it is that's screwing around in Loon, Vermont. And I wanna know by tomorrow night." Kingfish looked at me. "What's your girlfriend's name?"

"Pearlman," I said. "Ruth Pearlman."

He turned back to Tommy. "And have Collingwood tell Martino that I want evidence. He'll know what I mean. And I want it all to go to this Mayor Ruth Pearlman. *Capice?*"

Tommy nodded and started for the door. "I'll call him on the cellular," he said. "It's upstairs in my room."

When Tommy's footsteps had faded I looked at Kingfish. "I'm amazed," I said. "Granted, we don't exactly have the best brains working on it, but this has been going on up here for months. What makes you think you can find out overnight?"

"Tell Max, Ralphie. Tell him how good Martino is."

Ralph shrugged. "Marty's the best."

Kingfish stuck the cigar in his mouth and put his hand on my shoulder. "You know that expression, Max, 'The long arm of the law?' "

I nodded.

"It's chicken shit, my friend, compared to the reach of La Famiglia d'Antella."

CHAPTER ⚓ ELEVEN

All I wanted was to call Ruth back and tell her the good news about d'Antella's help, but he'd made me promise not to say anything, either now or after it had been accomplished. "I get enough criticism from my people, Max," he said. "Solving this little problem here in Loon stays our secret. Nobody's to ever know. Not your mayor girlfriend. Not Stormy or Bendel. Nobody. *Capice?*"

So, after dinner, I lit a cigarette and Spotter and I walked slowly up the access road in the heat to the mailbox, got the mail, and the *Loon Sentinel*. The story about MacMillan's visit to Whitefork Lodge was just about as bad as I'd expected. It was front page, top, under a banner headline that read "MACMILLAN AND KENDALL UNCOVER MAFIA AT WHITEFORK LODGE." There was a picture of the two of them posed at the access-road chain with the CLOSED FOR REPAIRS sign in the background. A smaller picture of d'Antella was inset into the article.

Everyone but Tommy and Stormy gathered in the dining room to find out what it said. She was cleaning up the kitchen and he was taking his turn at the monitor because Ralph thought he was experiencing a mild case of carpal tunnel syndrome.

It was hot. Every surface was sticky. The toilets were

sweating. The fan I'd put in the dining-room window didn't seem able to pick up the heavy, humid air and move it.

Connie was chosen reader. She sat at the table under the hanging lamp in her tight shorts, dabbing a wad of tissue at the damp skin inside the neck of her blouse, and read the story out loud. It began with a quote from Mac-Millan:"Following an anonymous tip, Acting Sheriff Billy Kendall and I found Vincent d'Antella and his cohorts . . ." She looked up and smiled. "Cohorts?"

Kingfish laughed from the fireplace where, as a favor to Ralph's sinuses, he was leaning on the mantel, blowing cigar smoke up the chimney.

Connie resumed reading, ". . . found Vincent d'Antella and his cohorts lurking in the woods at Whitefork Lodge under the guise of fly-fishing for trout. They were all heavily armed with modern automatic assault weapons, and upon further investigation of the lodge itself, Deputy Kendall observed what can only be described as a high-tech communications center in one of the building's rooms. Concerned for our safety, we left the property, but not before I warned Whitefork Lodge owner Max Addams of the risks inherent in harboring guests like d'Antella and his gang." Connie looked up. "Is this guy a jerk, or what?"

"We don't need your commentary, baby," Kingfish said. "Just read."

She frowned at him and then looked back at the paper. "Ah, let's see . . ." She ran her finger down the page, searching for her place. ". . . Here it is," she said. "That's all from the MacMillan guy anyway. This part is just the newspaper talking . . ."

"Read it."

She gave Kingfish another dirty look. "Keep your pants on, Fishy. I'm reading already." She wiped the perspiration from her upper lip, looked back at the paper, and read: "It seems unthinkable that any Loon citizen, much less

Mr. Addams, who, as we all know, has access to everything happening in this town through his 'connections' in city government, would choose to jeopardize his neighbors for financial gain. It's almost unbelievable to think that as we struggle to strengthen our law-enforcement personnel to solve this crime wave gripping our community, Mr. Addams selfishly chooses to bring more criminals in . . ."

"Oh, for Chrissakes," I said.

"Wait, Max," she said, "there's more." She looked back at the page. "Mayor Ruth Pearlman, who held a special press conference today to address this very issue, claims she has attempted to dissuade Mr. Addams from bringing Vincent d'Antella to Whitefork Lodge since he was first contacted by the crime boss more than a month ago. When asked why she chose not to inform members of the Sheriff's Department of d'Antella's impending visit, she declined specific comment, saying only, 'Mr. Addams and I have terminated our relationship.' " Connie looked up at me again. "You did?" she asked.

I shook my head. "That's just politics," I said.

"Connie, please," Kingfish said. "Will you finish reading that thing?"

"Here, let me help," Bendel said, pulling up a chair, sitting beside her and taking the paper. Their shoulders touched. She smiled and pointed to where she'd left off. He carefully hooked a pair of gold-rimmed glasses over his ears and read, "To this reporter, the solution seems obvious. Whether Mr. Vincent d'Antella has, as Deputy Kendall calls it, set up a command center or not, he and his kind have no place in a small town like Loon. Not today. Not tomorrow. We are simple, law-abiding, uncomplicated people. My advice to Max Addams and the staff of Whitefork Lodge is to send the bums packing." Bendel looked up. "That's it."

Connie dabbed at the sweat on his forehead.

I looked at Kingfish. He was smiling. "They've sure

got a surprise coming, don't they?'' he said.

Ralph laughed.

Connie and Bendel, not knowing why, joined in.

I didn't. I was mad. I excused myself and went directly out into the hallway to the telephone and called the *Sentinel*.

All Gordon Miller had to do earlier after interviewing MacMillan was to walk down to the lodge, meet Kingfish, and see for himself. But no. He chose to write a news story that was irresponsible, inflammatory bullshit. And he wasn't going to get away with it.

I asked to speak with him and the operator who answered asked my name and then asked me to please hold. By the time she came back on the line, I had watched Bendel and Connie go out the front door, down the steps, and across the lawn toward the workshop, listened to two songs by Natalie Cole and was halfway through a third. ''Mr. Miller's in an editorial meeting, sir,'' the operator finally said. ''He asked if he could call you tomorrow?''

''No, he cannot call me tomorrow,'' I was barely able to keep from yelling at her. ''Tell him I expect him to return my call before he goes home tonight.''

''I'll tell him, sir,'' she said, completely unruffled by the tone of my voice. ''Is that all?''

''Just tell him to make sure he calls.'' I hung up.

When I returned to the dining room, Kingfish was talking to Ralph. ''I think we're going to need to be extra observant for the next twenty-four hours.'' He tossed the cigar in the fireplace and walked to the table. ''Something like this''—he picked up the newspaper—''can get people real excited. You know what I mean?''

Ralph nodded. ''Yes, sir, I do.''

''Forget that automatic wake-up thing. I want you or Tommy on that monitor every minute all night.'' He saw me in the doorway. ''Hey, Max, what do you say we all have a little of that brandy of yours, go out on the porch in the air, cool off, and watch the sun set?'' He smiled.

"You certainly look like you could use it."

"I think I could," I said, and while he went to the sideboard and poured our drinks, I went into the kitchen to get Stormy. I wanted her to stop the sulking and join us like she used to do.

The kitchen was empty but smelled like chicken cooking. Stormy usually started something for the next day after cleaning up the evening meal, and a twelve-quart aluminum stockpot with its flat lid slightly askew steamed on a back burner. On the counter to the left was a cutting board with a partially diced bunch of celery, a knife, and three halved yellow onions. Three-quarters of a cigarette smoldered in the half-full ashtray beside that.

I put out the cigarette and peered out the window above the sink. Stormy, her fists in balls and her caftan swirling around her ankles, stomped up the yard toward the lodge from the workshop. Spotter trotted beside her. She pushed in through the back door and slammed it shut behind her. I heard Spotter yelp. She pushed the loose hairs from her face, smoothed her apron, turned, and saw me. "Damn fool," she muttered, coming to the sink, pushing me aside, and running water on her hands.

"Who? Spotter?" I backed up to the island. "Me?"

"None of you." She shook the water from her hands and wiped them on her apron. "It's Bendel." She moved back to the cutting board and resumed chopping the celery.

I watched her violently hack away at the celery for a couple of seconds and then said, "I'd hate to see you lose a finger. Want me to do that until you cool down?"

"It's done," she said and scraped the pile of celery shrapnel into the stockpot. She threw in the onions the way they were, lowered the flame, then turned and faced me. She was breathing hard and flushed. "I just moved his things into that room in the workshop."

"You what?"

"You heard me, Max Addams. I threw him out."

"Why?"

"Ohhhh, Ben-del," she said, doing a pretty good imitation of Connie's ditsy Marilyn falsetto, "this vest is so heavy. It might crush my breasts. Oh, Bendel. What kind of a rod do you have? Oh, Bendel. I just love the feeling of this grip in my hand." Stormy shuddered and grit her teeth. "Oh, Bendel," she spat out in her own voice. "You're such an old fool!"

I laughed. "I thought you said you weren't the jealous type."

"This ain't funny." She pulled a Camel from her apron pocket and stuck it in the corner of her mouth. "And this ain't just Connie. I wish it was just that bimbo." She produced an old steel Zippo. "Her I can handle." The lighter clinked open and snapped shut as she lit the cigarette. "It's Bendel, Max. He's different. And don't tell me you don't see it."

I shrugged. "All I see is you two not getting along like you used to."

She shook her head and exhaled a long stream of smoke. "I've had it." She studied her hands.

"C'mon, Stormy. They'll be gone in . . ."

"No." She stomped her foot. "That's not all of it. I think he's been messin' around ever since we was married. Here at the lodge. When we was in Italy, even. Down in New York . . ." She sucked on the cigarette. "Francesca warned me. At the weddin' no less. Said, 'Stormy, there'll always be somebody else in Daddy's life.' " Bendel's thirty-year-old daughter, Francesca, had been Stormy's maid of honor. "Told me to watch out. Said that's why her momma left him." Francesca was the product of Bendel's second wife. Stormy was his third wife. "Oh, he'll be faithful at first, Francesca said. But, once it wears off, watch out."

I sat hard on a stool. "Are you sure?"

"Some things a woman just knows, Max." She threw the cigarette in the sink where it hissed like snake. "This

Connie. He ain't just flirtin'. I can see it. It's just a matter of time . . ."

"Stormy," I said, "it's her, not him. Even Kingfish said that she's a . . ."

"You ain't seen him with her, Max."

"Of course I have," I said. "And we've had a lot of clients up here like her. You know that. And you know as well as I do, you have to go with it. You play along. You try not to offend them." I reached out and lifted her chin. Her eyes were wet. "You've had one or two flirts over the years, too. Remember that little optometrist from Massachusetts who fell in love with you? What was his name?"

She nodded and smiled faintly. "Walsh. Dr. Jack Walsh."

"You played along with him, didn't you?"

"I wasn't married then," she said. "And he didn't mean nothin' by it anyways."

"Neither does Connie," I said. "And neither does Bendel. He's just playing along."

"Still . . ."

"Do you have proof of the other stuff? New York? Italy? Do you?"

"Not exactly." She shook her head. "But you know he don't call when he's away like he use to. And when he does, it don't feel right. I just know."

"Have you said anything to him?"

" 'Course, I've said somethin'. I ain't one to mope." She wiped at her eyes with the hem of the apron.

"And?"

She laughed. "He just said I was crazy."

"Look," I said. "Rayleen'll be back tomorrow and I'll put him on Connie. Okay?"

She nodded.

"Meanwhile, the way the lake was looking this afternoon, I'd say it's going to be good for fishing tomorrow. I'll let Bendel take Kingfish out in the big canoe in the morning. And maybe I can help Rayleen with Connie."

"I don't like bein' embarrassed, Max."

"I know. Who does?"

"I feel like a fool. You shouldn't have to change things around just for me. Everybody's gonna know. What's Kingfish gonna say?"

"He and Bendel have already hit it off," I said. "Don't worry about it. This is probably the way it was meant to be in the first place. It'll work out fine."

"We'll see," she said, grinding out the cigarette. "But I still ain't lettin' him sleep with me. Not 'til I'm sure, anyways."

We have some pretty remarkable sunsets out over Sweet Lake during fly-fishing season and the one we were all watching now was easily a ten. We were all bathed in its intense red light. Perhaps it was the unusual humidity in the hot air out over the mountains beyond the lake or maybe one of those things that doesn't have an explanation, but we all agreed that the red ball of sun seemed literally to be simmering in the water.

"I can almost hear it sizzle," Connie said from her perch on the porch rail. Her blouse was now held with only one button, and if she hadn't been clutching Quincy to her chest, I'm sure the sunset would have had competition.

"It looks like it's bleeding to me," Ralph said, as he came out the screen door carrying his nightly Alka-Seltzer on the rocks. He slid into an empty rocker. He was right. Except for the motionless black reflections from the trees on the far shore and "V" wake of a solitary loon, the lake looked like a puddle of blood.

Bendel, only a silhouette against the red, was out in the yard with one of his cameras on a tripod trying to capture it for the calendar.

Stormy seemed a lot better. She had changed to a pair of slacks, pulled her braid up on her head, and put on eyeshadow and lipstick. She was barefoot and appeared elegant in a rustic sort of way as she blew cotton candy–pink cigarette smoke into the still air.

Kingfish, alternately smoking and dipping a fresh cigar in his brandy, was doing the same thing from his rocker next to mine.

"What happened to those peeper things we heard the other night," Ralph asked. "I don't hear them anymore."

"They only last a few days," I said, sipping my brandy.

"I don't know what peepers are," Connie giggled, "but I've never heard so many frogs. It's like Surroundsound at the movies. And what was that? A loon?"

I nodded. Over the chorus of frogs the loons had begun their maniacal laughter, adding a sort of macabre touch to the gory look of lake.

Quincy yipped and strained in Connie's arms as, tail wagging, Spotter walked slowly up through the red yard, sniffed at Bendel's tripod, and continued to Stormy, where he sat between her legs facing the lake. She hugged his head to her bosom. "Too bad you can't see color, you old fart," she said to the dog.

"Who said dogs can't see color?" Connie asked.

"Anybody who knows dogs," Stormy hissed back.

"Well, I don't believe it." Connie kissed the top of Quincy's head. "Dogs see lots more things than you know."

"Dogs ain't the only ones," Stormy mumbled.

"I think the lake's going to be good tomorrow morning," I said to Kingfish. "There were rises all around the edges during dinner."

"I saw."

"I think I'll let you and Bendel try it. I'll work with Connie tomorrow."

Kingfish nodded. Connie looked out at Bendel, who was still taking pictures even though the best of the sunset was gone. She didn't say anything.

The phone calls started a little after nine. Stormy's

knees cracked as she got to her feet to answer the first one. I could hear her say, "Hello, Whitefork Lodge," and was sure she was going to call me to the phone saying it was Gordon Miller. But there was only silence for about ten seconds and then I heard her hang up.

I looked at her as she came back out onto the porch. "Who was it?"

"Somebody who says they're gonna burn the lodge down again," she said, sitting heavily on the step. "Unless Mr. Kingfish here goes back to Rhode Island."

I looked at Kingfish. "I guess we aren't the only ones who read tonight's newspaper."

He nodded and blew a perfect blood-red circle of smoke into the still air. "Told you, Ralph," he said, "Told you it would stir them up, didn't I?"

"Yes, sir."

The second call came a few minutes later. This one I answered. "Get those fuckin' dago murderers out of Loon," a man's voice shouted before I could say anything. Then he hung up.

I didn't get to the screen door before the phone rang again. It was a woman's voice this time. "May I speak to Mr. d'Antella?" she said, pronouncing d'Antella "dant-eller." I told her he was busy and asked if I could take a message. She said, "Yes. Tell the murderer to go back to greaser land where he came from."

There were five more calls, essentially the same. After the last one, Stormy unplugged the phone.

I'd have to wait to talk to Gordon Miller tomorrow.

By the time the clock in the hallway bonged eleven, only Kingfish and I were left on the porch. Connie and Ralph had gone up to their rooms. He was relieving Tommy at three. After putting away his camera equipment, Bendel talked quietly with Stormy far enough out in the yard that we couldn't hear them. Finally they went their separate ways; she stomped to the cabin and slammed the door and he moped off to the workshop, his chin on his chest.

Neither Kingfish nor I spoke until the lights went out in the cabin and then the workshop. "Told you Bendel should watch his ass, Max," he said, flipping the butt of his cigar out into the yard. Its lit end arced like an orange tracer through the dark, landed with a shower of sparks, and died.

"They'll straighten it out," I said.

"Is that why it's me and him on the lake tomorrow?"

"More or less. Hope you don't mind."

"I just hope it's not too little too late," he said.

"Me too."

We finished our brandies in silence. The loons had stopped calling to each other, the frog chorus had quieted, and cool air was filtering down through the trees behind the lodge from the mountain. Spotter snored beside my rocker. I heard a toilet flush upstairs and then a door close.

"Guess I'll hit the sack too, Max," he said, getting slowly to his feet and stretching.

"Not everyone in Loon is like MacMillan or those people who called tonight," I said.

"I know, Max."

"I called the editor of the newspaper tonight," I said. "With all the crank calls, he didn't get a chance to call back but when I talk to him tomorrow, I'm going to demand he give me equal space."

Kingfish only smiled.

"And thanks for what you're trying to do for Ruth."

"You mean the thing with Martino?" He laughed. "Hell, it's been a while since I threw my weight around. It's kind of fun."

After he went up the stairs, I cleaned up. I emptied the ashtrays and carried the glasses to the kitchen. The brandy was gone and I tossed the bottle in the recycling bin by the back door.

While I was rinsing the glasses, I thought I heard bare feet come down the stairs and go out the screen door, but when I went out into the hallway and looked, no one was there. Only Lyle's carving of the mother loon and its chicks stared back at me from the dining-room table. *Who says you don't have eternal life?* I thought, as I returned to the kitchen, put the soap in the dishwasher and turned it on. Then I turned out the lights and went back out onto the porch in the dark. I closed the screen door quietly behind me.

I could still faintly smell Kingfish's cigar. Spotter was twitching in his sleep by the rocker and I walked quietly to the far end, unzipped my fly, and began peeing in the rosebush.

When I bought my first car, other than telling me never to miss a payment, my dad gave me one piece of advice. "You don't need to be a mechanic to keep a car running right," he said. "Just learn how your car sounds. And then always listen to it. Know its special noises so well that when even the smallest one of them changes or a new one is added, you'll hear it. Then find out why." I've been a listener to things ever since and I've applied this sensitivity to sounds to Whitefork Lodge. I know every one of them. I can lie in bed at night and, through sounds alone, inventory the condition of the lodge. I know the "whump" of the furnace when it turns on, the "rattle" of the refrigerator when it's making ice, and the "ticking" of the water pump coming on. There are three creaks in the stairs when the outside temperature goes below freezing. In a southwestly breeze the upstairs french windows "groan" as they shift in their frame. The "scraping" noise on the roof is a hemlock branch clawing at the cedar shingles over the reading room when the wind changes to the northeast. And even though the walls and floors of the new lodge are thicker than those in the original, I know which toilets are being flushed, which room's dresser drawers are being opened and closed, and as a result of Ruth's playful insistence that it's "bad luck" not to "christen" every room, I know the unique voice of every bed.

So, as I stood there peeing, I knew the staccato squeak I heard coming from the workshop's open windows were the rusty springs of the old twin bed on the other side of the thick log wall.

And I also knew what was making them squeak.

Overhearing someone getting laid is nothing new up here. On many early mornings Stormy and I have stood in the kitchen drinking coffee and have attempted to ignore the sounds of lovemaking above our heads. And as she always says as we go about our business, "We're all adults, ain't we? 'Sides, it's romantic up here." As usual, she's right. In fact, I always feel flattered that the casual ambience we've tried so carefully to create inspires more than just joyful camaraderie on the water.

Tonight, however, I had a horrible sinking feeling as I stood there listening, and when I looked over at the cabin, I saw Stormy standing in the dark doorway—just a silhouette in a pale floor-length nightgown, but nevertheless, Stormy looking out across the lawn at the workshop. She couldn't see me, I knew. But I knew she heard what I heard. And I knew she knew what it was.

And as a muffled "yip yip" blended with the squeaks, Stormy quietly closed the door. My heart broke for her. I knew she knew, as I did, who it was with Bendel.

Much later I was awakened by the sound of bare feet on the porch, the front door opening and closing, and footsteps running quietly up the stairs. My bedside clock read 3:05.

At 5:05 I was awakened again. This time, a faint thump then a clank came from the back of the lodge. I sat up. It sounded like it was in the kitchen. Or maybe the garbage shed at back of the lodge. Spotter raised his head and growled faintly.

I sighed. *Festus*, I thought. *It's only Festus. All this heat, he must smell the dead woodchuck.*

I flopped back into the pillows and went to sleep.

CHAPTER TWELVE

Getting up at six when Spotter nudged me to go out was difficult. I sat on the edge of the bed with my head in my hands. Too many cigarettes, too much brandy, and the noises in the lodge had made for a poor night's sleep. I felt like hell.

Spotter whined and I pulled on my robe. I had just put my hand on the doorknob when I noticed the folded slips of paper lying on the floor. They had obviously been slid under the door. I picked up the papers and, after letting Spotter out, went back to my room and put on my reading glasses.

The top page was a note from Stormy. "MAX—HAVE TO GO. GOT TO THINK," it said. "EGGS, HAM, COLD HOME-FRIES IN REFR. USE THE ORANGES! DON'T FORGET SPOTTER'S HEARTWORM PILL. COOKED CHICKEN & BROTH IN STOCKPOT FOR SUPPER'S CHICKEN & DUMPLINGS. RECIPE ATTACHED." It was signed simply with an "S." Attached with a paper clip was a stained and dog-eared recipe card for "STORMY'S 3-STEP CHICKEN & DUMPLINGS." I stuffed the note in my pocket and quickly went across the hall to the dining-room window and looked out at the turnaround where we all park our cars. My Jeep was gone, too. How I had slept through the sound of it starting and driving off I don't know.

I went into the reading room. Ralph was at the monitor. He looked up and yawned. "You're up early, Max."

"Were you here when Stormy left?"

"Yeah. I gave her our key for the chain."

"What time was that?"

He yawned again. "Five or a little after."

"She say where she was going?"

He shook his head.

"She carrying anything? A suitcase?"

He shrugged. "I don't know, Max. I was watching the monitor, for Chrissakes. She came in here and asked if I'd unlock the chain. All she had then was a purse and a bottle of whiskey. Bourbon, I think."

"She was drinking?"

"No." He laughed. "She was just carrying it. In fact, she put it in her purse while I was getting the key."

"And she didn't say anything?"

"Nope."

I looked at the monitor. "You wouldn't have her on tape, would you?"

"When she was leaving? Of course."

"Can you run it?"

While he rewound the VCR, I lit a cigarette and paced.

"Here she is," Ralph said, sliding his chair to one side so I could see. "The headlights help, but remember, Max, a lot of it's greenish because it was still dark when she left."

It was a medium shot of the upper end of the access road.

"What's that?" I pointed to what looked like black plastic trash bags lying on the ground. Cans and bottles were spread out near the one that appeared broken open. "It looks like garbage."

"Yeah." Ralph nodded. "About one this morning some idiot threw it out of a pickup. Probably more reaction to the newspaper story." He paused the tape. "Tommy was on when that happened. Want me to rewind? I think the guy's license plate is readable.''

"No. I want to see Stormy. Let it run.''

He pushed "Play." My Jeep, the top still down, came into view. Stormy was at the wheel. She stopped, climbed out, and, walking into the headlight beams, went to the chain, bent away from the camera, and began working with the lock. I studied the inside of the Jeep. Even though it was a very dark green inside the seat area, it wasn't difficult to make out the shape of a small suitcase in the back and her purse on the passenger seat.

"What's that thing lying on the seat there behind the suitcase?'' Ralph put his finger on the monitor screen and traced the shape. I leaned on the desk and squinted at the screen. "It looks like maybe a big umbrella,'' he said.

I shook my head. "I don't know what it is.'' It looked like her garden hoe.

Stormy finally got the chain unlocked, tossed it aside, and climbed back into the Jeep. I could see her ram it in gear and then she pulled forward, turned left on Route 16 toward the Starlight, and disappeared out of frame.

"Damn,'' Ralph said, "she didn't relock the chain like she said she would.''

"I'll take care of it.'' I wanted to clean up the trash anyway. "Listen, do me a favor, huh?''

"What do you need, Max?''

"I need you to keep this our secret for now. Obviously Bendel and Stormy have had a fight. Probably over Connie . . .''

"It figures. Did I call that one, or what?''

"She'll be back,'' I said. "Meanwhile, I don't think it would do anyone any good if we made it public. You know?''

"Hey.'' He smiled. "Long as it doesn't threaten the old man, I'm game.''

"Actually, I think it would upset him if he knew.'' One thing you learn when you run a business that deals with the public in as familiar a way as we do at Whitefork Lodge, you don't air your personal dirty linen in front of them.

Ralph nodded thoughtfully. "I think you're right, Max. So where do we say she is?"

"I'll think of something." I went to the doorway. "Meanwhile, this is just between you and me. All right? Let me talk to Bendel first and then whatever story he and I use, just play dumb. Okay?"

He yawned while he nodded.

"I'd better put the coffee on and see what I can rustle up for breakfast."

"Not on my account, I hope." He turned back to the monitor. "This monitor's given me a wicked headache. I'm going back to bed for a while as soon as Tommy relieves me."

I made the coffee and then went to my room. By the time I'd yanked on a pair of jeans, a crewneck sweater, and stuffed my bare feet in a pair of sneakers, I was shaking with anger. This was Bendel's fault. I wanted to go down to the workshop right then, yank him out of bed, and tell him exactly what I knew and what had happened.

But I couldn't.

Instead, I went to the kitchen and pushed inside through the swinging door. It was Stormy I cared about. She had told me how embarrassed she was. Someone might overhear me if I confronted Bendel, and I wasn't going to make it any worse for her by creating a scene. Besides, there was a good chance that he knew nothing about her leaving. And if he didn't know that she was gone, then he didn't know she knew about his little tryst last night.

I lit a cigarette and leaned on the counter. No, it was between her and him. And until she returned, he was going have to believe, like I had decided everyone else was going to believe, that Stormy had been called away in the middle of the night to help Merriam Martin.

On the chance that she might just have gone home, I

went back out into the hall and called her number in Loon. After twelve rings, I hung up and dialed Rayleen's apartment at the bowling alley. There was no answer there either.

I wished I knew more about recovering alcoholics. What pushed them back to the bottle? Was what she and I had heard coming from the workshop last night enough to do it?

I went back into the kitchen. I could hear the sounds of people moving around upstairs, and as I took a dozen eggs from the refrigerator, I heard Connie and Quincy come down the stairs and go out the front door onto the porch. Her voice came floating down the acoustically perfect hallway. "Now go pee-pee," I heard her say. "Mommy's right here." I heard a couple "yip yips" and then it was silent. I took a big bowl from the cupboard and began cracking eggs into it. I was whipping the eggs with a fork when I heard Bendel's voice approach the porch. "Good morning," he said, accompanied by the sound of his boots thumping up the steps.

"Hi," Connie answered. There was a long pause. I held my breath and then, in a very low voice, I heard her say, "I almost came back out last night."

"I wish you had," he whispered back.

"It was wonderful," she said, "You were . . ."

He cut her off with a "Shhh."

I heard footsteps on the stairs and Kingfish's voice boomed down the hall to me. "Bendel, how are you this morning?" The screen door slapped shut as Kingfish went out onto the porch.

"Good morning, Kingfish," Bendel said.

"You look especially radiant this morning, Constance," Kingfish said. "You must have slept well."

I heard her say, "Thank you, Fishy." And then they were quiet for a second. I could hear Quincy's collar jingle.

Finally Kingfish said, "Look at those trout rising out there."

To which Bendel replied, "It's going to be good on the lake this morning."

"Max up?"

"He's somewhere around."

I put down the bowl, quickly went out the back door and around to the front of the lodge the long way. If they had found me in the kitchen, Bendel would know I'd overheard them.

"Hey, Max," Kingfish said when he saw me come around the corner of the lodge.

Bendel raised an eyebrow. "Where were you?" he asked.

"Checking the garbage shed," I said, joining them on the porch. "I thought I heard Festus out there last night. I was wrong."

"Who's Festus?" Kingfish frowned.

As I told him about the bear, Connie scooped Quincy into her arms.

"And Stormy only wounded him?" he said, with a laugh. "Way that woman shoots, it must have been deliberate."

I smiled. "We did have at least one visitor. Someone threw a few bags of trash up at the end of the access road."

They all frowned.

I shrugged. "I guess when the town wackos couldn't get through by phone they drove over to make their statement."

Connie made a face. "They threw garbage?" Quincy was struggling to get down, so she set him at our feet.

"Is it a real mess?" Bendel asked.

"Not that bad." I shook my head. "If we get it cleaned up before any animals get into it."

"I'll take the wheelbarrow up there and clean it up before breakfast," he said.

"I'll help," Connie said.

"What sort of feast does Stormy have planned for us this morning." Kingfish rubbed his hands together and looked down at Quincy, who was sniffing our shoes. "I could almost eat this little rat."

"Fishy!"

"Stormy's not here this morning," I said.

"She's not?" Bendel said. "Where is she?"

"Merriam called real early this morning," I said and looked at Kingfish. "That's Lyle Martin's wife. She said she needed help. Stormy took my Jeep."

Bendel glanced quickly at Connie.

"Nothing serious, I hope," Kingfish said.

I forced a laugh. "Nothing, except that until she returns, you're going to have to eat my cooking."

"I can cook, Max," Connie said.

"Since when?" Kingfish said.

She blushed. "Well, I can sous chef."

I declined Connie's assistance, told them the coffee was ready in the dining room, and returned to the kitchen. I looked at my watch. It was seven. I wished I'd listened to Stormy years ago and bought a portable telephone. I wanted to call Ruth in the worst way. I needed to tell her what was going on. I need her advice. Her father had been an alcoholic. Maybe she would have an idea where Stormy would go. But I couldn't call her from the hallway without everyone hearing.

I was squeezing orange halves on our electric juicer when Rayleen's truck rattled into the yard, pinged several times with preignition, and backfired. Five minutes after that he limped through the swinging door into the kitchen.

His cap bill was pulled defiantly down on his forehead. He waited until the door swung shut behind him, and then, put his hands on his hips. "Didn't say nothin' to them out there, Max," he said, "but what's this bull 'bout Stormy goin' overta Merriam's? I took Merriam downta her mother's in Montpelier yesterday afternoon."

I put down the orange. "I told everyone that because I don't know where she went."

"What'd'ya mean you don't know where she went? What about Bendel?"

I shook my head and pointed to a stool. "Sit down, Rayleen. We've got a problem."

He pushed the cap back on his head and sat on a stool and I told him what had been going on since he left. When I got to last night's incident in the workshop, he stood and yanked his cap back down to his eyebrows. "I'll kill the son'bitch," he said. "That there daughter of his warned Stormy at the weddin'. She said this was gonna happen, Max. Just out and told Stormy the man was a skirt-chaser. Said, no way he'd ever change."

"I don't care about Bendel," I said. "Sit down."

He sat. "Damn!"

"I found this"—I handed him the note—"under my door this morning."

I was quiet while he read it. "Just like her, ain't it?" He gave the note back. "Don't wanta go nowhere's 'til she knows everybody's eatin' right."

"She took a bottle of bourbon with her."

His eyes widened and he looked at the ceiling. "Lordy, Lordy." He leaned on the island and put his face in his hands. "This's happened once before, Max."

"When her husband and child died?"

He looked up and nodded. "When Big Jim and the baby went, she lost it. Disappeared. Didn't even go to the funeral." He sighed. His eyes looked frightened. "Took two weeks to find her. Finally dug her outta one of them cabins over at Lake Champlain. Nasty as a boozer gets, she was. Had a huntin' knife. Thought she was gonna kill me 'til she recognized my face. Never seen nobody so mean drunk. Before or since."

"Do you have any idea where she might have gone this time?"

"You call home?"

I nodded. "Nobody answered."

"That don't mean she ain't there." He sighed. "But, hell, she coulda gone anywheres."

"Maybe we should call the Sheriff's office."

"No way. Stormy wouldn't want that little snot-nose brat Billy Kendall knowin' nothin' 'bout this." He stood. "I'll go lookin' for her myself, Max."

"But where?"

"Dunno exactly. She's got your Jeep, right?"

"Yeah. And a suitcase."

"I'll call some of them AA buddies of hers. Maybe they can help. I'll check with Pauline at Ruth's office too. Stormy 'n' her been close now and again."

"You'll have to use a phone somewhere else. I don't want any of these people knowing about this."

"Neither would she." He stood. "I'll find her, Max. If she's thinkin' 'bout drinkin' again she won't go far."

"What if she already is drinking?"

"Don't wanna think 'bout that."

I took out my wallet and handed him the lodge American Express card. "You can get cash with this at most ATMs," I said. "The PIN number's the same as our telephone number."

He put the card in his shirt pocket and looked at me. His pale blue eyes were filling with tears. "I just wanta kill that Bendel," he said, wiping his sleeve quickly across his eyes. "She's a good woman, Max. She'll be fifteen years sober this October. She don't deserve this kinda pain."

"I know. But don't forget, it's their problem, not ours."

"If Stormy's drinkin' again, Max, gonna be everybody's problem." He went to the back door. "I better leave this way." He opened it. "I see that Bendel's face right now, I might not be able to control myself."

"Call me," I said.

He nodded and was gone. I leaned on the stove and stared at the blackened ham steaks in the frying pan. Hang in there, Stormy, I thought. Wherever you are, hang in there.

Breakfast was an ordeal.

As I sat there at the head of the table watching everyone good-naturedly eat my runny scrambled eggs and over-cooked ham steaks, every look, gesture, and smile shared by Bendel and Connie was magnified by my knowledge of what they had done. And what it appeared to have caused. They had all the sickening mannerisms of new-lyweds and, it seemed to me, were less cautious about displaying their affection now that Stormy wasn't present. I could barely eat and twice had to actually leave the table on the pretense I'd forgotten something in the kitchen or I would have yelled, "Stop it! For Chrissakes, stop it!"

Of course, I could have so easily stopped it. And, in a way, I suppose it was unfair to Bendel for me not to take him aside and tell him about Stormy. But I needed every-thing to appear normal. Kingfish had paid handsomely for it to be that way and now, with his offer to help Ruth, a lot was riding on him. I just had to grit my teeth and watch Bendel continue to make a fool of himself. As usual, Kingfish simply seemed to ignore them anyway. All he cared about was where we were going to fish as soon as breakfast was over.

"The lake looks like it's going to be good," I said and then reminded them all of the changes I wanted to make in who spent time with whom today.

I didn't expect any major disagreement—not at the ta-ble anyway. But after we were finished, Bendel joined me in the kitchen. "Stormy put you up to this, didn't she?" He set his and Connie's dirty plates on the island.

I shook my head and squirted dishwashing liquid into the sink.

"What's wrong then?" he asked.

"Nothing's wrong." I turned and looked at him. "I'd just like a break, is all."

"Why don't you have Rayleen take Kingfish?"

"Rayleen's doing something else for me."

He nodded slowly. "All right," he said. "You're the boss."

I didn't comment and began putting the cooking utensils in the sink as he turned and left.

By the time I'd cleaned up, got the dishwasher running, and gone to the porch, Bendel and Kingfish were already in the Old Town and pushing off from the dock with four rods, their vests, a six-pack of Loon Lager, and several Cuban cigars piled between them. They didn't seem to be concerned about waiting for Tommy and I didn't see him anywhere. Kingfish, who was in the bow, saw me come out onto the porch and waved. "*Arrivederci*, Max," he yelled. "Don't let Connie give you any crap."

I waved back. "Take him over to the beaver dam," I shouted to Bendel and then watched them paddle away from the dock out onto the windowpane stillness of Sweet Lake, jabbering and laughing in a combination of Italian and English.

Although the Whitefork River with its variety of water and beautiful trout is what brings the fly fishermen to Whitefork Lodge in the first place, Sweet Lake is really the jewel of the property. Formed as a result of hundreds of generations of beavers' almost insane dedication to dam-building, the fifteen acres of deep, clear, cold water is home to not only some of the largest brook trout on the property, but two pairs of loons, osprey, several species of ducks, and lately a large armada of year-round Canada geese, who, I guess, are too lazy to migrate any farther south or north. The forest of mixed hardwoods and conifers surrounding the jagged granite shoreline hides white-tailed deer, moose, black bear, fox, and a small pack of noisy eastern coyotes. Sweet Lake is irresistible. No matter what kind of fishing our guests come for . . . even the purists who initially claim they only want to fish the river with dry flies . . . eventually they all end up either to their armpits wading the shore, in canoes out on the lake, or simply casting like children from the dock.

"You're angry, aren't you, Max?" It was Connie, and holding Quincy under one arm, she stepped out onto the porch. Her platinum hair was pulled back and held in place by two red barrettes that matched her lipstick, her low-cut halter top, and the sandal thongs that coiled halfway up her calves. A white leather skirt with big red buttons came only to mid-thigh.

"Angry?" I looked away. I didn't want to talk to her. Not now.

"About Bendel and me." She walked to the steps, leaned over, and put Quincy out in the grass. "You're mad, aren't you? That's why you changed everything."

"He is married, you know. And Stormy's my friend. They're both my friends." 'I don't like what I've seen,' I wanted to say, 'and heard,' but I didn't.

"He's not happy."

I narrowed my eyes and glared at her. "Since when?"

"Bendel's a free spirit, Max. You can't tie a free spirit down."

"He tell you that?" I was trying hard not to but I was getting angry.

"I just know." She gave me a Marilyn look. "I'm the same way."

I took a deep breath. "Look, Connie," I said, "let's get something straight. Whitefork is a fishing lodge, not Club Med. This isn't the first time something like this has happened here and it probably won't be the last, but this time someone I care a great deal about is being hurt. And hurt badly. If I didn't like Kingfish so much, I'd throw you out."

She looked stunned.

"Do us all a favor, huh? Stay away from Bendel for the rest of the time you're here."

"You can't tell me what to do." She said it through her teeth.

"Oh, yes I can," I said. I was mad now. "This is my lodge. We follow my rules." I gestured to her clothes. "And if you still want to learn to fly-fish, which I'd be surprised you do without Bendel to teach you, put on some clothes appropriate for the mountains and meet me on the dock in thirty minutes." I left her standing there and walked down into the yard. Quincy yipped and snapped at my cuffs and, for a split second, I considered place-kicking him to the other side of the lake.

Tommy came running out of the workshop waving his automatic rifle. "Kingfish! Bendel! Wait!" he yelled. "You're supposed to wait for me. Kingfish, I want you to wear a life jacket." Tommy looked up at me for help. "Max?" he yelled. "Where do you keep the life jackets?"

I trotted to the workshop and showed Tommy the six life jackets and four cushions we have hanging from the ceiling beams. He grabbed one of each and started for the door. "Good move on the switch, Max," he said. "I think Ralph was getting pissed at Bendel, the way he's been carrying on with Connie." I followed him out to the dock, where I held the canoe while he climbed in. "If you want to know the truth," he said, picking up the paddle, "it pisses me off too a little. Not at Bendel. I mean, the old man. No matter who it is, he just looks the other way."

"As far as I'm concerned," I said, "it's over."

"Let's hope." He pointed out at the canoe carrying Bendel and Kingfish. "Look at them. Best of buddies. I'd hate to see that ruined." He dug the paddle deep and the canoe lurched forward, gliding smoothly out onto the water and into the fading "V" wake from the bigger canoe.

As I stood on the dock watching Tommy close the distance, I glanced quickly up at the porch. Connie was gone. Although slightly vindicated by Tommy's remarks, I still felt like a shit. I hadn't meant to come down on her that hard, but my concern for Stormy, the way Ruth was treating me, MacMillan and Billy Kendall, the newspaper article, the trash on the access road, and the phone calls all seemed to hit me when she stepped out onto the porch in that ridiculous outfit and opened her pouty, little red mouth.

Out on the lake, Tommy was now drifting twenty or thirty feet to one side of the big green canoe holding the older men. Bendel was still paddling slowly in the stern, but I could see the flash of Kingfish's rod as he cast out across the flat water. Their voices, now unintelligible, floated across the water. I heard Tommy laugh just as the first booming gunshot echoed across the lake. Bendel seemed to stiffen in his seat. His paddle slid from his hands and floated away.

What I was seeing . . . what was happening . . . didn't register at first. Then a small geyser of water erupted just ahead of the canoe, followed instantly by the explosion of a second shot.

Kingfish dropped his rod, turned, and was beginning to stand up when another shot echoed, blowing off his toupee and violently knocking him backward to a sitting position on the gunwale. He appeared to look down at his stomach. The canoe instantly tipped violently and would have overturned but a fourth shot simultaneously slammed Bendel forward onto the gear stacked in front of him and blew Kingfish over the side and into the water on his back.

Even from my distance, I could see the crimson instantly begin to bloom in the water that closed over him.

The sky was suddenly full of wheeling, frightened, quacking ducks and honking geese and Tommy's rifle now chattered from the smaller canoe as he fired into the woods to my right, methodically raking the trees like a man watering a lawn. And then I was aware of Connie screaming and Quincy barking and Ralph yelling from somewhere behind me. "Get down, Max! Get down!"

I threw myself on the dock and, through my arms,

watched as Tommy dove from the small canoe into the spot where Kingfish went down. To my right I saw Ralph dodge professionally up into the thick tangle of trees behind the workshop, working his way from tree trunk to tree trunk into the darker trees. The big green Old Town rocked and slowly turned in circles with only Bendel's shoulder showing above the gunwale and his left arm dangling over the side. His hand trailed in the growing slick of red on the still water.

It became quickly obvious that neither Tommy, Ralph, nor I were in any danger of being shot, and after five minutes of lying on my stomach, I got up, yelled at Connie to go call the police, and grabbed a life jacket from the workshop. I put it on and, taking off my trousers and shoes, swam awkwardly out into the cold lake to the Old Town to help Tommy.

He had hauled Kingfish up from under water and lifted him as far out as he could, so now the top half of the old man's body lay in the canoe. His pelvis and scrawny legs still hung in the water. I could see one of his shoes was missing. The canoe had swamped in the activity and only the gunwales and upturned ends showed above the lake's surface. I knew that, because of the floatation chambers in each end, it wouldn't sink. But I also knew that in water this cold Tommy and I had to get to shore or risk hypothermia. "They're both dead, Max," Tommy said, treading water behind the canoe. His face was ashen. His lips already turning blue. "It happened too fast . . . I . . ." He coughed and spit. "I . . . I didn't even see . . ."

"We've got to get out of this water," I said, grabbing the bow of the Old Town. My legs were cramping. "I'll swim this canoe back. Can you push that one?"

He nodded and began to kick furiously and the red canoe carrying Kingfish slowly began to move. I did the same and, as best we could, we headed for the dock.

CHAPTER 🐟 THIRTEEN

It was slow going and by the time Tommy and I had the canoes and bodies to the dock, Ralph and Spotter were waiting for us. Connie was there too, but she was useless as she paced the water's edge wailing "Fishy! Fishy! Fishy!" hysterically.

The three of us dragged the bodies up into the grass and laid them side by side. On his back, Bendel appeared to be asleep until you saw the blood-soaked front of his shirt and the two finger-size holes in the fabric. I could only look at Kingfish once. He was on his stomach and the back of his head had been torn away by an exiting bullet.

I expected Ralph to come unglued as soon as Tommy and I got the bodies to the dock and I wasn't disappointed. Just like when Stormy killed the woodchuck, he vomited. Tommy, as cold as I knew he must be, efficiently squatted by Bendel's body and studied the exit wounds in his chest. "You see anyone?" he asked Ralph. "Anything at all in the monitor?"

Ralph wiped his mouth with the back of his sleeve and shook his head. "I didn't see anything. Just heard the shots." His face was pale and bleeding from several scratches where, obviously, branches had slashed at his face. His hands trembled on the automatic rifle.

"There was only one shooter," Tommy said. "That I'm positive of."

Ralph nodded and gingerly touched a cut on his chin.

"Sounded like a large caliber." Tommy touched the bloody hole in Bendel's shirt. "Maybe thirty-ought-six or thirty-thirty. Deer rifle probably." He looked up at Ralph. "You hear how spaced out the shots were? Like cocking time in a lever-action or bolt?"

Their conversation seemed ludicrous. I was wet and so cold I was shaking. Connie was on her knees between the bodies, moaning, her short white skirt smeared with blood. She had rolled Kingfish to his back. Spotter was sniffing Bendel and whining. And a killer was getting away while they calmly discussed guns and bullets. I put my hand on Connie's shoulder. "Did you call the police?"

"I told her to hold off, Max," Ralph said. His hand was at his mouth as if he might throw up again. "This is Vincent d'Antella. There are things we have to do first."

Tommy nodded. "Nothing the cops can do for anyone right now."

"Except get in the way," Ralph said, looking at Tommy. "You have the cell phone with you?"

Tommy nodded and wrestled it from the large pocket on the thigh of his soaked trousers. "It's useless." It was dripping wet. "Go call Collingwood from the lodge. We'll get the bodies out of this sun and into the workshop."

Ralph started up the yard, stopped, and turned. "Max? You think Stormy'd mind if I took a couple spoonfuls of that Pepto-Bismol she has in the downstairs bathroom?"

I shook my head.

Connie, her forehead now on Bendel's shoulder, was still moaning. Tommy grabbed her arm and jerked her to her feet. "Your boyfriend's dead," he said, putting his face an inch from hers. "So's your meal ticket. Now, get a grip, huh? And give Max and me a hand."

Tommy and I dragged the bodies into the workshop. Connie scuffed after us, carrying Bendel's hat and Kingfish's toupee. We laid the bodies on the floor beside my Harley. "Get a sheet from the bedroom," Tommy said to Connie. "It'll keep the bugs off."

"I . . . I can't," she cried, horrified, glancing from Bendel to the little bedroom and back again. "Please, no."

I got the sheet and we spread it over the bodies.

Whether it was finally seeing the two shapes under the white that way or just the adrenaline wearing off, I'm not sure. But all of a sudden, it hit me and I had to sit down. I had spent a lot of time with Bendel over the past few years. We had shared laughs and stories and a love for Whitefork Lodge, the outdoors, and beautiful fish. He was fun to be with, and at a time in my life when real men friends were few and far between, he had been one. And now he was dead and I couldn't help but think it was all my fault. I leaned my arms on my knees and hung my head. Ruth had warned me. Stormy had warned me. Even MacMillan had warned me. And I hadn't listened to any of them. I had been too eager to finish the rooms. Too eager to capitalize on the popularity created by "The Movie." Ruth had been right that day in her office. I was oblivious to everything and everyone except how it or they might affect my life, my livelihood, and my own image of myself. I shook my head and stared at a carpenter ant crossing the bare concrete floor between my bare feet. No, I wasn't responsible for Vincent d'Antella's death. His days obviously were numbered anyway. It was Bendel's murder I could have prevented if I'd simply said no to Donald Collingwood.

"Collingwood's on his way." Ralph stepped into the workshop doorway. "He'll be here sometime tonight. Meanwhile, he says go ahead and call the local cops, Max." He looked at Tommy. "We're to hide the videotapes we've made since we were here," he said to him. "Look at them first. Check one more time to see if there's anyone. Then put in a blank and say the recorder didn't work. He doesn't want the cops to have any of it."

Tommy stepped up to me and put his hand on my shoulder. "You'd better get a hold of Stormy, too, Max. She should probably know before that redneck deputy does."

Oh, God, I thought. *What's going to happen when Stormy finds out?*

After changing my wet clothes, my first call was to Ruth. I wasn't sure what I was going to say, but I needed to hear her voice. Connie had carried Quincy upstairs. I could hear her sobs as I listened to Ruth's private number ring at City Hall.

"Mayor Pearlman's office." It was Pauline.

"It's Max, Pauline," I said. "I need to talk to her. It's very important."

"Sorry, Max," she said. "She's out at the dam this morning. They're dedicating that new fish ladder." Ever since landlocked salmon began coming back into the Whitefork River, the only obstacle to their successful run upstream to spawn had been the antiquated fish ladder on the Whitefork Dam. Our local chapter of Trout Unlimited had lobbied hard and raised funds for the ladder's reconstruction. While Ruth was campaigning for governor, MacMillan had pledged matching funds from the town's treasury and the new ladder was built. Earl came off like some kind of environmentalist, but anyone who knew him and the bait draggers he fished with knew he had done nothing more than use taxpayers' money to assure himself plenty of lox with his bagels every morning. "Governor Perry's here for the ceremonies, too," Pauline added.

"Well, please have her call me just as soon as you can," I said.

"Is everything all right, Max? You don't sound like yourself."

"Just have her call. Okay?"

Pauline promised she'd tell Ruth first chance she got and we hung up.

My next call was to the Sheriff's office. That was easy. I simply told the guy who answered who I was and that I was reporting a double murder. He took it from there. "We're on our way, Mr. Addams," he said with more enthusiasm than I thought was necessary. "Please try not to touch anything and don't leave the premises."

I started to tell him that we'd had to touch the bodies to get them from the lake, but the line was dead.

In less than thirty minutes there were more squad cars jammed at angles around the front of the lodge than I thought there were in the entire state of Vermont. Not only were the three Loon County Sheriff's squad cars and their big four-wheel-drive Bronco with the three-foot-high stars on the doors there, but seven state police cruisers arrived with their blue, red, and white lights strobing and they were now parked across the lawn, wheels cocked and doors wide open. A cacophony of static and two-way-radio talk filled the air from ten blaring cop radios.

A small troop of five heavily armed state troopers wearing bulletproof vests had gone into the trees where Ralph and Tommy indicated the shots had come from. I could hear some of their conversation filter down to where I stood in the hot sun on the lawn with Ralph and Tommy waiting for Billy Kendall, two of his deputies, and the state-police lieutenant who seemed to be in charge to come back out of the workshop after viewing the bodies. Four more uniformed troopers and one too-young-looking sheriff's deputy had taken up posts on the porch and down by the cabin. They all held short pump shotguns and their eyes flitted around the yard as if they expected more shooting any second. I doubted any of them had a safety on, so I didn't make any sudden moves. Connie, with Quincy in her lap, sat in a rocker on the porch. She'd changed to long, baggy khakis and a sweatshirt and had washed the makeup from her face. She was the picture of the grieving widow. It was obvious she'd been through things like this before.

"Damn," Ralph said, shielding his eyes with his hand. "I wish I had a hat. I have a couple spots on my forehead that look like melanoma already."

"I wonder what's taking them so long," Tommy said. "It's only two bodies."

I could hear the telephone ringing in the lodge. Connie put Quincy down and went in to answer it. When she came back out she called to me, "Max, it's for you. The mayor."

It was cool in the hallway. A state-police trooper moved to the screen door after it shut behind me. I looked at his broad back as I picked up the phone. "Hello, Ruth," I said. I knew I sounded glum, but I just couldn't seem to put any energy in my voice.

"Oh, Max. I just heard. Are you all right?"

"I don't know yet. It's pretty terrible."

"It's awful. Bendel was such a wonderful man. How's Stormy? Does she need me? You want me to come out there?"

"Stormy's gone," I said and, lowering my voice, told her everything that had happened.

"Oh, my God, Max. What if she is drinking?"

"Exactly."

"Have you checked her house?"

"I called," I said. "Rayleen's out looking for her."

"What can I do?"

"I really don't know. Maybe you can check around with some of Stormy's friends in town."

"I'll get Pauline on it immediately," she said. "Her sister's husband is in Stormy's AA group. What about you?"

"Me?" I said.

"If I know you, you're already blaming yourself."

"I should have listened to you."

"Don't talk like that," she said.

"It wouldn't surprise me if I was a suspect. Probably all of us are."

"Are the state police there?"

"Yeah. Plus Kendall and his posse."

"I have the governor here today, so if they try to arrest you, Max, or anyone else at the lodge, I want them to call me first. Okay?"

"I thought you weren't taking sides in this thing."

"That was politics. This is personal. Stormy, Rayleen, and Bendel are like family. I love Stormy and . . ." Her voice cracked and she was silent for a few seconds. When she spoke again, I could hear the tears in her voice. "I'm the mayor and I'm not going to let anything else happen to the people I care about."

"Thanks," I said.

"Max, I should come out there. You shouldn't have to deal with this alone."

"No," I said. "Not now. I'll be fine. There's nothing you can do. Come out later though. Okay?"

She sighed. "You sure?"

"I'm sure. Right now, just see what you can do to help find Stormy."

The state trooper in the doorway turned. "They want you back outside, Mr. Addams," he said, opening the screen door.

"I've got to go, Ruth."

"Don't forget what I said about calling me. If anybody even takes out a pair of handcuffs just . . ."

"I hope it doesn't come to that." I hung up, went out onto the porch, and started down the steps. Ralph, Tommy, Billy Kendall, and the state-police lieutenant were coming up through the yard toward me.

"Stay there, Max," Billy Kendall said, pointing his big finger at me. "We're all comin' in."

The Vermont State Police lieutenant's name was Conklin—Samuel Conklin. He was about my age but taller, leaner, and probably in a lot better shape. His dark brown uniform looked tailored. His hair was in a brush cut like Billy's, but it was silver in color. His eyes were such a light blue that, depending upon how the light hit them, they looked all white. He needed a shave and the stubble on his square jaw was white too.

"I'll bet he's 'Whitey' to his friends," Ralph whispered as we were all ushered into the dining room.

Conklin stood in front of the fireplace in the dining room. His Smokey hat lay on the mantel. He had a clipboard in his hand. A trooper with a shotgun stood on his left. Billy Kendall stood to his right, like a soldier "at ease." His hat was in his hands behind his back. No doubt excited to be a part of a "big-time" investigation, Billy had obviously cut himself shaving this morning. Several small, freshly scabbed cuts and nicks showed on his square jaw and neck.

The rest of us were sitting on the far side of the dining-room table against the windows, Tommy and I in the middle, a sniffling Connie and a squirming Quincy on my left, Ralph on Tommy's right.

". . . and from our preliminary look," Conklin was saying, "it would appear that Mr. d'Antella and Mr. . . . ." He looked at Billy.

"Domini, sir," Billy said. "Bendel Domini."

". . . and Mr. Domini were struck at the same time by bullets from the same weapon. And, until the search team I have in the woods returns, it would appear that only one assailant is responsible." He looked at the clipboard. "Mr. Addams? You say you were on the dock watching Mr. Marchetti and the victims out on the lake when the shooting started?"

I nodded.

"Yes or no, Max," Billy growled.

"Yes," I said.

Conklin glanced at Connie. "And you, Miss Roth?"

He looked down at the clipboard. "You were on the lodge porch?"

"Yes."

"Watching?"

"Yes."

"And you, Mr. Garrett."

"Yes?"

"Why weren't you watching?"

"I was in there," Ralph pointed toward the reading room, "doing my job."

"Which was?"

"Monitoring the security cameras."

Conklin nodded thoughtfully and studied the clipboard for a couple seconds. Then he looked at Tommy. "Mr. Marchetti?"

"Yes?"

"Can you offer an explanation why you weren't shot?"

Tommy shook his head.

I was getting tired of this. They'd been at the lodge almost two hours now. "What's the point of that question, lieutenant?" I asked.

Billy glared at me, but if he was going to say something Conklin didn't give him a chance. "The point is, Mr. Addams," Conklin said, "everyone in this room is assuming that Vincent d'Antella was assassinated. That this was a mob hit and Mr. Domini just happened to get caught in the middle. The fact that Mr. Marchetti wasn't harmed or, as far as we can tell, even fired upon, is quite unusual." He looked back at Tommy. "Isn't that so, Mr. Marchetti?"

Tommy shrugged. "Maybe someone thought Bendel was employed by Vincent too."

"Perhaps," Conklin said. "Nevertheless . . ." A woman trooper came into the room. She wore a bulletproof vest with STATE POLICE stenciled on the back. She was from the group I'd watched go into the woods. She handed Conklin a small plastic bag. It rattled and the window light reflected from the three or four brass rifle cartridges inside. She whispered something in his ear and then stepped back and took a pose similar to Billy's.

Conklin unzipped the bag and extracted one shell. He looked at the end and then held it up in the light. "This cartridge casing," he said, "along with the others in this bag, were found about fifty yards from the lake up in the trees." He looked at Tommy. "About where Mr. Marchetti indicated he thought the shots came from." He handed the cartridge to Billy Kendall. "What caliber is that, deputy?"

Billy looked. "Winchester, thirty-thirty, sir." He handed it back and Conklin returned it to the plastic bag and gave it to the female trooper.

"It's rather strange," the woman said. "It's such a large caliber."

Conklin frowned at her. "Although out of order, the officer has a point." He looked back at us. "I've studied hundreds of mob killings and, with the exception of shootings where it was intended to look like a hunting accident, large-caliber heavy firearms are the exception." He looked directly at Ralph. "Is that not true, Mr. Garrett?"

Ralph nodded.

"What's he know?" Billy said.

Conklin glared at him and then continued, "Today's modern hired killer prefers lightweight, easily disassembled and disposable small-caliber weapons."

"I still don't see your point," I said.

"Mr. Addams." He frowned at me. "What I'm saying is, right now, evidence seems to indicate that Vincent d'Antella and Bendel Domini were not the victims of a planned mob hit. It appears that they were killed for a different reason."

"Might not even have been d'Antella they were shootin' at," Billy said.

Conklin spun around. "Deputy Kendall!" he said

through his teeth. "When I want your observations or comments, I'll ask for them."

Billy snapped to attention and blushed. "Yes, sir."

Conklin turned back to me. "Did Mr. Domini have any enemies that you know of?"

I shook my head.

"Anyone who might have been angry with him?"

I shook my head again. "He was a good man."

Conklin ignored the comment. "Mister Domini's wife"—he looked at the clipboard—"Anita? Yes, Anita." He looked back at me. "You said she's in Montpelier with her brother, Rayleen?"

"Yes," I said. I didn't think the truth would help anyone. "She doesn't know about this yet."

"This Rayleen? He works for you too?"

"Yes."

"When do you expect their return?"

"As soon as they find out about Bendel's death, I suppose." I hoped.

Conklin looked at Ralph. "Mr. Garrett?" He looked at the clipboard. "You say there was no indication of trespassers from any of the three cameras you were monitoring?"

"That's right, none."

"I noticed video-recording equipment in there," Conklin said. "I assume you'll be able to play back the footage recorded before and after the murders."

Ralph shook his head. "It's broken," he lied. "We just found out the record function wasn't working when we went to look after the shooting ourselves. We never needed to look at anything until now and . . ." A siren interrupted Ralph and we turned and looked out the window as two more state-police squad cars roared into the yard, the doors flying open before they had skidded to a stop.

"Ah," Conklin said. "That will be our forensic team." He walked over to the table, leaned on it, and looked at

Ralph and Tommy. "I'm not going to bullshit you two," he said, narrowing his eyes. "I've spent my career trying to put people like you and Vincent d'Antella away. So, just remember, nothing would make me happier than to find out you punks were behind this. Nothing." He looked over at me and straightened. "None of you are under arrest, Mr. Addams. But you are restricted to the premises until I say otherwise." He turned and started toward the dining-room door. Billy and the female trooper fell in behind. "Deputy Kendall and his people will be leaving," he said over his shoulder. "But the forensic team and myself will be here for another three or four hours." He stopped at the screen door and looked back at us. "Please find somewhere inside out of the way until we're through." Then he pushed through the door with Billy, the female trooper, and the guy with the shotgun right behind. I could hear Billy begin to whine and argue for staying even before they were down the steps.

"Assholes," Ralph muttered.

I went looking for Spotter. I hadn't see him since all the squad cars arrived.

He wasn't under my bed where he usually hid during a thunderstorm, nor was he in the kitchen. I found him outside the back door, lying in the grass beside Stormy's garden. His front paws and muzzle were in the dirt. "There you are," I said, sitting on the steps. I patted my knee. "Come here, boy."

He rolled his eyes toward me and exhaled. He didn't move.

"You know it's my fault, don't you?" I took out a cigarette, lit it, and looked at Stormy's garden. It was dry. The pea sprouts hung limply from their strings on the trellis. "We'll have to water this later, won't we?" I said.

Spotter closed his eyes.

I looked down at the yard and the workshop. Three state

troopers wearing rubber gloves had pulled the canoes up into the grass. They were carefully picking over them, putting things in small plastic bags, sealing them, and writing on the outside with black marker. Even though the sun was bright, I could see the windows in the workshop light up as flashbulbs went off inside. I could hear voices from the woods beyond. A slight breeze was coming across the lake, corrugating the surface. I could smell the water.

If only I had just told Bendel that Stormy was gone, that she'd taken a bottle of bourbon and left in my Jeep. He would have gone after her and he wouldn't be lying in there on the concrete now.

Conklin was right. These people were bad, pure and simple. Tommy and Ralph were nothing more than thugs. What had made me think that they were anything but common gangsters? What had made me think I could have people like that at the lodge and not suffer some sort of repercussions?

As much as I disliked MacMillan, he had been right, too. So had Stormy and Ruth. They warned me. And I hadn't listened. And now, a sweet, gentle man was dead. Oh, sure, Bendel had his flaws. Who didn't? But nothing he had done deserved what happened to him. Nothing.

As I reached down into the grass beside the steps and snubbed out my cigarette I felt my fingers touch something small and metal. I peered into the shadow and saw a spent brass cartridge casing. There were two others, partially obscured in the deep new grass near it. I picked them up, held them in my palm, and studied them. They glinted in the sunlight. They were the shells Stormy had ejected from the Winchester when she'd shot the woodchuck. Almost absentmindedly, I picked one up between my fingertips and squinted at the letters and numerals imprinted in a circle on the end. It read "WINCHESTER .30–.30 CAL." I tipped it in the light to make sure. These three spent cartridges were the same as the ones Conklin's people found in the woods.

I went back inside the kitchen, turned, and looked up at the gun rack above the door.

Stormy's Winchester was gone.

CHAPTER ♦ FOURTEEN

I sat on a stool at the kitchen island and stared at the empty gun rack.

Where the hell was the Winchester?

The last time I had seen it was when Stormy had shot the woodchuck. Could she have taken it with her this morning when she left? As protection, maybe? It was dark out. And the Jeep's top was down. It had never occurred to me to look to see if it was gone. Maybe it was the unidentifiable shape Ralph and I had seen on the backseat.

Or had Rayleen taken it? He and I had been in the kitchen when he left to look for Stormy. I hadn't paid any attention to him as he went out the back door—the ham steaks were burning—had he snatched it from the gun rack on his way out?

But why would he?

I dumped the three cartridges on the butcher-block top of the island and one by one set them up on end in a line. I could still hear Billy Kendall's comment during Conklin's questioning. "Maybe it wasn't d'Antella they were after," he'd said. And I distinctly remembered seeing the first shot hitting Bendel.

I couldn't believe what I was thinking. Could Stormy have been so angry . . . ?

It was ridiculous.

Or was it?

I'd never known her as a drinker, but what had Rayleen said about how vicious she became?

And what about Rayleen himself? The Lord's Workers violently opposed those who broke the Ten Commandments. I could only imagine the brainwashing they'd attempted along with the dunkings at the Sacrament of the Tears ceremony.

Both Stormy and Rayleen know the area well enough to slip in through the woods without the cameras seeing them. It would explain why Ralph hadn't seen anyone on the monitor.

I shook my head as if the movement would dislodge the thoughts. Stormy or Rayleen murderers? It was too bizarre. Talk about jumping to conclusions. Along with Ruth and my daughter, they were the two people I respected and trusted more than anyone in the world.

I stood, scooped the cartridges from the island, and put them in the breast pocket of my shirt. There was only one way to get this out of my head. I had to go down to the workshop, whether Conklin liked the intrusion or not, and talk to the forensic people. I was entitled to know what they knew. And maybe . . . just maybe, without being too obvious, I could find out what kind of thirty-caliber rifle they thought fired the bullets that killed Bendel and Kingfish.

"Just the man we wanted to see," Conklin said when he saw me step into the workshop's doorway. "C'mon in, Max."

One step into the room and I understood his sudden friendliness. It was Gordon Miller and photographer Rusty Granger from the *Loon Sentinel*. They must have arrived while I was in the kitchen. Gordon had Lieutenant Conklin backed up against the workbench with a handheld tape recorder. Rusty, his face obscured by a waterfall of long hair, was reloading his twin-lens reflex using the seat of the Harley as a table.

When Gordon saw me, he came at me with the tape recorder in his outstretched hand. "Max," he said, a big smile growing on his face, "Boy, you really got yourself a big problem this time . . ."

I planted my feet. "I thought you wanted me to get rid of Vincent d'Antella, Gordon."

"Hey, c'mon, Max." He frowned, stealing a look at Conklin over his shoulder. "That's not funny."

"No, Gordon, you c'mon." I grabbed him by the shirt-sleeve and walked him out of the workshop.

He stumbled but didn't fall. "Jesus, Max. Hey!"

I yanked him out onto the dock, where I traded my grip on his sleeve for a fistful of shirtfront. I put my face in his. "Does the lieutenant know about those inflammatory things you wrote about d'Antella the other day?"

His eyes were wide.

"He know how you told me to get rid of him?" I took the recorder from his hand.

"That recorder's private property, Max." He tried to grab it back. "Give it . . ."

I batted his hand away and gripped his shirt harder, lifting him to his toes. "If I was a cop, Gordon, I might wonder if maybe you didn't hire someone yourself to come out here and shoot these people. Or maybe it was you and MacMillan, huh?"

"Let me go, Max. Please."

I released my grip but I didn't get out of his face. "So, what do you think, Gordon? You think I should show Lieutenant Conklin the newspaper from the other night?" I punched my finger into his chest. "Huh?" I punched again. Harder this time. "What do you think, Gordon?"

"That hurts, Max."

"Not as much as those bullets must have hurt Bendel." I jabbed my finger into his chest again.

"Stop it, Max! What do you want from me?"

"I want a public apology for your article the other night." I jabbed him. "I want it in the paper tonight."

"All right! Jesus! All right."

"That's not all."

"But . . ."

"I want you to hold this story for twenty-four hours."

"What?" His eyes got even wider. "I can't do that. This is big news, Max."

"Of course you can, Gordon."

"But . . . but we have the exclusive to . . ."

I jabbed him hard. "Who's going to scoop you, Gordon? Who's going to find out unless you let it out?"

"But, why?"

"Stormy doesn't know about any of this yet."

"What? Why not?"

"She's not here." His heels were at the edge of the dock and I grabbed the front of his shirt again. "And I don't want her to find out about her husband's murder through your piece-of-shit newspaper."

"I can't just . . ."

I pushed him backward, he started to fall and would have gone in the water if I hadn't grabbed his shirt again. "You'll hold the story, Gordon"—I held him out over the water—"until I call and tell you Stormy knows. And if you don't wait, not only am I going to put Conklin and the Vermont State Police all over your ass, but I'm going to call the *Burlington Free Press* and every other damn newspaper I can think of and blow your big exclusive out of the water."

"All right!" he screamed. "Okay. Okay. I'll wait."

I stood him up and stepped back. "All you need to remember, Gordon, is tonight's the apology"—I gave the recorder back—"tomorrow's the story on the murders."

He looked at the recorder in his hand. The red recording light was still blinking.

"And, as long as this thing is still on," I said, "I want this on record too. Bendel was my close friend. And Vincent d'Antella was a gentleman." I turned and went back into the workshop.

This time Conklin frowned as he saw me enter. "I'd prefer you to stay up in the lodge, Addams."

"You owe me, Lieutenant," I said, walking over to where he stood by the bodies.

"Owe you for what?"

"For getting that newspaper jerk out of your hair, is what."

He sighed and nodded. "Yeah, so?"

"So, I want someone here to tell me what they think happened. I have a right to know. It was my friend who was killed and this is my lodge."

Conklin looked down at the man and woman squatting at the bodies for a few seconds. Then he looked back at me and nodded. "All right," he said, motioning to the woman. "Cynthia?"

She stood. "Yes, sir?" She began peeling off her rubber gloves.

"This is Max Addams," he said as Cynthia stepped over the corpses. "Max, this is Inspector Cynthia Brown." We shook hands. "Max owns Whitefork Lodge. Mr. Domini there was a friend of his and an employee. Cynthia recently joined our forensic team from Boston Homicide." He smiled. "Tell him what he wants to know, will you, Cynthia?"

"I'll try." Cynthia and I walked out into the sun and sat on the bench beside the door. She was quite pretty, in an Irish sort of way. A constellation of freckles from her chin to her hairline was broken only by a small upturned nose, cupid's-bow lips, and wide-set green eyes with laugh wrinkles at the corners. Her short red hair was starting to gray. The brown uniform, however, wasn't her color, nor did it fit very well, and as we talked she pulled at it here and there. "Where would you like me to start, Mr. Addams?"

"Do you know what kind of gun was used yet?"

"Only that it was a rifle and that is was not an automatic or semiautomatic."

"Meaning?"

"You know we found cartridges up in the woods, right?"

I nodded.

"Well, there are marks on the casing brass of those cartridges that indicate they were lifted mechanically from a magazine or clip into the rifle's chamber."

"Like a lever-action?"

She nodded. "Certainly, that's one possibility. But there's also bolt-action. Even pump-action. We won't know exactly until we get the cartridge cases back to the lab and are able to run more conclusive tests with similar weapons."

"How long will that take?"

She shrugged. "A couple of days, I would imagine."

"I saw it happen," I said. "Granted they were quite a ways away, but to me it looked like my friend was hit first."

She nodded. "You have a good eye, Mr. Addams. Although we'll be better able to determine the exact impact sequence of the bullets when we get the bodies back to the lab, it appears right now that Mr. Domini not only took the first bullet but the third and the last as well."

I had seen the last bullet hit and drive him forward on his face. "The third bullet hit him?"

"Yes. It hit his ear and although it only took a piece, we have been able to find enough of that tissue on the shirtfront of Mr. d'Antella . . ." She cleared her throat. ". . . at the entry point of his abdominal wound . . . to pretty conclusively indicate that bullet number three hit Mr. Domini first." She paused and studied my face—I think to see how I was handling this information.

"Go on," I said, taking out my cigarettes and offering her one.

She declined. I lit one for myself and she continued.

"The first bullet was fatal to Mr. Domini. It entered his back, went through his heart, and exited just above the canoe's waterline. The second bullet missed both men."

I nodded. I remembered seeing the geyser of water.

"The third bullet I just told you about."

"The ear . . . ?"

"Yes." She frowned. "Bullet number four is the strange one."

"Strange?"

"Well, maybe strange isn't the right word, but it's the bullet that makes some of us question who the intended target was."

Oh, Jesus, I thought. "Who?"

"Yes. We, of course, approached this double homicide on the theory that Mr. d'Antella was the target. And the first three bullets seem to follow that theory. I mean, if you think about where they went, it's a sort of zeroing in kind of thing."

"Zeroing in?"

"Yes. It's common for someone firing from a great distance. Not familiar with trajectory and the effects of gravity and wind, they shoot once to see how close they are and then zero in. Each shot gets closer to the actual target until . . ."

"Then Bendel was hit first by accident?"

"That's what we thought." She shrugged. "Now, I'm not so sure. You see, the bullet that killed Mr. d'Antella . . . bullet number four . . . the one that entered his eye . . . would never have done so if it hadn't entered Mr. Domini first and deflected off his ribcage as he was thrown forward." She could see the confusion on my face. "Let me put it another way, Mr. Addams. From what I've seen here today, it is very possible Mr. d'Antella just happened to get killed as the shooter zeroed in on Mr. Domini."

It was just what I didn't want to hear. I leaned my head back against the workshop's rough log siding.

"I'm sorry if this upsets you, Mr. Addams," she said.

I sighed. "Bendel was a friend. His wife is a friend."

"I'm sure it's of no consolation, but there's one more possibility we're examining."

I looked at her.

"The shots could have been deliberately and expertly placed. Someone could have wanted them both dead."

I sat up. "When will you know for sure?"

"Like I said about the kind of rifle, it'll take a day or two to be positive." She smiled. "Anything else?"

"No way to tell how many people did the shooting or what sex they were, I suppose."

"Oh, yes, we'll know all those things. They're accumulating a lot of evidence up at the shooting site," she said. "We already know that whoever it was walked in to the site from the north, where it appears he or she parked a vehicle in the parking lot of a roadhouse called . . ."

"The Starlight?"

"Yes. The Starlight." She smiled. "Right now, it appears there was only one assailant. Determining the sex will take a lot more equipment than we have here."

There was the sound of glass breaking inside the workshop. Like a small bottle had dropped on the concrete floor. "How do you do that?" I asked.

"How do we determine sex?" She peered around me, trying to see into the building. "As you probably know, that portion of the woods is quite dense. We've found small traces of blood in several places. We think that whoever did the shooting probably scratched up their hands or face pretty badly getting in there in the dark. DNA will tell us the sex." There was another tinkle of glass from inside. "I think I'd better get back, Mr. Addams. If that's all you need to know, I mean."

"You've been very helpful," I said, shaking her hand again. "Thank you."

She left me sitting there with my back to the log wall. Three mallards whistled overhead and, in quick, skidding splashes, landed out in the water. They ruffled their feathers and glided toward the far shore.

As I looked out at the lake I couldn't help but see Bendel and Kingfish die all over again. I saw Bendel hit by the first bullet, stiffen in his seat, and drop the paddle. Kingfish turned and the next shot missed. I saw the water geyser. The third shot hit Kingfish and he sat down on the gunwale almost tipping over the canoe. He looked puzzled and stared at his stomach. The fourth shot hit Bendel. He flopped forward a split second before Kingfish was knocked into the water.

I was more confused than ever. Who could have possibly wanted both of them dead?

By noon, Gordon and Rusty from the *Sentinel* had gone. Spotter had decided he could mope in the shade just as well as in the sun at the garden and had moved to the front porch with Tommy, Ralph, Connie, and Quincy.

Bendel and Kingfish's bodies had been taken away to Loon General Hospital, where they'd be kept in the cold room until the county medical examiner got back day after tomorrow. He was in Florida vacationing with his family. Lieutenant Conklin, Inspector Cynthia Brown, and the rest of the crew who had stayed were packing up their things and about to leave. They had several cartons full of small labeled plastic envelopes of evidence and even two large trash bags of leaves and twigs from the ''shooting site'' up in the woods.

I was sitting on the edge of my bed with what was left of a cold Loon Lager when the telephone rang. There were three empties on the floor at my feet and I knocked two of them over as I went out into the hallway to answer it.

It was Rayleen.

''You have her, Rayleen?''

''Don't get excited, Max,'' he said. ''I'm just checking in. Actually, I kinda hoped she was there.''

"I wish she was," I said. How was I going to tell him about Bendel and Kingfish?

"What's the matter, Max? You don't sound too good. Somethin' you ain't tellin' me?"

With as few of the gory details as possible, I told him how Bendel and Kingfish had been shot out on the lake this morning. "They're both dead," I said.

"Oh, Lordy," he said. "Oh, Lordy, Lordy, Lordy."

"I've got to ask you something, Rayleen."

He sighed. "What, Max?"

"Did you take Stormy's Winchester from the kitchen?"

"Hell no. What would I want with that old thing? Why? Is it missin'?"

"Would Stormy have taken it with her when she left this morning?"

He was silent.

"Dammit, Rayleen. Would she have taken it?"

He was silent again for a few seconds. Finally he said, "Most likely. Our daddy give her that Winchester on her sixteenth birthday. Only thing that woman cares more about 'n that gun is that old dog, Spotter."

"Do you think she's been drinking?"

"What's with all the questions, Max?"

"Bendel and Kingfish were shot with a thirty-thirty," I said.

"Oh, Lordy . . ."

"Do you think she could shoot someone?"

He sighed. "Wouldn't be the first time."

"What?"

"It was years ago, Max. Long 'fore you got here. Harry Lipser. Was a big real-estate man in Loon. He's dead now. But when he was alive, he went 'n' raped his sec'tary. Ginny Prentiss, her name was. Pretty little girl. Knocked her up too, I guess. Anyways, nobody knew it was rape 'til later. 'Til after she killed herself and left it in a note. Stormy was still drinkin' hard then, and when she heard, she went berserk. Went downta Harry's office with the

Winchester and blowed off three of his toes. Was gonna shoot off his balls, I think, but someone knocked the barrel down.''

"So she could she have . . . ?''

"Killed Bendel? It's possible. After what he done? If she'd been drinkin' and if there weren't nobody there to knock the barrel down. Stormy's the best woman shot in this county.''

"Jesus.''

"You betcha. Stormy 'n' that there Winchester got quite a history in this town.''

"We've got to find her, Rayleen.''

"Well, I'm gonna check on one thing,'' he said. "Doubt it'll pan out, so I didn't mention it before.''

"What?''

"Glen Morse, he's on the bottlin' line overta the brewery. Well, he told me he thinks he mighta seen your Jeep hightailing it up the new dam road when he was out for a smoke break.''

"What time was that?''

"Maybe an hour ago. But don't get your hopes up, Max. I ain't.''

"You going up there now?''

"Yep.''

"Where are you?''

"That Mobil station in Stoneboat.'' Stoneboat was the small town ten miles north of Loon.

"What are you doing in Stoneboat?''

"Stormy 'n' me useta come up here to the falls when we was kids,'' he said. "She's always liked it, so I thought maybe she come here.''

I peered out the screen door toward the yard. Conklin and his crew were just about finished packing up the squad cars. "You want me to try and join you? If you're going up to Monday Lake, you might need some help. It's a big place.'' It was. The Whitefork Dam was two miles across and one hundred and fifty feet high. The resulting three-hundred-acre body of water that had built up in the valley behind it was called "Monday Lake" because that was the 'day the dam had been finished and the valley had begun to fill. Other than Lake Willowby over near Burke Mountain in the Northeast Kingdom, Monday Lake is the only sizable body of water in northern Vermont. As a result, its shores are studded with docks and cottages. In the winter, ice-fishing shacks, snowmobiles, and cross-country skiers litter the surface. In the summer, power-boats, waterskiers, sailboats, canoes, and swimmers keep the deep, cold water churning with whitecaps. Right now, however, Monday Lake is still and except for a few cottages owned by fishermen, the one hundred and seven miles of jagged shoreline is dark and quiet.

"No," Rayleen said, "you stay there, Max. Don't make much sense you coming out unless I find she's up there somewheres and I have a problem 'cause she's got a snoot full. I'll look around a bit. See if I can spot the Jeep. If I need ya, I'll find a way to call."

"Rayleen?"

"Yeah?"

"If she did do it, tell her I'm on her side. Ruth will be too. And then get her back here as soon as you can. We'll figure out what to do next after that."

"Hoped you'd say that, Max."

He hung up just as Conklin stomped up onto the porch with his Smokey hat down across his eyebrows. He said something I couldn't understand to Ralph, Tommy, and Connie, squinted in through the screen door and knocked on the frame.

I put the phone in its cradle, went to the door and stepped outside. The squad cars were revving their engines. One trooper, a big bear of a guy whose trousers were too short, was standing at the bottom of the steps. Spotter was sniffing the thin white socks at his ankles. "You leaving, Lieutenant?" I asked Conklin.

He nodded. "But you aren't, Mr. Addams." He looked

at the others. "None of you are." He looked back at me. "You're all to stay here on the lodge property until the reports are in." He gestured to short pants. "Sergeant Feder here will be staying with you just to make sure you don't forget."

"How long do we have to wait?" Connie asked. Quincy had been struggling in her arms since I came out onto the porch.

"Two, three days," he said. "We're only taking the evidence into Loon for now. It'll be stored at the sheriff's office until tomorrow. Then, it goes down to our lab in Montpelier. Who knows? If the lab isn't loaded up"—he glared at Tommy and Ralph—"we might be able to make an arrest as early as day after tomorrow."

"I assume I can have visitors," I said. "And my staff will be returning any time now."

"Yes," he said. "And, in that regard, when Mrs. Domini returns, I'd appreciate it if you would call me. I'm staying at the Loon Hotel tonight. As investigating officer, I'll need to be there when she identifies the body."

I looked at Sergeant Feder and pointed to the workshop. "You can use that bedroom down there. Meals, if you want to call them that, will be served up here in the lodge."

Feder looked at the workshop and scowled.

After Conklin and the others left, Sergeant Feder went down to the workshop, I'm sure, to see if it was going to be as bad as he envisioned. I didn't give a shit whether he liked it or not, but if Stormy had been here, she would have followed him down there with an armload of clean sheets and a towel and put wildflowers on his bedside table after she made the bed.

The Stormy I knew was like that.

CHAPTER ✎ FIFTEEN

"**Y**ou busy, Max?" Connie peeked around the kitchen door.

"Just trying to put together something to eat." I was rooting through the cupboards trying to find the peanut butter. I thought I'd set it, some jelly, and after it thawed, a loaf of Stormy's whole-wheat bread out on the counter for anyone who felt like eating lunch. For my part, Loon Lager seemed to be all I needed and now, working on my fifth bottle, I was feeling a nice little buzz.

"Can I help?" She clicked into the room in the candy apple–red stiletto heels only a second ahead of a wall of musky perfume and slid a thigh up on a stool at the island. Now that the police were gone, she had changed back into her Marilyn Monroe persona, complete with skintight black toreador pants and a barely buttoned, white puffy-sleeve blouse. She brushed the wave of hair away from her eye and gave me one of her best MM looks. "I'm sorry, Max," she said. "I know you think this is all my fault." She sighed dramatically. "And, I suppose, to a large extent it is."

"Maybe this will teach us both to say no more often." I put the bread in the microwave, set it for defrost, and turned it on.

She gestured to my cigarette. "May I have one of those?"

"I didn't know you smoked." I slid the pack and the lighter across the island to her.

"I've been trying to stop." She stuck one in her mouth and lit it, exhaling through her nose. "But now . . ." Her eyes began to fill and she tipped her head back to keep the tears from running down her face. It didn't work and one escaped, taking a gray line of mascara with it almost to her white collar before she caught it.

I ripped off a square of paper towel and handed it to her.

"Thank you." She sniffed and blotted her eyes. "I saw you talking with that policewoman down by the workshop earlier." She gently blew her nose. "Did she say they knew any more about who might have done this?"

"You should have asked Lieutenant Conklin while he was here," I said.

She shook her head. "He frightens me."

"The woman didn't really tell me anything I didn't already know."

"What do you think happened?"

"You saw the same thing I did."

"No I didn't, Max." She wadded the towel in a small ball. "I went back inside to see if I could find Ralph."

She was right. I had felt bad about chewing her out and turned around to look at her on the porch. She hadn't been there. "That's right," I said. "You weren't there."

"I was looking for him when I heard the gunshots. I was back in that room where the monitor is when it happened. I ran out onto the porch but by then it was over and Ralph ran out from behind the workshop yelling for you and me to get down and then he ran back up into the woods again."

I didn't doubt her. Like when JFK was assassinated, we'll all always remember exactly where we were when it happened.

"But why did you lie to the police? You told them you saw the whole thing."

She blushed. "I was afraid it might get Ralph in trouble for not being at the monitor."

"Trouble? With who?"

"Mr. Collingwood when he comes."

I drained my beer but didn't comment.

"Well," she said, hanging the cigarette in the corner of her mouth and sliding off the stool, "I just wanted to apologize and maybe see if you knew anything." She tossed the little ball of paper towel on the island. "Do you think I could have one of those beers?"

I took a Loon Lager from the refrigerator and opened it. "You want a glass?"

"No, thank you." She shook her blond hair, took the bottle, and, hips rolling, pushed out through the door. I watched it slowly swing back and forth, half expecting her to reenter, dangling her blouse in front of her. She didn't and a few seconds later I heard the screen door slap shut as she went out onto the porch.

The microwave "dinged" and as I put the now-warm loaf of bread on a cutting board with a serrated knife, Tommy entered the kitchen.

"P and J?" He gave me a half smile. "You can't cook, can you, Max?"

I shrugged and got another beer. "Let's just say, I've kind of lost my incentive."

"I know. I thought Bendel was a neat guy." He picked up the serrated knife and sawed two slices from the loaf of bread. "The old man too. Believe it or not, I really respected him. He took a lot of crap and never backed down. Mostly, he refused to deal drugs. He was a real old-fashioned kind of guy. And, pretty unusual in today's world, he was a man of his word."

"I suppose," I said and sipped the new beer.

He unscrewed the jar of peanut butter. "You'll see, Max, when Martino comes through tonight."

"Still?" I had assumed that Kingfish's offer to help Ruth had died with him.

"Nothing's changed, Max." He dug a knife in the peanut butter and scooped out a large wad. "We're the old-style famiglia. Dead or alive, right now Vincent d'Antella's still capo di capi. Whatever the old man asked to have done gets done." He carefully spread the peanut butter on the bread. "Nothing changes that."

"I wish finding out who shot them was that simple," I said.

"It's already happening." He smiled, as he scooped jelly on the other slice. "If the shooter was from inside the organization, we'll know by tomorrow."

"And if it isn't? If someone else did it?"

"Then it's not our problem." He shrugged, carefully putting the two halves of the sandwich together. "Let the police figure it out." He pressed the sandwich flat between his big palms. "If they can."

"Seems a little callous, if you ask me. You say you respected him and he was a man of honor, but if the killer isn't one of your own, you don't care? I don't get it."

He held the finished sandwich up and admired it. "Vincent d'Antella was seventy-eight, Max. *Time* magazine called him a dinosaur and they were right. He was. He refused to step down. He could have retired to Montana. Fly-fished every day for the rest of his life. But no. He had to do it the hard way. And he made enemies. Inside the family and out. He knew the risks. And now he's dead. If it was a coup, we should know. To the victor go the spoils and all that. If it was just some jealous spouse, then, hey"—he smiled, and took a big bite—"we got more important things to worry about."

"You know about Stormy?"

"Yeah." His voice was thick with peanut butter. "Heard you talking on the phone."

"Ralph and Connie hear too?"

"Nah." He shook his head and chuckled. "They been

too busy accusing each other." He swallowed. "He thinks she arranged it 'cause he thinks the old man put her in his will. She thinks he did it because he was jealous she was banging Bendel." He took another bite. The sandwich was two-thirds gone.

"That must have been what she was intimating to me a few minutes ago in here," I said.

"Don't listen to them." He gave me a look of disgust. "They're nuts."

"What do you think?"

He slowly shook his head and swallowed. "I don't know what to think. Like I told you back that day we were putting up the cameras, it could be anybody."

"But do you think it could have been Stormy?"

"I've seen her shoot. Why not?" He stuffed the remaining third of the sandwich in his mouth. "What he did, I woulda, I was her."

I didn't seem to be able to sit still. I was nervous. The beer buzz wore off, and instead of it being replaced by a nice, nap-inducing weariness, I became more wired than ever.

I hooked up the hose and put a sprinkler out in Stormy's garden. I turned it on, sat on the back steps for a while, smoking a cigarette and watching the metronome of water sway back and forth in the sunshine.

When I finished the cigarette I wandered out to the front porch to join the others. I could see that Sergeant Feder didn't seem to be able to relax either. He was pacing the width of the yard in front of the lodge in the hot sun like a sentry. Perspiration had soaked through the back of his uniform shirt and was beginning to show around the brim of his Smokey hat. Every now and then he would stop, stare at the group on the porch for a few seconds, and then resume pacing.

"He's afraid of us," Tommy said.

"Yeah. And when he stops, he counts," Ralph said.

The scratches on his face had been tattooed with orange Merthiolate.

"If he drops from heatstroke," Connie whispered, "do we have to give him mouth-to-mouth?"

"You'd love it and you know it," Ralph snapped.

"When is Collingwood going to get here?" I asked Ralph.

He shrugged. "Tonight," he said. "But he might be here now. He was going to make arrangements for the old man's body. He could be in town."

I looked at Tommy. "How is that information your friend Martino is pulling together for the mayor going to get to her office?"

"What information?" Connie said.

"None of your business," Ralph said.

Tommy gave them a dirty look and then looked at me. "I don't know, Max. Martino used to be CIA until he found out the old man paid better. Those guys are like ghosts."

"Yeah," Ralph said. "Ghosts."

The conversation about Martino and the CIA dribbled down to small talk, which finally became almost intolerable to listen to, much less partake in. I felt like I was in some sort of dead spot in time. A lull. I was becalmed. I ached to do something. Anything. I wanted to help look for Stormy or see Ruth or anything to get me away from the lodge, Sergeant Feder, and these people.

When the phone rang, I almost ran to get it.

It was Ruth. "Any news about Stormy?"

"None."

"How are you holding up? Billy Kendall told me that you can't leave the lodge."

"I'm going crazy," I said. "When did you see Billy Kendall?"

"I called him in here to my office. He isn't doing anything now that the state police are in charge. I've got him and several deputies looking for Stormy also."

"You didn't tell him about the thing with Bendel and . . . ?

"Of course not, Max. But I had to tell him something, so I said she had become distraught over Bendel's death and might be drinking. That we are all afraid she might hurt herself."

"Did you tell him she might have a rifle with her?"

"Yes, of course."

"Oh Jesus, Ruth . . ."

"Max, I can't just send law-enforcement people out without apprising them of the situation. You might not like Billy Kendall, but most of those deputies are nice, decent men with families."

"But, what if she gets violent and . . . ?"

"Max, I thought you wanted to find her."

"I do, but . . ."

"No one is going to arrest her. This is Stormy we're talking about. Everyone in town likes her. No one wants to see her hurting or hurt."

I sighed. Ruth was right. Twice, since I've owned the lodge and known her, Stormy has been approached by people in town to run for office. The last time was when Earl MacMillan announced he was running for City Council president. She would have beaten him too had she done it. But, at the last minute, she backed out. "I'm too old to be in the line of fire," she told her supporters. "I work better when I'm snipin' at the bad guys from around the edges."

"I saw Rayleen," Ruth said.

"Where?"

"He was coming out of Judy Bowman's."

"What were you doing there?"

"We had a lunch for the governor at the Loon Hotel, and after we saw him off, I walked back to the office . . . you need air after those things . . . now Rayleen has Judy looking for Stormy too."

"Oh God, I wish I could help."

"Rayleen was going up to the dam. He said someone told him that they thought they saw your Jeep up there."

"I know. He told me last time he called. I'm waiting to hear from him now."

"He'll never find a phone up there, so I gave him my cell phone to use. I told him to call me as well as you no matter what he finds. That way I can be a kind of clearinghouse for information."

"Good."

"Do you want me to bring anything when I come out there tonight?"

"It would be nice if you were able to bring Stormy."

"I know," she said, lowering her voice. "Do you still think she might have done it?"

I told her about my conversation with Inspector Cynthia Brown.

"That doesn't tell me Stormy did anything," Ruth said. "The theory that someone might have wanted both of them dead is what I find interesting."

"But what's the connection between Bendel and d'Antella?"

"I don't know, Max," she said. "But I've got to go. I've got two other calls waiting."

"If it's anything to do with Stormy, call me right back."

"Of course." We hung up

I had barely taken three steps away from the phone and it rang again. I grabbed it. "Ruth?"

"No. It's me." It was Rayleen.

"Find her?"

"Not yet."

"Where are you?"

"Up top a the dam," he said. "You can hear me, Max?"

"Of course I can hear you. Why?"

"Amazin' things these little phones. Ruth give me her

cellulite phone to use. Told me I can call from anyplace and, by God, guess I can.''

"It's a *cellular* phone, Rayleen.''

"Whatever," he said. "What I wanta know is why you didn't tell me you told Billy Kendall that me 'n' Stormy was down in Montpelier with Merriam last night? Billy stopped me over on Hooker Hill Road. Couldn't lie my way outta it 'cause I didn't exactly know what the lie was that got me into it. The suspicious little shit's been more or less followin' me ever since.''

Ralph and Connie came into the hall and, without so much as a glance my way, started up the stairs. Quincy was headlocked in the crook of Ralph's other arm but managed a faint "yip" when he saw me.

"I'm sorry about putting you on the spot, Rayleen," I said, watching them get to the top landing. "But it doesn't make any difference now. Billy's helping us. Ruth has him and his deputies out looking for Stormy too.''

"Oh, Lordy.''

"Now what?''

"Just better hope Billy don't find her first. If she's been drinkin', we could be lookin' at another body with thirty-thirty holes in it. Stormy midwifed his momma when he was born. Told me, she knew the kid was bad 'fore he was even all the way out. Said she considered smotherin' the little rat.'' He sighed. '' 'Course, who knows if she meant it. Was pretty drunk the night she told me that one and . . .''

"I don't want to hear any more, Rayleen," I said. "Okay? I don't care what she said or who she shot or what she used to do when she was drunk. Right now, dammit, stop talking and find her!''

He was so silent I thought he'd hung up on me.

"Rayleen?''

"Sorry, Max.''

"No, I'm sorry." I sighed. "I didn't mean to bite your

head off. It's just that here I sit and I can't do a goddamn thing about anything.''

''Come out here to the dam then,'' he said. ''I'll wait for you.''

''That's one of the problems,'' I said. ''I can't. I'm under some sort of damn house arrest. All of us are.''

''The hell.''

''No, seriously. They even left a guard.''

''You didn't do nothin', Max. Just tell the guy you're leavin'.''

''We'll see,'' I said, finally feeling very tired. ''Meanwhile, let me know the minute anything changes. Then you won't be able to keep me away.''

''Right,'' he said. ''And, sorry again, Max. I always been too mouthy for my own good. 'Bout time somebody 'sides Stormy called me on it.''

''Don't worry about it. Just keep me informed.''

We hung up and Tommy stepped into the hall. He had been listening again. ''If you want to leave, Max,'' he said, ''maybe I can help you do it.''

''How?'' I peered by him out the door. Although the cadence was slower, Feder was still pacing. Beyond him, bull's-eyes of rising trout were appearing all over the lake. ''How can you help?''

He shrugged. ''That guy''—he thumbed toward the sergeant—''is a pussy. I could take him out in two seconds.''

I shook my head. ''Nobody else gets hurt if I can help it.''

He laughed. ''I don't mean kill him.''

''I know what you mean,'' I said. ''And I mean what I said. Nobody else is going to get hurt.''

''You can't just up and walk out of here, Max. I know Feder's kind. Conklin left him here because, given a chance, he wouldn't hesitate to shoot any of us.''

''I'm not going anywhere yet,'' I said. ''If Rayleen calls and needs me, then we'll talk about it.'' I pushed by him and went out onto the porch, down across the lawn, dodged around Feder to the lake's edge.

I squatted, scooped up a handful of water, and splashed it on my face.

I didn't realize Spotter had followed me until I felt his nose burrowing in under my arm. "Decided not to be mad at me anymore, huh?" I said, looking into his sad brown eyes.

He licked the water from my beard, then trotted a couple yards down the shoreline and "pointed" at a spot about thirty feet out. From what I could see, he was pointing at the only spot on the lake where trout weren't rising. He looked at me and whined faintly. Then he went back to his point.

Along with his other attributes, Spotter has what Stormy's always called "the Saint Bernard gene." I suppose it's as good an explanation as any, but instead of saving people from drowning, rescuing children from burning buildings, or carrying brandy to skiers trapped in blizzards, Spotter's method of salvation is different. Like the fish he sees when I can't, he seems to know when my stress level is reaching critical mass. More than once through our years together, Spotter has seemed to sense when I was troubled. I don't know whether he feels the bad vibes or what, but, whether it was the day after our big fire, the summer I thought Ruth was pregnant, a bad week on the river, or now, he seems to feel my pain and his solution is always the same: "Try catching some fish, Max."

I stood, walked over to him, and stroked his head. "Good dog," I said. "Maybe you're right. A couple of casts might help." I went to the workshop, quickly rigged my old Sage rod, and tied on a #14 tan elk-hair caddis with a green body. I held it up to the light to make sure the barb was crimped down and then walked back to where Spotter still stood. He gave me a quick glance over his shoulder, looked pleased, and resumed his point.

"You're sure that's the place?" I said to him, stripping some line to my feet and beginning to false cast above my head. I looked over my shoulder to make sure I wasn't going to hook Sergeant Feder. I wasn't. He had stopped pacing and was watching my line.

Spotter didn't move and kept his nose pointed directly at a ten-foot-wide smooth spot between two reappearing rise forms. My experience said, cast to the left rise form first, catch that trout, and then repeat the process on the trout rising on the right. Nothing I had ever learned told me to cast where no fish was showing when so many were. But then, it was Spotter's prescription, so I followed it to the letter.

When I had about thirty-five feet of line whistling by my ear in nice tight loops, I let it go, checked the line's forward progress with a quick lift of the rod tip, and watched the tiny imitation caddis fly drop gently to the water. I quickly stripped in the few inches of slack and held my breath. The trout on the right rose. Then the trout on the left rose. The wake of their rise forms spread, interlocked, and made my fly bob gently.

Just as I was about to strip in and cast again, the water opened up under my caddis fly and it disappeared. My line jerked taut and thrummed, the Sage bowed, and my reel buzzed as something long, heavy, and strong dove for the bottom with my fly in the corner of its mouth.

"Wow! Now that's a big one." It was Sergeant Feder. He was now standing a little to my right and behind me.

I ignored him and concentrated on the fish who, by now, knew he was attached to something and was doing everything in his power to free himself. My rod arched alarmingly as I palmed the reel, trying to slow him down. He could have simply kept going until I ran out of line, then snapped me off and been gone. Instead, he jumped, cartwheeling in the sunlight. It was a salmon. A beautiful, silver landlocked salmon. As he dove again, I reeled in, holding the rod tip low to the water, and this time I could feel him turn. I had him.

Two more spectacular cartwheel jumps and one long run and I kicked off my shoes and waded out into the cool water to meet him. I reeled him to my feet. He was well over three feet long and at least ten inches deep in the belly. He probably weighed fifteen pounds, by far the largest fish I'd ever caught at Whitefork Lodge. He was exhausted. His gills pulsed and his eyes rolled as I leaned and gently slipped the small hook from the corner of his mouth. Then I grabbed his tail and, after walking him out into deeper water, moved him back and forth until I could feel the slabs of muscle in his iridescent, steel-colored flanks tense and flex. I let him go and watched him hold motionless just below the surface, obviously for a second not understanding he was free, and then, with a flick of his tail, haughtily fin away and disappear into the dark, deeper water. And as Spotter knew it would, with the big fish went some of the tension of this long, long day.

"You just let something like that go?" Feder had his hat off and was wiping perspiration from his red face with his sleeve. "After all that, you let him go?"

I sloshed to the bank and picked up my rod. "Not everything gets killed here," I said.

Up at the lodge, the screen door squeaked open and Tommy stepped out onto the porch. He had the telephone in his hand, its cord stretched almost to breaking behind him. "Max?" he yelled. "I think this is the phone call you've been waiting for."

I dropped the rod and ran for the lodge. "Rayleen?"

"No," he said. "It's Stormy."

CHAPTER SIXTEEN

"Stormy. Stormy," I said, breathing hard from my run up the lawn. "Where are you? Are you all right?"

She didn't answer right away and instead I heard the clink of glass on glass and a gurgle of liquid. She was drinking. Finally she said, "Damned if I know." Her voice was thick, the words smeared together.

"Are you all right?"

"Jeep isn't."

"You had an accident?"

"Nah. It stopped. Damn thing stopped. Right over there."

"Where? Where are you?"

"Trout are risin', Max. Tell Bendel there are more damn fish risin' out here than I ever seen."

She didn't know he was dead. Therefore she didn't know he'd been shot. Therefore . . . the sigh of relief I let out ruffled the papers on the hall table. "No. I wanna tell him, Max. Put that skirt-chasing son of a bitch on the phone. He should see these fish. The Jeep can't. Only one eye on that baby. Put him on."

"Are you up at Monday Lake?"

"Are I where?" She giggled.

"Monday Lake," I said. "Is that where you are?"

"It's where Bendel ain't, that's for sure." She paused to slurp and swallow. "Put the little eyetalian flirt on the phone, Max. Time I chewed him out."

If I didn't know it was Stormy, I wouldn't have known it was Stormy. The voice was the same but that was it. "Bendel can't come to the phone," I said. "He . . . he's out looking for you. We're all worried about you. Where are you? I'll come get you."

"Been huntin'. Me and my Wish-chester. Shot some-body, I think. Once. Maybe, twice. Not sure if it was you or who." She chuckled. "Yoo-hoo."

My stomach tightened. "What do you mean you shot someone?"

"Blew his toes clean off. Shoulda been his dick so you can tell you-know-who to look out for his, by God." She sounded like she was falling asleep.

"Stormy!" I said. "Dammit! Where are you? I'll come and get you."

"You tell Bendel I'll be here waitin' for him to come, the old fart. Fish'll be . . . waitin' . . . Jeep ain't gonna see it . . . old Marilyn Monroe always fucked the best ones . . . didn't she . . . ?" I heard the clink of glass again and then silence. She hadn't hung up. She'd just stopped talking.

"Stormy?" I said. "Stormy? Hello?"

There was another clink, I heard her say, "Oh damn," and the line went dead.

I wanted to throw the receiver across the hall, but Tommy, who had stood to one side during the whole thing, took it from my hand, put it back in its cradle, and said, "No idea where she was calling from?"

"I think she might be somewhere out at a place we call Monday Lake. It's north of town." I shrugged. "She was talking about lots of fish rising."

"C'mon. I'll take you in the Thunderbird."

I nodded, went into my room, and quickly changed into a dry pair of jeans, my yellow long-sleeved T-shirt with the breast pocket, and not seeing my sneakers, pulled on the cowboy boots over my bare feet.

Tommy was waiting on the porch. Sergeant Feder was standing just out in the lawn with his hand on the butt of his service revolver. The holster was unsnapped. ". . . and my instructions are," Feder was saying, "that none of you go nowhere."

"Did you tell him about Stormy?" I asked Tommy.

He nodded but didn't take his eyes off Feder.

"Sergeant Feder," I said, starting down the steps. "This woman is in trouble. It was her husband who was killed out there with Vincent d'Antella today. She doesn't know yet. She has a drinking problem and we're afraid she might harm herself if we don't get to her right away."

"Call the sheriff," Feder said, drawing his revolver and pointing it at me. "Just don't come any farther, Mr. Addams." The gun was shaking slightly and he put his other hand on it. "I was told I could use this thing if I had to. And I will."

Tommy took a step down the stairs.

Feder swung the revolver in Tommy's direction. "I said, stay where you are."

Behind us, I heard the screen door open. "What on earth is going on out here, sergeant?" I didn't turn around but it was Connie doing her best breathy Marilyn Monroe impression. "Can't a girl get a beauty nap?" The screen door slapped shut and Connie's high heels tapped up behind Tommy and me as Feder's eyes bugged and his jaw literally dropped. Connie continued down onto the step between us.

I glanced at her and my jaw dropped too.

She was completely naked except for a choker of pearls, bright red nylons that only came midway up her white thighs, and the candy apple–red stiletto shoes. Vincent hadn't exaggerated. She did look better without her clothes. Her skin was like milk and whoever had refashioned her breasts deserved the Nobel. Someone also had carefully trimmed her pubic hair in the shape of a heart.

She put her hand on my shoulder to steady herself, lifted one long, red leg, and fiddled with the strap on a shoe. "Gosh, Max," she said, "I thought you advertised peace and quiet up here at Whitefork Lodge." She put her leg down, smoothed the top of the stocking, and hips moving like they had a life of their own, continued down the steps into the yard.

Feder's mouth was still open and his eyes had yet to move above her shoulders. "Please, ma'am," he said, shakily pointing the gun at her. "Just stop right there."

She didn't.

He pointed the gun away from her to his right and fired. The small explosion startled all of us. "That . . . that's a warning, Miss," he said, pointing the revolver back at her. "Next one will be . . ."

Connie stepped up to him, put one hand on his shoulder, and encircled the gun barrel with the fingers of her other. I could only imagine the look she was giving him as she lifted the snub-nosed .38 from his hand and tossed it out into the yard. His eyes looked like a puppy's.

Then she punched him out.

It happened so fast and was so unexpected, I didn't really even see it. One second she was standing there in front of him. The next he was flat on his back bleeding from his mouth and she was rubbing the knuckles on her right hand. "Damn cops," she said, walking to the gun, bending over, and picking it up. She turned, cocked a hip, and looked at us.

"Where did you learn that?" Tommy said.

"You learn a lot of things when you strip to drunks," she said, slowly walking back to the porch. "Never grabbed a man's revolver before, though." She shook the little gun and smiled. "Usually, I have to unzip a fly first." She stopped in front of us. "So, don't just stand there staring at me. Go!"

Tommy and I went to the Thunderbird. "I'll drive," I said. "I know the way."

"Nobody's driving this thing anywhere." He was bent over, staring into the car's grille. "Feder's damn bullet went right through the radiator."

I joined him at the front of the car. He was right. There was a hole in the grille and thick, greenish liquid was puddling below it on the gravel.

"Damn," he said. "Now what?"

I was already heading for the workshop. "My motorcycle," I said over my shoulder: "It hasn't been started in a while, but it works."

Tommy trotted after me and we went into the workshop, stepped around the bloodstains on the floor, and went to my Harley. The key was in it and I rolled it out into the sunshine.

Nineteen eighty-eight wasn't the best year for the Harley-Davidson Company. They were owned at the time by some company that made bowling balls, and the bikes turned out that year looked it. Instead of the heavy steel and iron you usually associate with a Harley, when I bought my Sportster it had a lot of cheesy plastic where it shouldn't have. Rayleen, who had completely rebuilt it, had attempted to replace as much of the plastic with as many new metal parts as possible. As a result, the fenders and teardrop-shaped gas tank, only put on a month ago, were still without paint and primered gray.

I had only ridden it once since he'd got the engine together and I unscrewed the gas cap.

Tommy peeked in at it. "You're empty," he said. "Where do you keep the gasoline?"

I shook my head. "The only gas we allow around here since the fire is the stuff we use for the lawn mower. But it's got oil mixed with it." I flipped the switch under the tank to open the reserve. "There's about two gallons in this thing's reserve tank." I pulled the choke, pushed the starter button, and the bike roared to life.

entment,

"How far will two gallons get you?" he yelled over the throbbing exhaust.

"Far enough," I shouted back. "I think."

He stepped back.

"You're not coming?" I patted the seat behind mine.

He shook his head. "I'm not riding bitch."

"Suit yourself." I shrugged. "If Rayleen calls, tell him to look for me around Monday Lake. We'll need his truck to bring Stormy home."

He nodded.

"And thank Connie."

He nodded again.

I stomped on the gear shift with the toe of my boot, let out the clutch, and fishtailing slightly in the lush grass, roared out across the lawn.

Connie was still naked. With Ralph now standing behind her, she sat on the top step of the porch pointing the revolver at Sergeant Feder, who was now sitting upright in the grass. Considering his angle of view, I doubted she actually needed the gun to keep him from moving.

Whitefork Dam is about five miles north of Loon. You can get there by several picturesque routes, but considering the amount of gasoline I had in the reserve tank and the fact that I was driving illegally without a helmet or motorcycle operator's license, once I got down into town I took River Road, which runs along behind the ugly, vacant redbrick mill buildings that cling to the granite ledge above the Whitefork. It was common knowledge that the Sheriff's Department seldom patrolled this area in the daytime and I hoped this afternoon was no different. I didn't need to be stopped now.

The river is wide, slow moving, and deep at this point, and as I raced along the backs of the buildings, the sound of my exhaust was almost deafening as it reverberated off the hundred-year-old brick. The wind tore at my beard and flattened my hair. I felt good. I was going to get Stormy and bring her home. My fears of her murdering Bendel had been unfounded. We would all help her grieve and then find her sobriety again. Life at Whitefork Lodge would return to the gentle pastime of catching and releasing trout, hearty meals, evenings on the porch, and later in season, quiet conversation in front of crackling fires in the big stone fireplaces.

The new Dam Road is a right turn just beyond the Big Bear Campground sign. I geared down, turned, and then throttled up the steep incline. The road had been resurfaced for the fish-ladder dedication ceremony Ruth and the governor attended earlier in the day and the brand-new jet-black ribbon of asphalt stretched straight out before me, climbing, it seemed, right into the blue sky.

At the top, where the road runs the length of Whitefork Dam, I stopped the bike and, with it rumbling between my legs, looked out across the expanse of blue water toward the mountains and Canada. The lake was corrugated with whitecaps and lapped at the gravel only three feet away on my left. Far below me on my right, white water shot from the sluiceway at the bottom of the dam. It was this nutrient-rich bottom release of cold water that made the downstream and my part of the Whitefork River such an incredibly fertile trout fishery.

Closed in the winter except to kids on sleds, Dam Road opens in March so that the several hundred people living around Monday Lake during the summer can get in to their cabins and cottages, drain the pipes, open the windows, flip mattresses, and sweep out the rodents who winter in the cupboards and crevasses. As I gave the motorcycle gas and it growled across the top of the dam, I could see the remains of bright red, white, and blue bunting still hanging from the safety railings around the viewing platforms surrounding the new fish ladder. If the circumstances had been different, I would have parked the bike and gone down to the ladder to watch the landlocked salmon fight their way to the top. Instead, I made a U-

turn, stopped, and looked back down the road toward
town, hoping to see Rayleen's pickup on the way. There
was nothing except one logging truck overloaded with
what looked like the better part of a couple acres of spruce
forest stacked on it.

I might as well try to find her myself, I thought, turning
the Harley back toward the far end of the dam. *Besides,
who knows, maybe I'll find Rayleen with her when I do.*

On the other side of the dam, after the steep descent,
the blacktop turns into the rutted, winding one-lane of
packed dirt that runs most of the way around the lake.
Some locals call it Monday Road, but officially, because
the post office doesn't deliver out here, it has no name.
Whatever it's called, it's a bitch to negotiate on a motorcycle and I had to slow down to avoid losing control in
the deep ruts and loose gravel. I was headed north, and
although I could see nothing through the thick trees, the
lake, cottages, and cabins were to my left. Every driveway
had a sign at its mouth identifying either the owners or
the primary activity when it was in use. I stopped at each
one and peered down its long, overgrown track looking
for the Jeep or Rayleen's truck. I could see nothing but
the corner of a small building and a patch of blue water
at "Pike Camp." There was no sign of the Jeep or the
pickup at "The Hendersons," "Trout Cove," "Bob's
Place," "The Last Best Place," "Lakeview," or "Ed's
Eden." The reflected light from something metal at "John
and Flo's" took me all the way down their driveway to a
rickety cabin partially on stilts in the water. The reflection
turned out to be from the sun on the shack's aluminum
foil–coated siding. I turned around and sped back out to
Monday Road.

Ten more driveways. Ten more dumb names engraved
in crooked, weathered signs half-buried in blueberry
bushes and poison ivy and I was about to turn around and
go back to the lodge. The only thing that had kept me
going was the definite evidence that two or more vehicles

had gone this way before me sometime during the day. Their tire tracks would disappear and reappear in the hard and soft places on the dirt road.

I carefully negotiated a bumpy, thickly overgrown corner and there, straight ahead beside a small shingle sign that read "Camp David" in fading white letters, was Rayleen's International pickup. It was parked just in the driveway off the road and I pulled in next to the driver's side.

I rolled forward and peered down the driveway, but because of the way the two wheel ruts curved away to the right through the trees, I could see nothing. Not even the lake. I looked back at Rayleen's truck and it was then that I noticed the windshield.

Surrounded by a spider's web of fractured glass, two neat bullet holes stared back at me like blood-shot eyes.

I quickly toed the Harley into neutral, kicked down the stand, and went back to the truck. I didn't want to look inside. I took a deep breath and peered in the open window. It was empty. Nothing but glass in tiny, gemlike shapes scattered all over the seat and floor and what I assumed to be Ruth's cellular phone on the dash.

I reached in through the window, grabbed the phone, and stuck it in my T-shirt pocket. Then I went back to the Harley, climbed on, put it in gear, twisted the throttle, and the two gallons of gasoline in the reserve tank ran out. The bike sputtered, bucked forward, and died. I pushed the starter several times and cranked it over, but it was no use. It was dead.

I left it leaning on its stand and walked up the driveway toward the lake, a place called Camp David, and, I hoped, Stormy and Rayleen in one piece.

I had gone about twenty yards when four booming rifle shots from somewhere just ahead broke the silence and vibrated through the trees around me.

"Oh, Jesus!" I said out loud, and ducking, began to run in a crouch toward the place where I thought the shots came from.

CHAPTER ❦ SEVENTEEN

I saw the Jeep before anything else. It was grille-first against a large white birch. The right-front fender was crushed back into the hood, which had been bent almost in half. The headlight was smashed and the tire on that side was flat. It looked like Stormy had just driven in until the tree stopped her.

Parked just beyond it and near the door to the small one-story green cottage was a Loon Sheriff's Department squad car. As usual the car door was wide open and the police radio was blaring. Since I didn't see a scoped deer rifle inside . . . or any rifle for that matter . . . I wasn't sure whether it was Billy Kendall's car or one of his deputies'.

"Stormy?" I yelled. "Rayleen?"

There was no answer and I walked around to the front of the cottage.

There is a look to what is known locally as a "Monday Lake Mansion." They are all, basically, little boxes with three or four rooms, no winter insulation, cheap siding, and always, not just on the water but half in it. Camp David was no different, and like so many of them the portion that sat out on stilts in the water was a screened-in porch. Also, like so many of them, water and weather had taken their toll and Camp David's porch looked like it was about to crumble and fall into the lake. I wanted to peek in, but all the windows had been nailed closed with sheets of plywood.

I called again and this time I heard Rayleen's voice through the wall. "In here, Max."

I went back to the side entrance, climbed the short flight of rickety steps, and pushed the door open. Since the windows were boarded up, my eyes had to adjust to the dim light inside, and when they did, I could see I was in a living/dining room kind of area toward the front of the square building. A small kitchen took three walls in a tiny alcove to my right. To my left was a round table and four straight-back wooden chairs. Beyond that, a moth-eaten whitetail deer head with crooked antlers hung between a shuttered-up dark picture window and a flimsy flush door that led out to the rotting screened porch on stilts in front. A twin-bed mattress, covered with a dirty pink chenille bedspread and stained pillows in an attempt to make it look like a couch, sat beneath the deer head. Several dog-eared issues of old *Playboy* magazines were stacked on a coffee table in front of it. Pictures cut from calendars . . . deer, fish, and naked women . . . were taped to most of the other walls. The place smelled of stale cigarette smoke, booze, and a backed-up toilet. Straight ahead, I could see a ripped recliner and a couch with a cheap pole lamp at each end. Rayleen was in the recliner. Stormy, the hem of her caftan up around her pale thighs, was lying on her back on the dirty couch. Her mouth was open. She was snoring loudly.

"Rayleen?" I said. "Is she . . . ? I only got one step toward him when a million bright lights flashed before my eyes, a painful, deafening crash resounded through my head, and the plywood floor came flying up at my face. Then everything went black.

I came to half lying, half sitting against the couch where Stormy lay. My head pounded painfully as I tried to sit up the rest of the way. The lights were on in the room now and they hurt my eyes. I tasted blood, and from what I could see, the front of my shirt was soaked with it.

"You okay, Max?" Rayleen whispered from the recliner.

I looked at him and for a second my eyes wouldn't focus. I nodded. "I don't know." I tried to pull my hands from behind my back. They were tied. "What the hell's going . . . ?"

"Shh," he said. "He went outside to use the radio. Makin' sure nobody comes out this way, I betcha."

"He? Who?"

"Billy Kendall, who else? The little shit hit you pretty hard."

"With what?" I actually felt a little sick to my stomach. Like I might have a concussion.

"Revolver butt."

I struggled against whatever was holding my wrists together.

"Don't bother, Max," Rayleen whispered. "I been tryin' for most of an hour and it don't do no good. He used Stormy's panty hose."

"Since when does she wear those things?"

He shrugged. "Since she thinks she's runnin' away, I guess."

"Is she all right?"

"For now."

"Drunk?"

He nodded. "She's been passed out since I got here."

"You okay?" His face was covered with dried blood.

He nodded. "Just some cuts from glass flyin' around in the truck when that little shit pumped a couple through my windshield."

"Jesus. What's going on?"

"Not sure. He ain't said much yet. Sure been busy, though. Just shot somethin' outside with Stormy's Winchester. Four times."

"I heard it."

"Been bringing in all kinds of stuff too." He nodded toward the table. "That's it over there."

I squinted at the table. From my place on the floor I couldn't see the top and could only make out the edges of a couple plastic bags, what looked like a hemlock bough, and the top half of a box of rifle cartridges. I could see that they were thirty-thirties.

I worked myself up into a sitting position. The nylon around my wrists was so tight that my fingers were already numb. "What do you think, Rayleen?"

"Think he might be plannin' on killin' us," he said. "I mean, why else . . . ?"

The door opened and Billy Kendall stomped inside. "Max," he said, with a cruel smile, "you're awake sooner than I thought." He closed the door. He was carrying Stormy's Winchester in one hand. The bunch of twigs, dead leaves, and small branches that he was carrying in the other he dumped on the table.

"What's this all about, Bill?" I asked.

He leaned Stormy's Winchester against a chair. "It's about earnin' respect, Max. Remember?" He dug in his breast pocket and pulled out four spent cartridges. "That day Earl and I were out at the lodge? Told me yourself, respect's what I need." He laid the cartridges on the table, came across the room, and squatted beside me. He was wearing pale latex gloves. "So, today's the day I get that respect, Max." He poked my forehead with an index finger. It hurt. "And, if I've got it figured right, I might even get your girlfriend in the process."

I twisted against the panty hose. "You're a loser, Bill," I hissed. "You couldn't get respect if they were giving it away at the hardware."

He grabbed me by the hair and punched me in the face. I saw stars again and heard a crunch as my nose broke. Instantly, warm blood ran down over my lips and chin to my neck and into my shirt collar. My eyes filled with stinging tears.

"The only losers around here," he growled, "is you and these two old farts." He stood and walked back to the table, where he pulled out a chair and sat with his back to us.

"You going to kill us, Bill?" I asked.

"Nope." He didn't turn. "Stormy's gonna kill you. Just like the drunk bitch killed that cheatin' husband of hers."

I looked at Rayleen and he slowly shook his head. He didn't understand any of this any more than I did.

"First, though," Billy continued, "I've got to get all this evidence right. And that means I've got to concentrate." He shot me a look over his shoulder. "So, shut up."

I licked the blood from my lips and tipped my head back to stop the bleeding. What the hell was going on? The questions raced through my mind. Did Billy think Stormy killed Bendel? Why did he want to kill Rayleen and me? What was that going to prove? How did he know about Bendel's infidelity? What was this "evidence" he was talking about?

I looked up at Rayleen. He had his eyes closed. I could hear Stormy snoring softly above me. I looked at the broad tan back of Billy's uniform shirt as he hunched over the table. There was a line of dark sweat down the center. This was like one of those frustrating dreams we all have every now and then, populated with people you know, doing things you can't figure out, and the harder you try to get it out of your head, every time you fall back to sleep, your mind goes right back to it.

Billy worked at the table for about an hour, then stood, stretched, and farted. He picked up something from the tabletop and came across the room toward me. It was one of those large Swiss Army pocketknives. The biggest blade was out. In his other hand was a sheet of facial tissue.

I twisted to get out of his way, but he wasn't coming for me, and straddling my outstretched legs, he leaned over me to Stormy on the couch. I heard her groan. He stood like this with his crotch hovering above my head for several seconds. I could smell urine on his trousers. Stormy groaned again. Louder this time.

I tried to hit his leg with my head but the pain from the movement made me dizzy. "What are you doing?" I shouted up at his crotch. "Leave her alone."

He didn't pay any attention to me and a few seconds later he straightened up and walked back to the table. The tissue was red with wet blood. He sat back down on the chair and, without turning, said, "Damn drunk didn't feel a thing, Max. Yet. Just took a little blood, is all."

"He cut her finger, Max," Rayleen said.

"Why?"

Billy looked over his shoulder and smiled. "You'll know soon enough." He turned back to whatever he was doing on the tabletop.

I looked down at the front of my shirt. Ruth's cellular phone was still in my pocket. I wondered if it still worked. I had fallen on it and now it was saturated with blood from my nose.

Another half hour went by. Rayleen looked like he was asleep. Stormy was still passed out and snoring loud. I couldn't feel my arms any longer. The were dead numb. My head hurt. My nose had swollen and, the way they stung, I knew my eyes were turning black.

Finally Billy pushed himself away from the table. "There," he said, sticking the knife in the tabletop. He turned the chair and, still sitting, faced us. "Wake up, Rayleen," he yelled. "It's story time and I'm only gonna tell it once."

Rayleen's eyes popped open and rolled frantically. When he saw me, he relaxed. "What's happening, Max?" His voice was hoarse.

"I'm what's happening," Billy said. "You're looking at the next sheriff of Loon County. Guaranteed. After that, who knows?"

"What makes you so sure, Bill?" I said. "You have to be elected, you know."

He smiled. "Oh, I'll be elected. By a landslide."

I sighed and shook my head in disgust.

"You don't believe me, Max?"

I looked him in the eyes. "No," I said. "I don't."

He reached behind himself. "Did you know that the staties left all the evidence they collected from your lodge at my office until they take it down to Montpelier tomorrow?"

I nodded. "Conklin told me."

He lifted a small plastic bag from the table and held it out. "Like this thing." He waved it back and forth. "Look familiar, Max?"

"Yeah." It was the bag of spent thirty-thirty cartridges that had been given to Conklin in the lodge dining room this morning.

"The shells in here aren't the ones that were in here this morning," he said. "These babies came directly from Stormy's Winchester."

I frowned but didn't say anything.

"Just put them there myself." He smiled and rattled the bag. "These were the four shots you heard when you came in here earlier." He put it back on the table and then, one by one, picked up four other shells and held them in his hand. "These are the ones that were found up at the shooting site, Max." He stuffed them in the breast pocket of his shirt. "I'm tossing them out in the lake before I leave here today." He patted the pocket.

"Why?" I said.

"Since the bullets that killed Bendel and d'Antella went completely through them, the only way forensics has of matching the murder weapon is through marks on the spent shells." He held up the plastic bag of shells again. "And these'll match Stormy's Winchester because, now, they're from Stormy's Winchester."

"You're tryin' ta make it look like Stormy did it," Rayleen said, "ain'tcha?"

"Well. Well." He smiled at Rayleen. "You aren't as dumb as you look, Rayleen."

"Question is," I said, "Why?"

"Why!?" Billy laughed. "I'm gonna solve this thing, Max, and Stormy has the motive I need. Her husband was screwing d'Antella's girlfriend. And everyone in town knows how somethin' like that would upset Stormy. Especially now she's gone back to drinkin'."

"How'd you find out about that?" Rayleen growled.

"What? Bendel doing the girlfriend? Or Stormy's drinking history? Shit, both were easy." He nodded toward Stormy. "Got files on that old lush's violent side all the way back to the door-to-door salesman she brained with a shovel."

I looked at Rayleen. He just shrugged and gave me a weak smile. "Didn't know 'bout that one," he whispered.

"As far as Bendel and the broad," Billy was still talking, "that was a piece of cake too. I've been using Pauline Tritch in the mayor's office for months now. Kiss an old lady's ass and she'll tell you anything. And that Pauline knows everything." He looked at me. "In fact, heard you had a scare the other day, Max. Thought you and Ruth were gonna be Mommy and Daddy there for a day or two, didn't you?"

I sighed. "What's going to happen, Bill, when they find the real killer?"

"They won't, Max. They can't." He was still smiling. "You see, I'm the one who did it. And I control the evidence." He watched our faces as what he said sank in, then kicked the big plastic garbage bag with his foot. "I even threw away all those twigs and leaves and shit they got at your place and refilled this bag with new stuff myself. All from right around here." He held up the bloody tissue. "Dribbled just enough of Stormy's blood on it to make sure the DNA matches the owner of the Winchester and not me.''

It would work, I thought. I remembered what Cynthia Brown had told me about the DNA they'd be able to get from the traces of blood the killer's cuts and scratches had left in the woods. "But why Stormy, Bill?" I asked. "Why not one of d'Antella's people. The bodyguards, for example. Why not make it look like it really was an assassination? That's what everybody's thinking anyway."

"Don't like the assassination theory." He shook his head. "Staties are anal enough. I don't need the fuckin' FBI crawling around here, also. Too many other things they might uncover." He smiled evilly again. "Besides, I'm thinking about the bodyguards for Lyle's murder."

"Lyle?" Rayleen strained to sit up, couldn't, and fell back on the recliner. "You killed Lyle too? You little shit."

Billy shrugged. "Didn't intend to but, hell, he saw me trashin' the bowling alley." He looked at me. "I couldn't just let him go, now could I, Max?"

"The crime in town?" I said. It was all coming together. "That's been you all this time, hasn't it?"

"Not in the beginning it wasn't. But when it started tapering off, Earl had me start it up again."

"MacMillan?"

"Well, it was actually Bernstein's idea first. But once I got goin', Earl liked my style. He really got into it. We'd all sit over in Bernstein's room at the Loon Hotel and decide what calamity was going to befall the tiny town of Loon next." He laughed. "It was great. Of course, Earl's main thing was the way the *Sentinel* was trashin' the mayor because of it." He shrugged. "That's why he made me temporary sheriff. Make sure nothin' got solved and the lid stayed on 'til, at least, election day."

"Somebody'll catch ya," Rayleen said.

"Somebody already did," Billy shot back. "Lyle Martin."

"How are you going to pin Lyle's murder on d'Antella's bodyguards?" I said. "They were out at the lodge when . . ."

"No they weren't, Max." He grinned. "I got me a piece of E-mail from the mayor herself that says they were in Loon buying fishing licenses that morning." He ran his hand over his brush-cut. "Plus I stole me some interesting odds and ends of theirs when Earl and I were out at the lodge that day. Not to mention that Rhode Island car I found abandoned out at the dam." He shrugged. "Just have to figure out how to use it all. And when, of course."

"So, what now, Bill?" I asked.

"Well," he said, "here's sort of the way I'm gonna report it to the *Sentinel* tonight." He sat back in the chair and folded his arms over his tie. "Based upon the evidence I've been able to accumulate, early this morning, Stormy here parked her Jeep down back of the Starlight by that big Dumpster of Skip's and drank herself mean. I'm gonna say I found an empty quart of Jim Beam in the Jeep and another one broken on the ground by the Dumpster." He lifted two empty bottles of Jim Beam bourbon from the table and held them up like an auctioneer. "Then I'm going to tell everybody how I think it happened. I'm gonna say that, just before sunrise, Stormy, who was now real drunk and real mad, took her trusty Winchester and a pocket full of thirty-thirty ammo and hiked in to Sweet Lake, where she set up about fifty yards from the water and waited. D'Antella's cameras didn't see her 'cause she knows the woods." He smiled. "Then I'm gonna say, I think she only wanted to kill Bendel 'cause of his screwing around, but when she saw d'Antella with him, well, pissed as she was, she shot 'em both . . ." He looked at Rayleen.

I think Rayleen had had it; his eyes were closed again.

"Hey, Rayleen!" Billy leaned and shook the old man's foot. "Am I boring you?"

Rayleen opened his eyes. "Huh? Wha?"

"You both listenin' now?" Billy looked back and forth between the two of us. "We're just getting to the best part."

"Get it over with," Rayleen mumbled.

"Let's see," Billy said, "where were we . . . ? Oh, yeah. I was telling you how I'd tell the *Sentinel* how Stormy killed both of them. Well, then she hiked out of the woods and back to the Starlight and hightailed it out here to Monday Lake just before the big dedication ceremony started and broke into . . ." He looked at Rayleen. "What's this place called?"

"Camp David," Rayleen said, rolling his eyes. "Belongs ta Dave Tesar and that redheaded fellow . . ."

Billy held up his hand. "Just the name, Rayleen." He continued, "Broke into Camp David, where she continued her drinking. She used that phone right there"—he pointed to the phone on the wall in the kitchen alcove—"to call you, Max. And Pauline." He smiled. "Which is how I really found out she was out here at the lake." He actually blushed a little. "Of course, I won't tell it to the *Sentinel* like that. To them, I'll say I was working on a hunch, coupled with good police work. Anyway, the way I'll tell them I think it happened from there is"—he looked directly at me—"you and Rayleen found out Stormy was here and came to get her and she shot the both of you." He smiled. "I was just cruisin' by and heard the rifle, but by the time I got down here to the cottage, your dead bodies were in the yard. And when I came in here, I found Stormy dead on that sofa there. Obviously, depressed from too much booze and everything she'd done, she put the Winchester in her mouth, hooked her toe on the trigger, and blew her brains out." He looked first at Rayleen, then at me. "And that's it. I solve the biggest murder case in the history of Loon, and as a result of all the good publicity and"—he winked—"a little boost from Loon's next mayor, Earl MacMillan, I beat Ralston in the next election and become the highest-paid sheriff in county history.'' He sat back in the chair and sighed. ''What do you think?''

''Think you're 'bout as crazy as they come,'' Rayleen said.

Billy's face turned dark and his little eyes got smaller. He stood and kicked the chair across the room. He didn't even have to say it; it was time to make it all come true.

He stepped across the room and grabbed Rayleen by the ankles and yanked him from the recliner. I winced at the sound Rayleen's head and bony back made hitting the bare wood floor. He was still conscious and, amazingly, his cap didn't fall off as Billy dragged him toward the back door.

''Lordy, Lordy,'' Rayleen moaned.

I was helpless. All I could think of to do was to keep Billy talking. Maybe buy time. Maybe someone else would show up. Meanwhile, ask him questions and, while he answered, try to think of a way out of this. ''What did Stormy do, Bill,'' I asked quickly, ''take off her panty hose and tie Rayleen and me up with it before she shot us? Or was it after she shot us?''

Still holding Rayleen by one ankle, Billy grabbed the Winchester by the barrel. ''Don't you worry, Max. That panty hose'll be at the bottom of Monday Lake with the cartridges from my rifle before I report this.'' He dragged Rayleen the rest of the way to the door.

As he fumbled with the ankle, the Winchester, and then the doorknob, I tried again. ''What about all this blood on my shirt?'' I yelled at him. ''This is nose blood. Won't that hotshot Inspector Brown woman know the difference? What's she gonna think? She supposed to believe that Stormy came outside and punched me in the nose before she shot me?''

That stopped him. I could see him thinking about the logic of it. He might have known the acronym DNA, but he didn't know shit about forensics.

Of course, neither did I. But I kept jabbering anyway.

"You surprise me, Bill," I said. "All this careful, detailed preparation and you're going to screw it up because of a nosebleed?"

He dropped Rayleen's foot, walked over, and stood, looking down at me. I could hear the breath going in and out of his nose. I wasn't sure whether he was going to kick me or punch me again, but I braced myself for either.

"Nose blood's no different that any other blood," he said.

"Who the hell told you that?" I said. "Of course it's different." I was really winging it now. "A nose is different than a heart, right?"

He nodded.

I shrugged as best I could. "So's the blood in them. Inspector Brown would see that in a second."

He didn't say anything for several seconds and just stood there looking down at me with the gears turning in his demented brain. Then he walked away and disappeared behind me and after a while I could hear him rummaging in drawers in what must have been a bedroom.

I looked over at Rayleen. "I got him out of the room," I said. "Now what?"

Rayleen was looking at me upside down. "How 'bout that phone in your T-shirt pocket?" he said. "If you can get over here, maybe I can dial it."

I immediately fell to my side, rolled over, and got on my knees. My head pounded. I couldn't stand, so I began carefully knee-walking toward Rayleen. "What was the last number you dialed?" I whispered, as I struggled not to fall over.

"The lodge," he said. "You wasn't there. Tommy told me you'd just left on the Harley."

I was almost to him. "Then all you have to do is push redial, right?"

"Wrong," I heard Billy say as his fingers dug into my hair and gripped. "Stand up, Max." I felt an excruciating pain on the top of my head as he lifted me to my feet, spun me around, and thrust a powder-blue New England Patriots' sweatshirt at me. "Put it on."

"How?" I asked. My hands were tied behind me.

He looked irritated, exhaled hard, and stepping over Rayleen, grabbed the Swiss Army knife. He spun me around and quickly sawed through the panty hose. When he spun me back, he had his revolver out and pointing directly at my chest. "Now, get that T-shirt off," he growled.

I tried to move my arms. They wouldn't move. They were dead numb. "I can't," I said. "My arms . . ."

Billy jammed the gun in my belly. "I said, take it off, Max!"

I tried again. "I'm not kidding, Bill. I can't."

"Dammit, Max." He grabbed my arms and thrust them vertically above my head. I held them there but if I hadn't been watching I wouldn't have known they were up. Worse, whatever feeling that was coming back stopped dead as soon as he shoved my arms up there. They waved slightly above my head.

"What the hell's wrong with you?" He jabbed the gun harder into my belly. "You fuckin' with me, Max?"

I shook my head. "My arms are asleep," I said. "They don't work." I was only going to be able to hold them up there for another few seconds. They felt like lead. My shoulder muscles weren't getting the message.

"Oh, for Chrissakes!" he said and, keeping the muzzle of the gun against my torso, stepped directly in front of me, reached over my shoulder, grabbed the back of the T-shirt, and yanked it up over my shoulders and head, then pushed it up my arms to my wrists.

The extra weight was all my poor dead arms could take. They dropped like logs, down over his head, by his shoulders and elbows, finally stopping at his forearms. He was suddenly pinned in an accidental bear hug between my dead arms, the T-shirt around my wrists, and my chest. I couldn't let go. His face was an inch from mine. "What the fuck?'' He struggled but my arms had his tight to his sides. I felt like one of those stuffed dolls with the long arms you can wrap around yourself. Where he moved, I moved. He shook, I shook. ''Goddammit, Max,'' he yelled in my face. ''Let go or . . .'' He kneed at my groin but we were too close. The revolver went off. And then in quick succession three more times, and I felt the floor vibrate as the bullets tore through the plywood between my feet. My ears were ringing and the air in the room was suddenly thick with the acrid odor of cordite.

I don't know whether it was the closeness of the gunshots or the fact that he head-butted me again and I heard my nose break for a second time, but I suddenly went crazy also. I jammed a boot heel on his instep and then lowered my head and, like a wrestler aiming his opponent at ropes, drove us across the room toward the front of the cabin. Together we were probably 450 pounds and we slammed hard into the flimsy front door, crashed through, taking it with us outside and onto the rotting porch floor, which collapsed, sending the two of us down eight feet into five feet of ice-cold lake. I think I heard the gun go off again as we went under the water.

I wanted to get away but I couldn't. I was on top. Some piece from the porch was pressing on the backs of my thighs. We were held pressed under and I couldn't let go. My arms still wouldn't work. His weight and mine and whatever it was pushing on my legs held my wrists locked and pinned beneath his back. I had the distinct feeling that we were going to drown like this. I tried to roll but he misinterpreted it and countered the opposite way, struggling under me, trying to head-butt me. He wasn't trying to escape. He was trying to hurt me. Kill me. His head thrust violently up at me again and I arched my back and lifted mine out of range and my face popped above the surface. The porch floor, plus the door, plus his girth was enough to put my head out of the water. I gasped and took a lung full of air. I breathed. I kept my back arched and face away from his lunging head.

I knew what was happening. The last thing I am is violent, but I had no choice. I was pinned as much as he was. He was underneath and I was on top.

Billy now struggled frantically beneath me. His legs kicked, his head twisted. I could feel his chest heave, his belly flex, and his groin push against mine. Now he wanted up. He wanted to breathe. He wanted free, but I knew if I let him, he'd shoot me. Or drown me. And then he'd kill Rayleen and Stormy.

Now I hung on deliberately and tears of anger and frustration stung my eyes. "Stop it, Bill! Stop it," I yelled at the water. "You're making me do this . . ."

And then I felt the water resonate with his gargled scream. I looked away, out across the surface of the lake at the mountains with their soft, pale spring colors and hugged Billy Kendall beneath me in what had become a death grip until he didn't struggle or jerk or twitch anymore and the frothy, oily bubbles of his last breath were no longer clustered around my chin.

CHAPTER ☙ EIGHTEEN

There is nothing that tastes more like summer than a ripe tomato straight from the vine and still warm from the sun.

As far as I'm concerned, you haven't lived until you've stood with your toes in the soft, warm dirt in the sweet smell of a garden with chest-high dark green plants all around and let that juice run down your chin and over your bare chest.

"I can't believe I took off my blouse to eat a tomato, Max." Ruth chuckled and bit into the big red orange fruit cradled in her two hands. The warm juice exploded around her lips, ran down her chin to her neck, and, as she broke into laughter, split into two rivulets at her breasts and began to drip from the pink nipples.

I stooped and caught the juice in my mouth.

It was Labor Day weekend. In two months the fishing season would be over for another year, the days would shorten, crackling fires would warm the dining room and scent the chill air, and Sweet Lake would come alive with the reflected fiery colors of autumn.

Right now, however, the heat of summer buzzed around the lodge and hung in the trees. The Whitefork River, tired and low, only gurgled through shallow, shadowed runs, and the trout hovered in the cooler bottom water of the deepest pools. A frog could hop across Sweet Lake on lily pads and by midday their flowers studded the green with delicate spots of yellow, white, and purple or at sunset hung like leis from the wet shoulders of partially submerged, quietly feeding moose.

The lodge was empty for the weekend. Not by accident, but by choice. I had canceled our Labor Day–weekend guests' reservations and refunded their money months ago. We all had something personal that needed done these three days.

Considering the way the season started, it was a wonder we'd stayed open at all.

Loon County's Acting Sheriff, Billy Kendall, was pronounced dead on the lawn at Camp David only seven hours after he had killed Bendel Domini and Vincent "Kingfish" d'Antella on Sweet Lake with four shots at fifty-seven yards from his scoped Marlin bolt-action thirty-thirty. Billy's responsibility for the murders on Sweet Lake was supported by the paraphernalia found on the table at Camp David and the spent thirty-thirty rifle cartridges in his uniform shirt pocket.

The scandal that erupted in the hours following Billy's death still numbs the town of Loon four months later. His inferences and allegations to myself and Rayleen about City Council President Earl MacMillan and crime consultant Avery Bernstein were scoffed at by many until the morning after Billy's death, when Ruth unlocked her office door at City Hall and found three large cardboard cartons sitting on the rug in front of her desk. They contained photographs, taped telephone conversations, letters, receipts, telephone bills, notarized statements, fingerprints, videotapes, dates, times, and places that conclusively proved that, at the very least, Earl and Avery were guilty of interfering in criminal investigations, obstructing justice, and conspiracy to defraud. And if Merriam Martin agrees to allow Lyle's body to be exhumed, Earl and Avery face accessory-to-murder charges as well.

Although I'd been instructed to keep the source of the material anonymous, Martino had decided otherwise, and attached to one of the cartons was a note that simply read, "Compliments of Vincent d'Antella: a man of honor and generosity."

In his digging, Martino had also found documents that Ruth felt could link Earl to the hunting/shooting death of Gordon Miller, Sr. I'm not completely clear on the details, but I hear the state's attorney general is investigating the connection between Earl's Scotch Hill Dairy Farm, the use of cancer-producing chemicals to increase milk production, and an editorial exposé Gordon Senior was writing at the time of his death.

Further investigation by Lieutenant Conklin and the Vermont State Police, however, found that in the case of Bendel and Kingfish, Billy acted alone and neither Earl nor Avery knew anything about it.

In her testimony at the first of several hearings, Inspector Cynthia Brown said that Billy's work was so thorough and his plan so well thought out, that there was no way she nor any of her colleagues would have known that the evidence from Whitefork Lodge had been tampered with or altered.

Had my arms not fallen asleep, Billy's plan would have worked.

I never did see Collingwood that day, but was told that after Billy's guilt was clearly established by the state police, Kingfish's body was released and he had accompanied it back to Rhode Island.

Tommy and Ralph were gone by the time I got back to the lodge that night and have simply disappeared back into the dark world they came from. I did receive a postcard from Sicily about a month and a half after they left. I can't decipher the pencil scrawl of Italian and there's still a difference of opinion between Ruth and me as to what it says. We do agree, however, that the signature *"Il Nipote"* means "The Nephew."

Other than Ruth, Connie benefited the most from the events of those few horrible days. She was able to make the incredible publicity work for her and I read all about her new life and home in Hollywood in a recent *People* magazine that some guest had left at the lodge. Although theoretically still in mourning, she has already been linked romantically with several movie stars and producers. The article, which was peppered with pictures of her and Quincy, also claimed she had been cast in the title role in a soon-to-be-made-for-cable movie about the life of Jayne Mansfield.

Ruth refuses to fire Pauline Tritch. In fact, she gave the woman a small raise and a cubicle with a door. Her explanation is simple. "Pauline made a mistake, Max. She's apologized and promised never to reveal confidential information again." She smiled. "Keeping her happy is my guarantee. She knows too much about all of us to ever be let go."

Understandably, there's turmoil in the Loon County Sheriff's Department. With Billy dead and Sheriff Benjamin Ralston not healing down in Montpelier, there's a definite lack of leadership. At Ruth's request, Lieutenant Samuel Conklin has stepped in temporarily and the gossip in town is that if he can find a house his wife likes, he might just be willing to stay.

Like Conklin, Judy Bowman has stepped in to fill a gap also. She was voted temporary president of the Loon City Council to replace MacMillan and already appears to be not only good at the job, but is considering an official run for the office in this November's elections.

The murders, Billy's death, and the collapse of Earl MacMillan's good-old-boy-network was a wakeup call for Gordon Miller, Jr., and his *Loon Sentinel* newspaper. The possibility that his father might have been murdered has also seemed to make a difference. In the past four months, Gordon's writing style has matured. His choice of headline is less sensational. No longer does he use information

254 aÞ David Leitz

without verifying its accuracy. His long-overdue tribute to his father was very moving and his three weeks of editorials on MacMillan and the misuse of public trust have been nominated by the American Smalltown Newspaper Association for the prestigious P. L. Tungston Award for responsible community journalism.

Over the years, when asked whether she feared starting drinking again, Stormy had always said, "Don't think I got another drunk in me. This old body just couldn't take it again."

I'm happy to say, she was wrong.

She did have one more drunk in her. And because it only lasted twelve hours or so, her body withstood the abuse.

We brought her back to the lodge in an EMT ambulance, put her in the bed in my room, and waited. Ruth's doctor, Sondra Ross, was nice enough to come all the way down from her home in Stoneboat and look Stormy over. "She's better than most women her age," Sondra told us in the dining room after the examination, "but be gentle when you break the news to her about her husband's death. Although she says she doesn't remember, I think she's understood a lot of what's already happened."

Hearing that, Rayleen and I briefly considered not telling her about Bendel until morning. I was afraid the news of his death might just push her over the edge again and this time we'd lose her forever. Ruth wouldn't hear of it and I, of course, was chosen to break the bad news.

Stormy was propped up in my bed as I walked into the room and quietly closed the door. I'd never seen her hair unbraided and it spread out across the pillows around her head like Christmas tinsel.

I sat on the edge of the bed and looked at her.

She smiled, reached out, and patted my hand. "I remember more than I let on," she said, "especially after Billy hit you in the face." She reached up and touched my nose. "It all right?"

I nodded. Actually, it still hurt like hell. It was swollen and both of my eyes were black.

"You look kinda like a prizefighter." She smiled. "You saved my life, didn'tcha?"

I shrugged. "Only by accident."

"You got a cigarette?"

I nodded and gave her one.

She broke off the filter, stuck it in the corner of her mouth, and I lit it for her. After she'd taken a deep drag she said, "He's dead, isn't he?"

I nodded.

"How?"

"Billy Kendall shot him and d'Antella out on the lake."

"This morning?"

"Yeah."

"Was it quick?"

"Like a heart attack."

She sighed and looked at the ceiling. Her eyes teared but she didn't cry. Finally she said, "I'd like to go out and sit on the porch a while, Max." She handed me the cigarette and I snubbed it in the ashtray. "You help me?" She slid out from under the sheet and put her bare feet on the floor.

I grabbed the afghan from the foot end of the bed, threw it around her shoulders, and walked her out into the hallway, through the screen door, and out onto the porch. After getting her situated in a rocker, I started back inside.

"Don't go yet, Max," she said, grabbing my sleeve.

"I thought you wanted to be alone."

"I do. In a minute."

I went back and sat in the rocker next to hers, got our chairs rocking in sync, and stared out at the lake. The moon had already gone down and the loons had finished calling for the night. Only the big bullfrogs remained and their deep-throated croaking bounced around the shore.

"Where is he?" she finally asked.

"In town. At the hospital."

"They want me to identify him?"

"I think so."

"I'll do it tomorrow. You come with me?"

"Sure. I'll even do it for you it you rather not . . ."

"No. I gotta see him. He needs to know I forgive him."

"He knows, Stormy."

She reached across the space between our rockers, took my hand in hers, and squeezed it. "I gotta see his face when I tell him."

She sat out there on the porch all night. And the next morning, after a cup of coffee, Ruth and I took her to see the body. We sat in the hall while she went into the cold room alone.

She was in there for an hour, but it was worth it. Whatever it was she and Bendel talked about, when she came out, she was the old Stormy again. "Let's go," she said, striding out down the hall ahead of us, her caftan billowing around her boot tops. "I got funeral arrangements to make, an AA meetin' to attend, and if I don't have a cigarette in thirty seconds, I'm gonna have me a nicotine fit."

Bendel's funeral was small and Catholic. Stormy had him cremated and the empty casket at the front of the church was, as the pastor put it, "Just to give the friends and family something to focus on through the service." I thought it was a ridiculous and unnecessary expense until Rayleen explained, "It's a rental, Max. I been to ten funerals in this here church in the last fifteen years and that there casket's been in every one of 'em."

My daughter Sabrina and her husband David drove up from their home in New York City. As a surprise, they brought my two-year-old granddaughter Elise with them.

Neither Ruth, Stormy, nor I had seen Elise in almost a year, and the giggling little demon with golden ringlets and bright blue eyes bounced from one pair of arms to another all afternoon. And as small children so often do, her ignorance of what was going on put a perspective on things that no church sermon could ever accomplish. By the time the three of them left the next morning, all of us were cheerful and optimistic.

Bendel had loved the dog days of summer and so Stormy asked that we set aside Labor Day weekend to scatter his ashes in the river he'd grown to love so much. I agreed.

And now here we were on Labor Day weekend and Ruth was giggling among the tomato plants in the garden and playfully slapping my hands away from her breasts and attempting to get her blouse back on.

At the sound of Rayleen's truck, she buttoned up and we walked hand in hand from the garden to the front of the lodge to greet Rayleen and Stormy. They had just returned from a trip to town to pick up ice for the small party we were having after the ceremony.

Only our closest friends were invited: Judy Bowman and her husband Bob, Skip and Lo Ming Willits from the Starlight, Loon Hotel owner John Quinn and his life partner Simon Hill, Merriam Martin, Pauline Tritch, Loon Lager brewers Tom Davies and Art Currier, and, of course, Spotter.

By two o'clock everyone was on the porch laughing and telling "Bendel stories" over cold bottles of Loon Lager. Along with a couple cases of traditional "Loon Necks," Tom and Art had thoughtfully brought a six-pack of the new nonalcoholic version of Loon Lager they were just beginning to sell in the Middle East, so even Stormy had a beer bottle in her hand.

At two-thirty, we set down the beers and, with Stormy carrying the brushed-aluminum urn, we all moved into the yard for the short walk to the Whitefork River.

Just as I was issuing last-minute instructions, a long black Cadillac limousine came down the access road and pulled up between our group and the front of the lodge. It had tinted windows and Rhode Island license plates.

The driver's side door opened and a young man, who reminded me of Tommy, jumped out, opened the back door, and held it.

Donald Collingwood was the first one out. As usual, he was tan, composed, and dressed impeccably in a suit and tie. He smiled at me and quickly turned and extended his hand to an old woman in a formless black dress. He helped her from the car, and when she was standing, he closed the door. Her face and white hair were carefully covered with a black veil and in her hands she carried an urn the size and shape of Bendel's, except it was made of blue pottery.

Collingwood walked directly up to Stormy. "Mrs. Domini," he said, "may I have a word with you? In private?"

Stormy nodded, handed Ruth the urn, and then she and Collingwood walked a few yards out into the yard, where they stood and quietly talked.

The rest of us tried not to stare at the old woman holding the blue urn while we waited.

A couple minutes passed and then Stormy and Collingwood walked back. They were smiling. "Everybody," Stormy said, walking to the old woman and putting her arm around her shoulders, "this here is Mrs. Vincent d'Antella." She smiled at the woman. "Violetta?"

Violetta smiled, nodded her head, and said, "Si, Violetta."

"Violetta doesn't speak much English, but Mr. Collingwood here has told me that Violetta wants to scatter her husband's ashes with the fish he loved to catch." She smiled. "And, I said, why not? Bendel never liked bein' out in the river alone anyways."

We all applauded. Then, with Collingwood holding Violetta's elbow and Spotter trotting at the front, we headed for the river. As we entered the trees, Rayleen, who was on the other side of Ruth, whispered something to her and she said, "Good question."

"What's up?" I asked her.

"Rayleen asked how Collingwood knew we were doing this today."

"That is a good question." I looked at Stormy. "Did he say anything to you about how they knew?"

She shrugged. "Only somethin' 'bout some guy named Marty told 'em. I never heard of him."

Ruth and I looked at each other and smiled. "Martino," we said in unison.

Stormy had chosen the Cobble as the place she wanted to put Bendel. She kicked off her boots and unceremoniously waded in until the hem of her caftan was floating. Spotter bounded in and stood beside her, looking up at the urn. I think he was trying to figure out how she was going to fish with it.

The rest of us, including Collingwood, sat on rocks and logs and took off our shoes and socks and rolled up our pants and dresses. Violetta kicked off her shoes, turned her back, and peeled her dark hose down from above her knees. She laid them carefully over a hemlock branch and removed the veil. She then turned, smiled at all of us, and waded into the current beside Stormy, her white hair like snow in the shaft of sunlight that illuminated both of them.

"Bendel would have loved this light," Stormy said, beginning to unscrew the lid on the urn.

We all waded into the water and, facing downstream, formed a half circle behind the two widows.

Stormy handed her lid to Rayleen and I took Violetta's when she had it off. Then we all stood there with the cold, crystal-clear water of the Whitefork swirling around our bare legs and listened to the gurgling laughter of the river, the birds, and the wind in the trees.

Finally, as though they had been planning it for months, Stormy Domini and Violetta d'Antella upended the urns containing the ashes of their husbands and two white smokelike clouds spread out across the water, combined as one, settled on the surface, and began to float away downstream.

Stormy and Violetta hugged. Spotter barked. Ruth and Rayleen cried.

Me? I watched the ashes mix with the sparkling water, swirl around the mossy rocks, tumble through a gurgling chute, and out onto the surface, a deep green pool below us. There, like a haze of breath on a windowpane, it slowly faded away.

As small brookies began to rise in the pool, I smiled and took Ruth's hand.

Even in death, Bendel and Kingfish were fooling the trout.

Bettina Bilby has agreed to board her neighbors' felines for a long holiday weekend: an expectant tabby, a pampered blue-eyed Balinese, a depressed ginger Persian with a cod-liver-oil addiction, and Adolf, an imperious mouser with a patchwork face.

But during a freak storm, a carrier pigeon is downed on the doorstep with a tiny load of large flawless diamonds. And Bettina's dilemma escalates as Adolf gobbles up one of the gems and a succession of elegant but shifty strangers prowl the gardens, offending the cats, and bringing in their wake back-door bloodshed and murder.

THE
DIAMOND CAT

Marian Babson

Spring has returned to the mountains of northern Vermont, and Whitefork Lodge owner Max Addams is ready for another tranquil season of fly-fishing and hospitality...until a lumber company begins clear-cutting trees and Max's trout start dying by the bushel.

Soon Max discovers it isn't just the trout that are turning belly-up. With one close friend found dead in the water, his livelihood at stake and the town turning against him, Max must reel in the killer before he becomes the catch of the day.

CASTING IN DEAD WATER

DAVID LEITZ